I tried to ignore Detective Nate Williams's grin.

"No curse. Unless you consider wacky mothers a special variety. My mother is convinced that she and her book club are going to drop dead from reading some ridiculous novel. She started in with me last night and wouldn't quit. Now she's calling me at work."

"I'm listening."

"There are about fifteen or so members in my mother's book club, and every year they give the librarian at Sun City West a list of their choices for murder-mystery reading."

"Okay, fine. So this book came as one of the suggestions from a book club member?"

"Uh-huh. It was part of the original list for the year."

Nate rubbed the bottom of his chin and leaned in. "What makes your mother so sure the book has anything to do with these deaths? From what I overheard, and believe me, I wasn't trying to snoop, it sounded like they were all unrelated."

"Three of the women died within days of each other and, according to my mother, each received a cryptic e-mail a few days before."

"What kind of e-mail? What did it say?"

"'Death lurks between the lines.'"

"What's this about a cursed book?"

Booked 4 Murder

J.C. Eaton

KENSINGTON PUBLISHING CORP.
http://www.kensingtonbooks.com

KENSINGTON BOOKS are published by

Kensington Publishing Corp.
119 West 40th Street
New York, NY 10018

All Kensington Titles, Imprints, and Distributed Lines are available at special quantity discounts for bulk purchases for sales promotions, premiums, fund-raising, and educational or institutional use. Special book excerpts or customized printings can also be created to fit specific needs. For details, write or phone the office of the Kensington special sales manager: Kensington Publishing Corp., 119 West 40th Street, New York, NY 10018, attn: Special Sales Department, Phone: 1-800-221-2647.

Kensington and the K logo Reg. U.S. Pat & TM Off.

ISBN-13: 978-1-4967-0855-7
ISBN-10: 1-4967-0855-5
First Kensington Mass Market Edition: July 2017

eISBN-13: 978-1-4967-0856-4
eISBN-10: 1-4967-0856-3
First Kensington Electronic Edition: July 2017

10 9 8 7 6 5 4 3

Printed in the United States of America

Dedication

To all of our friends at the Sun City West dog parks,

You kept bugging us to write a murder mystery about the dog parks, big and small. Well, we didn't stop at one book. You gave us so much "fodder" we had to do a series. Enjoy! And please remember—This is a work of fiction!

Acknowledgments

The Sophie Kimball Mysteries would never have seen the light of day if it wasn't for the folks behind the scenes who believed in us and supported us every step of the way. Our agent, Dawn Dowdle, at Blue Ridge Literary Agency and our Kensington editor, Tara Gavin, gave us those first breaks with *Booked 4 Murder*. We are, and will be, forever grateful to them for making J.C. Eaton a reality.

We are fortunate to have a topnotch team of "first responders" who review our drafts, catch our blunders and keep us on track. Thank you Ellen Lynes, Susan Morrow, Suzanne Scher and Susan Schwartz. Your eagle eyes are amazing. And to our "technical responders" Beth Cornell, Larry Finkelstein and Gale Leach, we could not have managed without your expertise.

Finally, to the original book club ladies in Sun City West who make solving domestic murders an everyday thing, we thank you for getting us hooked on cozies. Kenlyn Boyd, Polly Cameron, Audrey Ellis, Judie Ives, Ellen Janicki, Geri Lahti, Janet McNamara, Arlene Peterson, Louise Rossignol, Liz Walter and Gêne Stickles, keep up the sleuthing.

And to the entire Sun City West Community, thanks for giving us the inspiration. We love calling this place home.

Ann I. Goldfarb and James E. Clapp, writing as J. C. Eaton

Chapter 1

"I'm telling you, Phee, they were all murdered. Murdered by reading that book."

I tried to keep my voice low, even though I felt like screaming. I had gotten the full story last night, but apparently that wasn't enough.

"That's insane, Mother. No one drops dead from reading a book. Look, can we talk about this later? I'm at work."

"Then you shouldn't have answered your cell phone."

She was right. It was a bad habit. One I had gotten used to when my daughter was in college and had all sorts of would-be emergencies. Now it was my mother in Arizona who seemed to have a never-ending supply of issues—the plumbing in her bathroom, a squeaky garage door, the arthritis in her right hand, a bridge player from her group who was cheating, and trouble keeping her succulents alive. Today it was some bizarre story about her book club. I glanced at the bottom of my computer screen for the time and decided to let her speak for another minute or so.

"Like I was saying, all of us in Booked 4 Murder are going to die from reading that book. There's a curse on it or something."

"Honestly, Mother, you can't be serious. We went through this last night. Minnie Bendelson was eighty-seven, overweight, diabetic, and had a heart condition! Not to mention the fact she was a chain-smoker. A chain-smoker! Edna Mae Langford fell, broke her hip, and died from complications of pneumonia. And she was in her eighties."

"What about Marilyn Scutt? She was only seventy."

"Her golf cart was hit by a car going in the wrong direction!"

"That wouldn't have happened if she wasn't engrossed in that book. That's what I'm telling you. She died from that darn book. And now I'm petrified. Of course, I've only read up until page twenty-four. I was in the middle of a paragraph when I got the call about Edna Mae. That's when I stopped reading the book."

"Good. Read something else."

"I'm serious, Phee. You need to fly out here and find out how that curse works."

"How on earth would I know? And once and for all, there is no curse."

"You can't say that for sure. You need to investigate. With your background, that shouldn't be too hard."

"My background? What background?"

"Well, you work for the police department, don't you?"

"In accounting and payroll! I have a civil service job. I'm not a detective."

As if to verify, I picked up the placard in front of my computer. It read, SOPHIE KIMBALL, ACCOUNTS RECEIVABLE.

"You come in contact with those investigators every day. Something must have rubbed off by now. You've had that job for years."

"Look, Mother, I promise I'll call the minute I get home from work, but I can't stay on the phone. Do me a favor. Stop reading those books for a few days. Turn on the TV, listen to the radio, or find something other than murder mysteries to read. Maybe a good cookbook."

"Who cooks in Sun City West? This is a retirement community. I'm going out with friends for dinner. Call me after seven your time."

"Fine. And stop thinking about a cursed book."

My finger slid to the red End button just as Nate Williams approached my desk. He had been a detective in this small Minnesota city for close to two decades and was counting the days till his retirement. At sixty-five, he still looked youthful, even with his graying hair. Maybe it was his height or the way he sauntered about as if he didn't have a care in the world.

"What's this about a cursed book? Some new case and they called your department by mistake?"

I tried to ignore his grin.

"No curse. Unless you consider wacky mothers a special variety. Come on, hand over your receipts for processing. I'll make a quick copy for you. The machine's right here."

"So, what's with the cursed book? Sounds more interesting than the stuff I've got on my docket."

"Well, if you must know, my mother is convinced that she and her book club are going to drop dead from reading some ridiculous novel. She started in with me last night and wouldn't quit. Now she's calling me at work."

Nate took the receipt copies and let out a slow breath. "And you don't believe her?"

"Of course not. It's just her overactive imagination. When my father was alive, he kept her in check, but he passed away when they moved out west years ago. Now it seems she and her friends have nothing better to do than speculate on all sorts of stuff—the government, health care, economics, immigration. . . . You know, the usual things that retired people talk about."

"Hey, I haven't even turned in my retirement letter, so no, I'm not part of the geezer gossip group yet."

"Oh my gosh. I wasn't referring to you."

My face started to flush, and I quickly turned toward my desk to hide my reaction.

"Take it easy. I'm only kidding. So, what gives? What's this book club death threat all about?"

"Gee, Nate, you sound more and more like a detective each day. Quick, pull up a chair and I'll fill you in. I've got a break coming in a few minutes. Might as well put it to good use."

Working in this department for so many years, one of the perks was having my own office. Granted, it was tiny, just a desk, computer, and copier, but it was fairly private if you weren't bothered by the hallway traffic and constant interruptions. Nate had stopped by at a good time. Most of the workers were already making their way to the coffee machine for a fifteen-minute respite.

"Want me to run and get you a cup of coffee before we start?" he asked.

"Nah, I'm fine. You're the one who's going to need a cup of coffee or something stronger when you hear this lunacy."

"I'm listening."

"There are about fifteen or so members in my mother's book club, and every year they give the librarian at Sun City West a list of their choices for murder-mystery reading. To avoid arguments, the librarian selects a different book from the list for each month and makes it a point to acquire some copies for the library."

"Hmm . . . he or she isn't in the club, I presume?"

"Correct. It's a she, but that's all I know."

"Okay, fine. So this book came as one of the suggestions from a book club member?"

"Uh-huh. It was part of the original list for the year."

Nate rubbed the bottom of his chin and leaned in. "What makes your mother so sure the book has anything to do with these deaths? From what I overheard, and believe me, I wasn't trying to snoop, it sounded like they were all unrelated."

"Three of the women died within days of each other and, according to my mother, each received a cryptic e-mail a few days before."

"What kind of e-mail? What did it say?"

"'Death lurks between the lines.'" I couldn't tell if Nate was trying to stifle a laugh or clear his throat.

"Astounding. Sounds like a take on those old nineteen eighties urban legends where someone gets a mysterious videotape, they watch it, and within days they die."

"You think someone is trying to scare a bunch of old ladies?"

"I don't know what to think. But you were right. Your mother should stick to reading a cookbook or something."

"She never went near one when I was growing up, and she's not going to start now. Frankly, the only thing that's going to stop my mother from dwelling on this is if I fly out there and make a fool of myself investigating."

"Listen, kiddo, you'd never make a fool of yourself, no matter what."

"I don't know the first thing about investigating. I'm no detective."

"The heck you're not! The way you track down and verify receipts, hold everyone accountable for monies spent, and triple-check every bit of documentation that comes across your desk? If that's not detective work, then what is?"

"You know what I mean. What does my mother expect me to do even if I fly out there? Take out a pencil and paper and start acting like Sherlock Holmes?"

"Nah, he'd use an iPad by now."

"You do think this is absurd, don't you?"

"Yes and no. Coincidental deaths maybe, but not that e-mail. Keep me posted, Phee. By the way, what's the name of that book?"

"It had a strange title. *The Twelfth Arrondissement*. Whatever that means."

"It's a neighborhood in Paris."

"How on earth do you know that?"

"You'd be surprised at all the irrelevant facts I know. But this one is firsthand. I lived in Paris for a year when I graduated from college. Couldn't figure out what to do with the rest of my life and thought I'd take a crack at studying art. Needless to say, that dream evaporated and here I am."

"Yes, here you are!" came an unmistakable voice that bellowed down the hallway. "I was looking all over for you, Williams."

"Be right there, Boss. Gotta run. Remember, Phee, if anything turns up, give a holler."

"Sure thing."

I clicked the Refresh button on my computer and waited for the screen to adjust. Of all the crazy things. Why would the book club be reading about some neighborhood in Paris? It didn't sound like their usual cozy mystery. Then again, there was nothing cozy about this.

As hard as I tried, I couldn't stop thinking about that bizarre book and my mother's irrational fears. They plagued me the entire afternoon. I mean, who in the twenty-first century, other than my mother, her book club friends, and my mother's sister, Aunt Ina, would believe in curses? The only saving grace was that my aunt wasn't in the book club. She lived in the East Valley, miles from Sun City West. Compared to her, my mother was the epitome of rational thinking.

Once when my cousin Kirk and I were ten or eleven, we were having lunch with our mothers at some restaurant after a horrid morning of clothes shopping for school. Kirk accidently spilled the salt shaker and my aunt went berserk.

"Quick! Kirk! Take a pinch of salt and throw it over your left shoulder."

"I'm not gonna do that. I don't want salt all over my neck. It'll itch."

"If you don't throw it over your shoulder, you'll be cursed with bad luck. Pinch that salt and throw it."

Kirk refused, forcing my aunt to lean over the table and throw the salt for him. Unfortunately, she knocked over two water glasses in the process, both of them landing in Kirk's lap. What followed next was one of those memorable family moments they tell you you'll be laughing at ten or twenty years later.

In a rush to stand up, Kirk toppled backward, knocked the chair over, and landed on the floor.

"See, I told you," my aunt said. "Next time you'll listen to me."

Was *The Twelfth Arrondissement* my mother's spilled salt shaker? I tried dismissing it from my mind till the moment the workday ended and I set foot in my house.

Chapter 2

I barely had time to put my bag on the counter and kick off my shoes when my phone rang. The voice in my head screamed, *LET THE ANSWERING MACHINE GET IT,* but I didn't listen. I grew up in a household without an answering machine and you had to race to the phone or forever wonder what you missed. Old habits die hard.

"Phee, thank goodness you're home."

"We agreed I'd call you later this evening, Mom. I just got in."

"Thelmalee Kirkson is dead. Dead. This afternoon at the rec center pool. It was awful."

"Oh my gosh. Did she drown?"

"Drown, no. She doesn't even swim. I mean, *didn't* even swim. Just sunbathed and read."

"Heart attack?"

"No, bee sting. Out of nowhere. She got stung and died from anaphylactic shock before the paramedics could get there."

"That's awful, Mom. I'm so sorry. She was in your bridge group, wasn't she?"

"No, that's Thelma Morrison. Thelmalee was in my book club. When the fire department finally removed her body from the lounge chair, do you know what they found?"

Before I could catch a breath, my mother continued. "They found that book. *The Twelfth Arrondissement*. Facedown on the small table near her chair. She only had a few pages left. So you see, it *was* that book. It's put a curse on us!"

"For the last time, Mother. There is no curse. No book curse. This was a horrible accident. A fluke."

"Four perfectly fine book-club members dead in such a short time is not a fluke or a coincidence. Sophie Vera Kimball, you need to fly out here and investigate. I don't want you to get a phone call from my friends, or worse yet, the Sun City West Sheriff's Posse telling you that your mother is number five."

"I think you're overreacting. Besides, I can't just up and fly to Arizona."

"Knowing you, Phee, you've got plenty of vacation and personal days. I'm right, aren't I? Besides, you can get away from that awful Minnesota weather and enjoy the sunshine out here."

"The weather's fine in Minnesota. It's September, for crying out loud. You'll see me in December. Liked we planned."

"December is too late. Call me tomorrow to let me know what flight you're on."

"Mother, I am not—"

Drat! She'd already hung up, and I wasn't about to call her back. I took off my blazer and slacks, and slipped into my favorite worn jeans and an old sweatshirt. Then I grabbed some leftover lasagna from the fridge and popped it into the microwave. No sooner did I press the Start button when the phone rang again.

Unbelievable. Is there no stopping her from driving me insane?

I debated whether or not to answer and decided to let the machine get it. Nate's voice was loud enough to drown out the sound of the microwave. I quickly picked up the receiver.

"Sorry, Nate. Couldn't get to the phone fast enough. What's up?"

"Thought I'd give you a head start, kiddo. I looked up that book, and I have to say, it's really obscure. I mean, on the Amazon ranking list, it's got a really high number, and that's not good. Plus, it's not even listed with Barnes & Noble. No one's heard of it. No one's reading it. Except for your mother's book club."

"Who's the publisher?"

"It's self-published and copyrighted with the author. Also an unknown. So unknown the name didn't come up on Google."

"You didn't have to go through all of that trouble on my account. Honestly, my mother is just being overly dramatic about this. Although . . . she did call a few minutes ago to tell me another book club member died. She was stung by a bee and died of shock at the large recreation center pool."

"So that makes what? Four? Four deaths in less than a month with all of the people having a common relationship? If you ask me, maybe you should fly out there to investigate."

"Oh, come on. I don't have the slightest inkling of how to go about something like that."

"Want me to rent an old noir movie for you? It's

really quite simple. You interview, or in your case, talk with the people in the book club, library patrons, and witnesses who were there when one of the women died. Start to put together bits of information that seem to lead up to something. You know, follow the clues. Like I told you earlier today, you already know how to conduct an investigation."

"Nate, you don't really believe there's a curse related to that book, do you?"

"Logically, no. Then again, was it a curse that killed those archeologists who uncovered King Tutankhamun's tomb, or was it a coincidence?"

"I think it was a virus. Dust spores. Maybe you should be the one to fly out there and commiserate with my mother."

"Thank you, no. But I'll do one better for you. Do you remember Rolo Barnes who used to work in the IT department for us?"

"Rolo Barnes? The guy who looked like a black Jerry Garcia?"

"That's the one."

"Of course I remember him. Made payroll a nightmare for me. He refused to have direct deposit and insisted that his paychecks be even-numbered only. Boy did that guy have his quirks. Why?"

"Because no one knows more about cyphers and codes than Rolo. And, he owes me big-time for a matter that I'd rather not discuss. Anyway, I downloaded the e-book version of *The Twelfth Arrondissement* and sent it to him. He'll check to see if there are any codes or messages embedded in the text."

"Boy, things in your office must really be boring if this is getting your attention."

"I wouldn't say boring, more like routine. And

honestly, Phee, what detective wouldn't want to sink his or her teeth into a good old murderous curse."

"One who lives in this century and not the Middle Ages. Anyway, thanks for doing some of the legwork. If I do decide to hop a plane, you'll be the second one to know."

No sooner did I hang up the phone when the buzz of the microwave made me jump out of my skin. I half expected to turn around and see my mother standing there offering to pack my suitcase. Now I was the one getting unnerved. I was positive my mother was being totally irrational about this. Or was she? Nate certainly didn't dismiss it, and he'd dealt with all sorts of bizarre situations. Still, my mother lived in a senior community and well . . . the likelihood of someone passing away wasn't unusual, even if the cluster of deaths was.

I hated thinking about getting old and at approaching forty-five, I still considered myself years away from middle age. I had no gray hair and still looked decent in a high-waisted two-piece swimsuit, although I shied away from thongs and skinny bikinis.

I ate my dinner quickly, threw on a light jacket, and headed out for a quick walk before it got too dark. The river side of Sibley Park was only a few blocks from my house and strolling down the trail that bordered the water always seemed to help me unwind. The maples, elms, and oaks were starting to show the first signs of autumn, but the spruces and pines held steadfast to their greens and blues. In another few weeks they would be the only ones with any color left. Soon I'd need a heavier jacket. Then a polar fleece one. And then . . . Ugh. The heavyweight down coat that wouldn't come off until April. If I was lucky.

I had to clear my head, but, unfortunately, the walk wasn't working. All I succeeded in doing was giving myself more time to think about death, curses, and my mother's perpetual nagging. She wouldn't give up. When I returned from the park and turned the key into the front door, the annoying beep sounded from my answering machine.

Not my mother again! I swear I'll have the landline disconnected.

I glanced at the clock on the microwave: 8:37 p.m. Almost a quarter to seven in Sun City West. I pushed the button on the phone and sure enough, my mother's voice exploded like a cannon.

"One more thing, Phee. I know you think there's no such thing as curses or hexes, but I wanted to remind you about the summer when you were eight. You may not remember it, but I do.

Of course she remembers it. The woman must have an eidetic memory. She probably remembers everything I did or said. Yeesh.

I took a long breath as her message rambled on. I expected the machine to cut her off, but it didn't.

"The water pump went out on the car and cost us a fortune; then the dryer broke and was beyond repair, so your father and I had to shell out money we didn't have, and then that rotten storm swept through Mankato and the tree in front fell, taking our bay window with it."

I recalled the tree falling into the front window but pulled up a blank as far as the car and dryer were concerned. What any of this had to do with unexpected deaths in Sun City West was beyond me.

"For six weeks, we were jinxed. That was the only explanation. And you know when it ended? Well, I'll tell you when it ended, Phee. It ended with the tree. That was the third thing. Jinxes always come in threes. But this is different. This is a book curse. A curse! God knows when it will end. We've already had four. And that's why you have to come out here and figure it out. Four dead women aren't figments of my imagination. And you don't want your mother to be number five. Understand?"

I understood all right. The curse had reached me. Across the phone lines and into my living room. My mother would nag, demand, and whine like a fourteen-year-old girl whose cell phone was confiscated by the vice principal. Dinnertime or not, I pushed the Redial button on the phone. She picked up before it even finished ringing.

"So, did you make those reservations?"

"No, Mother, I didn't make reservations. I'm sorry those ladies passed away, but there's no such thing as a book curse. Only Wes Craven could have come up with something like that."

"Who's Wes Craven? Don't tell me he's someone you're dating."

"I'm not dating anyone, Mother. And never mind about Wes Craven. He was a director of horror films who passed away."

"I'll bet he was reading that book. Well, are you coming or not?"

She'd gotten me so rattled I mumbled the four possibly worst words in the world: "I'll think about it."

* * *

Seventy-two hours later, I was hoisting my carry-on bag into the overhead bin of the plane.

"You did the right thing," my daughter Kalese said when I called her from the airport. "Poor Nana Harriet must be scared out of her mind."

"Scared isn't exactly the word I'd use, but 'out of her mind' is getting close."

I gave the bag an extra shove and watched it teeter for a second before it landed on its side. Like the canvas carry-on, I was a pushover, too.

Chapter 3

Sun City West, Arizona

It was a three-hour flight to Phoenix, with no amenities, unless you considered a self-paid box lunch one. I opted for the Snickers bar in my bag and bottled water as I gazed out the window. At least I wasn't stuck in the middle seat. I was joined by two impeccably dressed whitehaired women who appeared to be in their late eighties or early nineties. Their pale blue tops with a hint of sparkle on the collars and their matching gray pants gave them a modern look. One of them wore a fringed navy scarf around her neck, while the other sported a large abstract necklace. The one with the necklace took a seat in the middle and smiled. Perfect dentures or excellent oral hygiene over the years. I made a mental note to keep flossing.

"Hi," she said. "Are you stopping in Phoenix or going on to Los Angeles?"

"Uh, hi. Phoenix. I'm visiting my mother."

"We're going to Phoenix, too. We're on our way back from a wedding in Minneapolis. Our great-niece. She's some sort of an engineer and married another sort of engineer. What is it they do, Gertie?"

The lady with the blue scarf looked up.

"Technical risk assessment for amusement rides. Whoever thought that could be a career . . ."

I leaned over and caught her eye.

"Yeah, the technology keeps changing every day."

"One thing I'd like to see them change is the size of these seats. It keeps shrinking every time we get on a plane. And before you say anything, Trudy, I haven't gained a single pound in fifteen years."

"I wasn't going to say anything."

It seemed odd to me that both ladies had nicknames for the same formal name—Gertrude. I thought about commenting on it but didn't want to be intrusive. I reached for the safety brochure in the front seat pocket when Gertie changed the subject.

"Has your mother lived in Phoenix long? Trudy and I have been Arizonians for over forty years."

"Um, at least a decade or more. Actually, she lives in the West Valley. Sun City West, to be precise."

"My goodness, what a coincidence. Isn't that a coincidence, Trudy? My sister and I live there as well. At The Lillian."

The way she articulated the words "The" and "Lillian" made me wonder if it was a place most people knew of. Most people being everyone but me.

"The Lillian?"

"Yes, I'm sure your mother is familiar with it living in Sun City West and all. The Lillian is a premier resort retirement hotel. It's located right in the center of the city with its own recreation center and amenities."

"I see."

Trudy leaned over again and I marveled at her tasteful makeup and choice of earrings.

"Gertie and I are twins, but you probably figured that out already. When we turned eighty-five we promised ourselves that on our ninetieth birthday we would sell our homes and move into The Lillian. It was time to treat ourselves. Gourmet dining, concierge service, housecleaning, linen service, private limousine drivers for appointments, and more conveniences than anyone could possibly imagine. We both have residences on the same floor, and Gertie still has her cat. That is, if Maybelle remembered to feed him."

Gertie shot a look at her sister. The same look teachers have been giving petulant kids for centuries.

"She remembered. She's not daft. I spoke to her this morning, and Mr. Whiskers is fine."

"Anyway, like I was saying, we've lived in The Lillian going on four years and love it. We should have moved in when we were young, in our eighties."

Young. Eighties. Wow.

"It does sound wonderful."

And please don't let my mother know about it or I'll get roped into doing the packing.

Suddenly a voice came over the loud speaker.

"ALL CARRY-ON LUGGAGE MUST BE STORED IN THE OVERHEAD BINS. IF YOUR LUGGAGE DOES NOT FIT, PLEASE SEE ONE OF THE FLIGHT ATTENDANTS."

Trudy turned to Gertie and grabbed her arm.

"If only Edna Mae had listened to us and moved into The Lillian, she'd still be with us."

Edna Mae. I'd heard that name. At least five times from my mother. *If* it was the same Edna Mae.

"Was she a friend of yours? Edna Mae?"

Gertie looked up, sighed, and touched her sister's wrist before answering.

"Edna Mae was a dear friend of ours. Generous and thoughtful. Also independent and stubborn. Not the best housekeeper either. Trudy and I tried to talk her into selling that place of hers and moving into The Lillian with us, but she'd have no part of it. Said The Lillian was for old people. Well, at her age she was no spring chicken either. Don't you agree, Trudy?"

Her sister gave a quick nod and continued with the saga.

"You got that right, Gertie. And her family tried and tried to talk her into moving out of her house. Edna was as blind as a newborn dormouse and was always bumping into things. Anyway, she fell in her own driveway, broke her hip, and died in the hospital shortly after that. Pneumonia."

It had to be the same Edna Mae. How many fall-in-your-driveway-break-a-hip-die-of-pneumonia Edna Mae's were there? And yet, oddly enough, no mention whatsoever about *The Twelfth Arrondissement*'s snappy little book curse.

Told you, Mom. This is a bunch of hooey.

"I'm sorry about your friend. That must have been awful."

"Awful and avoidable. That's why I'm glad we made the right decision to move."

The overhead speaker came on again.

"LADIES AND GENTLEMEN, WE WILL BE TAKING OFF IN A MATTER OF MINUTES. PLEASE TURN OFF YOUR CELL PHONES AND LAP DEVICES UNTIL WE ARE IN THE AIR. FASTEN YOUR SEAT-BELTS AND ENJOY OUR ON-SCREEN SAFETY VIDEO."

"I miss real people standing in front of us and talking," Gertie whispered. "Anyway, I intend to shut my eyes and get some sleep. Trudy will probably be doing the same thing. That wedding wore us out."

By the time the video had ended and the plane was speeding down the runway for take-off, Gertie and Trudy had closed their eyes.

The flight was too short for a movie, and it was just as well. The screens were always obscured by the light coming in from the windows, and the earplugs were painful. I took out my iPad, selected airplane mode, and started to tap a news App when I realized I had recently installed an App for Kindle but never down-loaded anything.

I'm not afraid of a silly little curse, am I?

I looked up *The Twelfth Arrondissement,* paid the $2.99 with my credit card, and waited for a second while it loaded. For a book that purportedly housed a curse, at least according to my mother, the cover was fairly innocuous. It was a lovely picture of a park with trees, grass, and a small bridge, not unlike Sibley Park near my house.

I wonder how many bodies they've uncovered there. . . .

Bracing myself for something straight out of Edgar Allan Poe, I slid through each page with trep-idation, expecting something horrible to jump out at me, but that never happened. Instead, I found myself immersed in some sort of tragic romance.

For a self-published book, it wasn't bad. No glaring grammatical errors and a solid plot with believable characters. I couldn't, for the life of me, understand what this book had to do with four curious deaths.

By the time the plane had started its descent into Sky Harbor Airport, I was halfway through the book and still breathing. No sudden drop in air pressure, no one screaming, and no curse. I shut off the iPad and looked at the craggy mountain ranges that surrounded the valley. The downtown skyline got closer and closer until the plane made its final descent and taxied to the terminal.

"That was certainly a good nap," Gertie announced as the pilot jammed on the brakes, forcing enough air pressure into my ears to last the rest of the day.

"Yeah, it was a nice, smooth ride."

"Speaking of rides, would you like our chauffer to drop you off at your mother's house? It's no trouble. Really."

"Thank you. That's so sweet of you, but I've arranged for a rental car since I'll need it for my stay."

I offered to help Gertie and Trudy with their carry-on bags, but they had arranged for wheelchair service. As Gertie pointed out, "It's such a far walk from the terminal to the baggage claim, our legs would never hold up." She had a point. I, on the other hand, faced what seemed like countless miles of moving walkways until I finally reached the highlight of terminal three—its steep escalator ride to the ground floor that resembled a trek to the bottom of the Grand Canyon. The artwork was spectacular, making it feel as if I was really on a descent into the canyon. Of course the moment I stumbled forward and caught myself, I knew otherwise.

The rental car kiosks were directly across from the baggage claim, and I secured the keys to my subcompact in record time. A white Honda Fit. It was destined to give my mother a real fit once she tried to squeeze into it, but I wasn't about to spend a fortune on rental cars. Besides, we could always take her oversize sedan if it turned out to be a real problem.

As I pulled out of the parking garage, I was nearly blinded by the bright sunlight. My eyes were accustomed to Minnesota's gray skies and not bright blue ones. Phoenix was actually a valley surrounded on all four sides by mountain ranges. A few cacti were visible from the road, but it was mostly palm trees that gave the area its notable look. Palm trees that were planted by Californians, according to my mother, who's still griping about it.

"If they wanted the state to look like California, they should have stayed there."

I chuckled to myself as I followed the signs to I-17 North and joined the rush-hour traffic. My mother had won this battle. It took me forty-five minutes to get to Bell Road, a major street that spans the entire length of Phoenix. From there it was another twenty miles to the West Valley, which meant another forty-five minutes in traffic. At least there were lots of options for a quick meal. I settled on one of my favorite places—The Black Bear Diner. It resembled an old Adirondack cabin with its knotty pine walls and tables, and was about as far removed from Southwestern style as anything could get. No matter how many times I visited Arizona, it never disappointed me with its juicy burgers or mile-high stacks of multi-grain pancakes. Today was no exception. By the time I wiped the warm burger juice from my lips, I was ready to face the traffic again, hoping it would thin out. It didn't. It took me close to an hour to get into my mother's development, or "the compound," as the residents referred to it.

I should have expected as much. September was a golden time for road construction in Arizona and it seemed as if every intersection was getting a make-over. My mother lived on the farthest side of Sun City West, near U.S. Route 60. Behind her, it was still desert—no malls, no housing, just coyotes, javelinas, and killer sunsets.

The glare was piercing my eyes as I turned off the main street and headed toward her block. Her section of Sun City West was Phase III, built in the mid-1990s. Unlike Phases I and II that began in the seventies and eighties, her phase didn't have the air-conditioning units on the roofs of the ranch-style houses, nor the rows of giant palm trees and fake grass lawns on each street. Instead, the developer let her area retain the desert ambience that brought people here in the first place, and she had central air-conditioning. Prickly-pear cacti and saguaros stood out on the gravel lawns. Unfortunately, there was no escaping the ceramic coyotes with bandanas or the quails sporting bow ties that seemed to be everywhere. So much for style.

A quick right turn and the light intensified. It took me a second or two to realize it wasn't the sunset. It was the pulsating lights from the combination of a sheriff's car, a fire engine, and an ambulance.

My God! Is it at her house? Has something happened?

Before I could get any farther, a deputy signaled for me to make a left turn onto another street. My mother's block was closed. At least from this direction.

Thankfully, I knew the neighborhood well enough to swing around the block and approach my mom's house the other way. A small crowd of people had gathered on the sidewalk, but it was impossible to tell which house was the one in question. I pulled over and parked. It wasn't my imagination. The emergency vehicles were situated in the middle of the block, right where my mother's house stood.

No smoke. No burning smells.

My mind didn't rule out the myriad of other reasons why the response vehicles were stationed by her house. *Heart attack. Home invasion. Stroke . . .*

In a flash, I raced out of the car, slammed the door behind me, and ran toward the house. Someone was yelling something behind me, but I was too distraught to turn around. It was only when I was a few yards from the ambulance that I realized it wasn't my mother's house. It was the house directly across the street from her.

"Slow down, Phee! You're liable to have a stroke!" My mother's voice drowned out every other sound on the street.

She rushed toward me, the color of her hair intensified by the lights. It looked reddish blond, if there even was such a color. Unlike me, with the soft highlights from my ash-brown hair, my mother hadn't seen her natural hair color since she was thirteen and discovered peroxide.

"Mom!" I turned and gave her a hug as we stepped out of the road and back to the sidewalk. "What's going on? For a minute I thought it was your house!"

"The house is fine. I'm fine. For now."

She was quick to stress the "for now." "I don't know the details. I heard it from Herb Garrett, who lives next door to Jeanette. Poor Jeanette. You remember Jeanette Tomilson, don't you?"

"Oh dear. Your neighbor died."

"No, no, Jeanette's not dead. But it was a close call."

I didn't say a word.

"So, like I was saying, I got this straight from Herb. You met Herb once, didn't you? He's right over there with one of the deputy sheriffs."

In the dusk with the lights flashing, it was impossible to tell which one was Herb. Rather than ask, I nodded in agreement as my mother went on.

"Jeanette had just come back from shopping and put all of her groceries away. You know, you have to do that right away or things will melt. Then she sat down to watch a double episode of *Family Feud*. It's much funnier since Steve Harvey took over the show. After *Family Feud*, she turned on one of those stupid sitcoms and must have dozed off. Then, all of a sudden, her smoke detectors came on. Well, not the smoke detectors, the other ones—the carbon monoxide detectors. And good thing Jeanette has one of those home alarm systems, because it rang straight into the sheriff's office and they dispatched a car."

"So it was a gas leak?" I asked.

My mother shook her head. "No, not a gas leak. It was her car. That new KIA she bought. It was still running with the garage door closed."

"What? Who leaves a car running in a closed garage?" I was flabbergasted.

"Well, certainly not Jeanette. She swore up and down she'd turned the engine off."

"Maybe she got confused . . . forgetful. You know."

"Jeanette wasn't befuddled. For heaven's sake,

Phee, she's only fifty-five! It was attempted murder. That's what it was. Herb spoke to her just before the deputy sheriff arrived. She had to turn her car off in order to use the house key to unlock the door that goes into her pantry. The house key was on the same ring as the car key. Someone must have broken in from the side door of the garage."

"That still wouldn't explain how they got the keys to start the car," I said.

"Who cares how they did it. Don't you see? Someone was trying to kill her."

"Don't tell me . . ."

My mother's voice was slow and deliberate.

"Jeanette Tomilson is in my book club. And she's a fast reader."

Chapter 4

We walked inside my mom's house as the response teams finished up outside. The fire department had opened the windows in Jeanette's house to air out the place, while the onlookers stayed to watch.

"Do you want something to eat?" my mom asked as I rolled my carry-on into the front foyer. A small flash of brown fuzz scurried across the room and ducked under the couch.

"What was that? Did you get a cat? A dog? Since when?"

"Oh my goodness. I forgot to tell you, didn't I? That's Streetman. He's a long-haired miniature chiweenie."

"A what?"

"Chihuahua-Weiner dog. Recent rescue. The owner went into assisted living and no one would take him. He's only two years old but has more behavioral issues than a fifteen-year-old boy in reform school."

"Um, I don't think they have reform schools

anymore, but . . . what kind of issues? He doesn't
bite, does he? Or pee all over the place?"

"No, no. Nothing like that. He's a bit neurotic,
that's all. You'll see what I mean. Give him time and
he'll warm up to you. Just don't go sticking your
head under the couch."

"That's the last thing I feel like doing."

I glanced at the couch and slowly took in the rest
of the place. The house looked the same as the last
time I visited. No noticeable changes in a year—the
cozy living room with its comfy sectional and floral
chairs, the round oak kitchen table that faced the
street, and my mother's latest assortment of Southwestern tchotchkes. It was as if I had never left.

"So, yes or no? Want a bite to eat?"

"I grabbed a hamburger on the way here, but I
could use a cup of coffee."

"I can brew a new pot or reheat the leftover coffee
in the microwave."

"Reheating's fine. I'll get a cup. Want some, too?"

A few minutes later we were munching cookies
and drinking whatever brand my mother had picked
up on sale. Streetman ventured from his hiding
place and positioned himself in front of my mother,
who bent over to pet him.

"So, now do you believe me about the book
curse?" She popped a small butter cookie into her
mouth, but not before breaking off a piece for the
dog. That done, she adjusted the strand of pearls
that hung over her embroidered teal tunic. Even
sitting in her own home, my mother refused to look
sloppy. She would never resort to wearing a T-shirt or,
God forbid, jeans. Nope, Harriet Plunkett, all five
foot four of her, was from a different generation.

One that was still struggling with her daughter's casual style. I could swear she was eyeballing my graphic tee.

What the heck. It was a long plane flight and the days of wearing white gloves are over.

"Like I told you before, Mom, I think these are all unrelated incidents. The fact the ladies are all reading that book has nothing to do with it."

"Then what about the e-mails we got?"

I had to admit, that part was baffling. Even Nate Williams felt the same way. We spoke about it briefly the day before I flew out west, and I could recall every word of our conversation.

"Call it whatever you want, kiddo, but sending an e-mail like that is harassment. If you can find out who sent it, you'll know if it was a prank or if someone had darker motives."

"And how, exactly, am I supposed to do that, Nate?"

"Same thing I told you a few days ago. Snoop around. Ask questions of the neighbors and friends of each of the victims. Think of it like filling in the edges of a jigsaw puzzle."

"What about the two ladies who died in the hospital? The HIPAA laws will never let me talk with hospital staff."

"Staff? No. But you can ask other patients and visitors."

"I simply don't have the inclination for this. I wouldn't know where to begin."

"It's no different from tracking down a bill that some police officer left on your desk with no name or information."

"Phee! Phee, are you listening to me?" My mother's

voice was like a razor. "I've been speaking for five minutes and you haven't said a word."

"Sorry, Mom. I must be tired. I'll go unpack my stuff in the guest room. Everything's still in the same place, isn't it?"

"Uh-huh. The only thing I changed was that awful pullout couch in my sewing room. I bought a daybed in case you ever visit with a gentleman friend."

"If I ever have a *gentleman friend*, I don't think he'd be sleeping in the daybed."

My mother shot me a dirty look but didn't press it, and I quickly changed the subject. Talking about my love life, or lack of it since a miserable divorce nineteen years ago, always made me uncomfortable.

"Give me a few minutes to freshen up and unwind; then we can talk about this so-called investigation you want me to conduct."

By the time I had unpacked and washed up, my mother was sitting at the kitchen table with a small notebook in front of her. Kinsey Millhone, Stephanie Plum, and Miss Marple would have been impressed.

"I have everything all written down for you, Phee. The names, addresses, and information about the ladies in my book club who were murdered, or nearly murdered in Jeanette's case."

"Mother, we don't know they were murdered."

"That's beside the point. As I was saying, I have everything organized for you. I wasn't sure if you wanted it alphabetically or by the date they died, so I have two versions. I hope you can read my handwriting."

I was half tempted to tell her an Excel spreadsheet would have been easier, but I decided against it.

"Um, gee, thanks, Mom."

"You can get started first thing tomorrow morning. Not that I'm telling you how to begin, but I do know Cindy Dolton takes her dog, Bundles, to the dog park every morning at six. She was Minnie Bendelson's roommate at the hospital before poor Minnie passed. I met Cindy when I stopped in to visit Minnie that first day and got an earful about Bundles and the dog park. Once they lift Streetman's suspension I'll be able to take him back there."

My eyes popped open.

"His suspension?"

"Apparently there were some issues with the previous owner. Streetman is neutered, mind you, but still has a propensity for amorous advances with female dogs. Some of their owners filed a complaint."

This dog is getting worse by the minute.

"I see."

"Anyway, I was sure Minnie would be out of the hospital in a day or so, and all of a sudden, she's dead. Like that. You can find out what Cindy knows when you meet her."

"Six a.m.? You said six a.m.? *That's* when she's going to be at the dog park?"

"You can't expect little Bundles to hold it past that hour, can you? Of course that's when you'll find her in the dog park. She'll be easy to spot. She has short gray hair, and Bundles is a small, curly-haired white dog. A poodle mix, I think."

"What about Edna Mae Langford? Oh, and before I forget, I met two ladies on the plan, twins actually, who were friends with Edna Mae. That is, if it's the same Edna Mae, and I'm pretty sure it is."

"Who were the twins?"

"Gertie and Trudy."

"I don't know them. Did they give you a last name?"

"No, but they said they live in The Lillian."

"The Lillian? They must be in their nineties."

"Um, yeah. I think they said ninety-four. Uh, is that the place people go for . . . um . . . their final decade?"

My mother's mouth literally fell open.

"I wouldn't quite put it so bluntly, but it's *the* place to go when you want to live the remainder of your life in opulence and comfort. It's styled after one of those fancy old European resorts. If it's still standing when I'm ninety, I'll consider it."

I gave her a nod. My idea of opulence and comfort was anything above a Motel 6. What have I been missing?

"Anyway, Gertie and Trudy told me they wanted Edna Mae to move to The Lillian."

"Edna Mae was too young. Still in her eighties."

Eighties. The pinnacle of youth. Must be the nineties are the cutoff for old age around here.

"So, uh, getting back to her death. She died in the hospital, too. Like Minnie. Of course, getting pneumonia is kind of common after breaking a hip. Strange, huh? And from what I remember about Edna Mae when I met her a few years ago, she used to be a heavy smoker. That probably didn't help. No book curse there, Mom. And it would be hard to make a case for foul play. Might as well strike that one off the list and save myself some time."

"With the pneumonia part, sure, but what about the accident itself?"

"Are you saying that someone caused her to fall in her own driveway? How? How could that have happened?"

"How? I'll tell you how. Edna went outside to get the mail and tripped over a small pile of those gravel rocks from her yard that wound up right in front of the mailbox."

"Mom, the birds are notorious for uprooting the gravel and small rocks. Every time I visit, I'm always sweeping the patio for you."

"Well, maybe it wasn't birds this time."

I sighed as I reached for her notebook.

"If I'm going to get started before six in the morning, this is going to be an early night for me. Let me see the rest of your list."

I scanned the names and information. My mother had compiled more data than the IRS and DMV combined. Listed were names, friends, relatives, hobbies, and miscellaneous comments, such as "Refuses to use the utensils in a restaurant. Brings her own disposable plastic ones."

Undoubtedly, retirement had given my mother a new occupation—busybody. I made a mental note to keep working until I collapsed at my desk or was carted off on a gurney.

There was nothing out of the ordinary about anyone on the list. One retired teacher, two retired bookkeepers, and two retired homemakers. Typical occupations for that generation. I was about to close the notebook when my mother added one more sheet of paper.

"Oh, this almost slipped my mind. I didn't get a chance to add this information to the notebook. It's still on a piece of scrap paper."

"What is it?"

"A list of their spouses and what they do or *did* for a living."

I scanned that list quickly and again, no surprises, unless I considered the large X across one of the occupations to be unusual.

"You have a big X across the pastry chef, Mom. What does that mean? Is he deceased?"

"No, that's for Jeanette's ex-husband. They've been divorced for years. Told me she couldn't wait to go back to her maiden name—Tomilson—and didn't plan on changing it anytime soon. She's got a boyfriend in the area but keeps it very hush-hush. He might be married for all I know. That could be a motive, you know. I mean, if he was married and his wife tried to kill Jeanette."

"Even if that were true, Mom, I don't know how that could possibly relate to the other deaths. Never mind. I'll get started in the morning and see what I can do. Remember, I'm only going to be here for a little over a week."

"Then you'll need to work hard. I'm not going to get a night's sleep until I have answers."

"Well, I intend to get them. I'm exhausted."

Every bone in my body started to creak as I stood. I was about to say good night when I suddenly realized something. "Mom, how do you suppose the person who sent the e-mails got your addresses? Are they listed somewhere?"

"The library has a list for the book club. And they're listed in the different clubs that people belong to. Minnie Bendelson's was listed with the Doggie Park Friends Club, Marilyn Scutt's was listed with the Lady Putters and—"

"Okay, I get the idea. Good night, Mom."

"Good night, Phee. Oh, and one more thing. Be

quiet in the morning. Streetman likes to sleep late. Gets grouchy if you try to wake him."

That made two of us, but it never stopped my mother from waking me up at all sorts of ungodly hours. I'd only been there for a little while, but I could tell already that the master of the house was four-legged.

Chapter 5

In spite of the AC set at seventy-eight and the ceiling fan at full blast above my head, beads of sweat trickled down my neck as I nodded off. I must have been so exhausted from the flight yesterday, the preparation leading up to it, and the dramatic welcome on the street from the local fire department that I slept like a corpse. The alarm on my smartphone sent a jolt through my body as I sat up. It was five-fifteen. I wanted to give myself enough time to take a quick shower, grab something from the fridge, and get to the dog park by six in order to find Cindy Dolton and Bundles.

Doesn't my mother keep anything decent in her fridge?

All I could find was some cottage cheese and milk. Suddenly, I remembered an earlier conversation with her.

"Who cooks? We all go out to eat."

That's wonderful, Mom. But this is breakfast. At an ungodly hour.

I'd have to look for a Starbucks or McDonald's if I

wanted a cup of coffee. Maybe later. I rinsed off in record time and headed out the door, careful not to make a sound. Last thing I needed was a grouchy Streetman.

With the sun rising in the east, I found myself squinting behind the wheel. Yep. My luck. I had to drive east into the sunrise to get to the dog park. It was adjacent to the tennis courts and less than a ten-minute drive. Ten minutes wondering if my vision would ever return to normal. Was this what it felt like to be snow-blind? I'd need to pick up some heavy-duty sunglasses if I planned on lasting the entire week.

At precisely one minute past six, according to the digital clock in my rental car, I had reached the dog park. *Gray-haired woman, small, white curly-haired dog.* At least nine or ten people milled about as an animated pack of small dogs ran all over the place. Small white dogs.

Great, Mom. All the dogs are small and white.

I unlatched the gate and stepped inside, making sure nothing on four legs would escape. *And yet another surprise. All of the women here have gray hair!* There were only two men in the park, and they were talking to each other. I approached them and asked if they knew who Cindy Dolton was. *And please do not tell me she has gray hair and a small white dog.*

"She's the lady over by the fence, near the large garbage cans," one of the men said.

I thanked him and walked over to her before she decided to join the other ladies who were seated on the benches or standing underneath one of the trees.

"Excuse me, are you Cindy Dolton?"

She eyed me as if I was about to serve her with a subpoena.

"Don't tell me you're from the Recreation Department. If it's about that incident last week with the Schnauzer, I want you to know it wasn't Bundles's fault. That dog started it by sniffing around Bundles's rear. Some dogs don't like having their butt sniffed."

"No, I suppose not. Don't worry. I'm not with the rec department. I wanted to speak with you about your roommate from the hospital, Minnie Bendelson."

Her demeanor changed immediately. "Oh dear. Are you a relative? It was so awful. That poor woman. So sweet. You know, I was in for chest pains following the gallbladder operation I had a few months before. Turned out it was just scar tissue. Well, anyway, they brought Minnie in because she was having chest pains, too, but not exactly like mine."

My God! How does Nate Williams stand this?

"Uh-huh," I muttered as she continued.

"Anyway, they ran some tests and she was starting to feel better even before the results came in and then BOOM! All of a sudden, she's dead. Talking to me one minute about her chicken casserole recipe and gasping her last breath the next. I'm still not over the shock."

"Was she doing anything else besides talking to you?" I asked.

Cindy Dolton looked at me as if I had lost my senses. "What do you mean? What else could she be doing? She was in a hospital bed."

"Was she drinking anything? Eating anything?"

"Now that you mention it, she'd just taken a bite

out of her salad. It was some sort of Asian chicken salad. You know, the food has gotten much better at the hospital. It used to be so bland. Now they have all sorts of salads, hummus, and dishes with names on them I can't pronounce. I buzzed the nurse immediately when Minnie couldn't breathe, but it was too late. They said she must have had a heart attack."

"What about an autopsy? Did they perform one?"

"Sweetie, at our age, unless the family requests it, they don't. Said she died from heart failure. I am so, so sorry for your loss."

"Um, actually, I'm Harriet Plunkett's daughter. You met her in the hospital. She asked me to look into Minnie's passing because it seemed . . . well . . . sudden, and Minnie was so liked. Anyway, I hope you and Bundles have a great day."

Just then, the doggie gate flew open and three Dachshunds charged inside. Cindy Dolton stood between them and Bundles like an armed guard in front of a vault. I took the opportunity to make a dash for my car and headed straight out of the parking lot toward the nearest coffee shop. I needed to jot down two questions once I got there. In my mind, they were already numbered.

1. Did Minnie Bendelson have any food allergies?
2. What ingredients were in that Asian salad?

If I could prove she was poisoned intentionally, then this was no book curse. It was an excuse for someone to commit murder.

Luckily, I didn't have to drive too far. Sunsational Coffee was wedged between a nail salon and a beauty parlor, in walking distance from the dog park. A chalkboard next to the counter listed the daily specials. Too bad I wasn't a fan of hazelnut; it was 50% off. Maybe other people didn't like it either. I opted for my usual—regular coffee and cream, no sugar.

After the first few sips, I began to feel more like myself. Now what? How was I ever going to find out what ingredients were in Minnie's salad? As far as food allergies were concerned, my mother should already have that information.

Unlike Mankato, Minnesota, where coffee shops didn't start to fill up until eight in the morning, this one was already crowded. Apparently there were lots of early risers in Sun City West. I found a small table adjacent to the doorway and sat down carefully, making sure not to spill the hot coffee all over the place. I glanced at my mother's notes again, trying to decide what to do next. The library seemed like a logical choice, but it didn't open for another hour. I reached into my bag and took out my iPad. Might as well put the time to good use and plod on with *The Twelfth Arrondissement*.

Okay, so the wealthy landlord found out his son was having an affair with the man's former mistress. It still didn't explain why someone murdered the family governess. *Not my problem! It's just a book. I have real murders to solve. Oh my gosh, am I listening to myself? I don't even know if these are murders. Get a grip.*

I was hoping there might be something in the plot, or maybe the setting, that would link to the unexplained deaths, but that was stretching it. I knew that the book had nothing to do with the sudden passing of four ladies and a near-death experience for the fifth. Still, I kept on reading, getting up once for a refill.

As I started to head back to my spot by the door, someone tapped me on the elbow and I jumped.

"Whoa! I must be losing my touch. You're Harriet Plunkett's daughter. Sophie, right? We met a few years ago when you and your daughter were visiting. Cute little thing. I'm Herb Garrett. I live across the street from your mother."

The stout, balding man standing in front of me looked vaguely familiar.

"That must have been quite a few years ago," I said. "The cute little thing graduated from college and is teaching."

"No kidding. What about you? Are you married?"

Is this guy going to make a pass?

"Used to be. I gave it up for Lent."

"Well, anyway, you sure picked a hot time to visit your mother. They won't turn the oven off around here until October."

"Yeah, well, I had some vacation days coming and thought I'd see my mom. I wasn't prepared for that dramatic scene on the street last night. Does that kind of thing happen often?"

"Emergency responses? Yeah, all the time. People fall. People have heart attacks. Lucky the hospital is close by."

"No, I mean the car left running in the garage. My mother told me that's what happened."

"Once in a while that kind of thing happens. Got a lot of old coots around here who are so scattered they forget one thing from the next. Usually it's food left on the stove or someone taking something out of the oven and forgetting to turn the oven off. But Jeanette's not like that. She's kind of young, if you know what I mean, and she's as sharp as a tack. No . . . if you ask me, there's something fishy about this. Boy, it's a good thing she has an alarm system for the house. Well, I'm headed to the bocce court. Nice talking to you, Sophie."

"You can call me Phee. Everyone else does."

"Nice yacking with you, Phee. Enjoy your visit and keep cool."

Herb headed out of the coffee shop with a large drink, pausing to wave at a few people. I returned to my seat and kept reading, waiting for the library to open.

When I finally exited the coffee shop, the wall of heat hit me as if someone were pushing me straight into an oven. I couldn't get to the car fast enough. I'd always visited during the holidays in December or April, never in late summer. In the thirty seconds it took me to get into the car, I realized one thing— no wonder people were up and about at six in the morning. Anything after eight was at your own risk.

The sun was brutal. I looked around the car for anything I could throw over the steering wheel so I wouldn't get scalded when I returned from the library. Thankfully I'd left a lightweight sweater on the passenger seat and immediately tossed it over the wheel as I opened the door. Staring straight ahead, the library's tall, stucco tower with its stylized clock came into view. Westminster Chimes, belting out the hour, seemed out of place, given the drab beige structure that housed the clock face. I shrugged and started to walk toward the building.

The library was only a few yards from my parking

spot, but the heat made it feel as if I were at the other end of the earth. Once inside the sliding glass doors, I had to stop and catch my breath before asking one of the volunteers at the counter for the librarian.

"I'll see if Miss Morin is at her desk," was the reply as a slender woman in her late sixties or early seventies started for the hallway.

In the meantime, I looked over the brochures on the counter listing activities, book talks, and speakers.

"Can I help you?" came a soft voice from behind me. I turned quickly, fixing my eyes on her name tag: GRETCHEN MORIN, LIBRARIAN. The woman appeared to be tall, in her mid-forties, with shoulder-length blond hair that was starting to reveal its darker roots. Wearing khaki slacks and a white tailored shirt, she looked more like a model for L.L. Bean than a librarian in a senior citizen community.

"Yes." I tried to keep my voice low as well. "I'm visiting here and heard about your book club. Since a group of us are starting one back in Minnesota, I was hoping you could give me some pointers about book selections."

"Book selections? That's usually up to the members of the club."

"Won't that be difficult if each person wants the club to read a particular book? I heard you had a solution for that."

"Let's move over to the table near the media area. We won't be in the way as patrons check out their selections."

I followed Gretchen Morin and sat at the wooden, rectangular table.

"I'd love to know how your library handles matters like that. You see, it will be a new club for my library, and I'd hate to have it get off on the wrong start if people are disappointed or disgruntled because their books weren't chosen for discussion."

Unbelievable. I can't believe what's coming out of my mouth. And I can't believe how smoothly it's coming out. Not bad for information-gathering.

If Gretchen Morin thought I was faking it, she didn't let on. "There are so many books out there . . . best-sellers . . . debut novels . . . not to mention the different genres. It would be impossible to please everyone. Sometimes, unilateral decisions are best."

"I understand." I leaned in closer so my voice wouldn't be too loud. "So, you make all the decisions about the books that are selected?"

"Me? Of course not. That's not what I meant. At the start of the year, each person in the book club offers a title for consideration. Twelve books are chosen randomly, with each one assigned to a different month. I compile the information and type the list for distribution. Then I make sure our library has at least three or four of those titles on our shelves."

"Chosen randomly?"

"Yes, the titles are written down on slips of paper and placed in a small index box on the main counter. I then draw the first twelve entries. That simple."

"And there are never any changes?"

"Well, yes. Once in a while when it comes to duplicate authors. The book club agreed that only one author per year would be selected. I mean, no matter how exciting Stephen King is, or how intriguing J. A. Jance is, the readers in the club want exposure to other authors."

"Is there any way of knowing who recommended a specific book?" I asked.

"No, it's done anonymously. That's because a few years back, when certain club members didn't like a book the group was reading, they made life miserable for the person who offered it for consideration."

"Really? That sounds so juvenile."

The librarian nodded in agreement. "Even adults can have their moments. Is there anything else I can help you with?"

"You said the file box is on the main counter. So then anyone could write down a title and submit it, even if they weren't in the club."

"I suppose that's true, but to my knowledge, it has never been an issue. Who wants to recommend a book for reading if they aren't going to be part of the discussion?"

Maybe someone who figured out a way to create a stir and shift the focus of attention like magicians do.

She started to get up from the table.

"Are the books always best-sellers or novels written by known authors?"

Gretchen Morin paused as if I'd asked her to ignore the "state secrets privilege." I could tell by the look on her face she was uncomfortable.

Make a note of that.

"Not always. Club members sometimes select local authors or self-published authors who they've heard about from the Internet."

"I see. Well, thank you so much, Miss Morin. You've been very helpful, and I'm looking forward to sharing your insights with our club once I get home."

"It's all part of my job. What did you say your name was?"

I told her the truth.

"It's Sophie. Sophie Kimball."

"Nice to make your acquaintance, Sophie Kimball. Have a good day."

She marched back to the hallway. All business.

A single thought kept jabbing at me—If *The Twelfth Arrondissement* was so obscure, then how on earth did anyone find out about it?

At that point, I had two options: try to find out what was in that Asian salad that Minnie Bendelson ate, or take a look at the gravel in front of Edna Mae Langford's house. I opted for the gravel since I had a funny feeling about it. At least I wouldn't have to talk with anyone. It was hard creating scenarios at the drop of a hat. I don't recall Nancy Drew ever doing that. Or the Hardy Boys for that matter . . .

Chapter 6

The steering wheel still burned my fingers in spite of the sweater I'd tossed over the wheel. I made a note to pick up one of those windshield screens at the gas station after I checked out Edna Mae Langford's place. She lived a few blocks from the library, near one of the newer recreation centers. I figured I could scope out her property and make it back in time to grab lunch with my mother.

For some reason, my mother had become fixated about eating at a certain time. Our conversation about it still played out in my mind.

"I like to eat lunch between eleven forty-five and one so I can eat dinner at five. Five-thirty the latest."

"That seems so early for dinner, Mom."

"I don't like to go to sleep with heavy food in my stomach."

When I was growing up, dinners were flexible. Now I had to abide by my mother's new military schedule. That meant having me finish up my so-called sleuthing before noon.

I found Edna Mae's street without any trouble.

Pristine gravel lawns. Cookie-cutter stucco houses. I half expected Rod Serling to pop up and announce, "A quiet street in the middle of a senior living community . . ." He'd be the only one popping up.

A mail delivery truck approached slowly from the opposite side of the street. The driver waved as he slowed down in front of a mailbox with a large metal roadrunner affixed to the top. I waved back as I got out of the car. Other than the mail delivery truck, mine was the only vehicle on the block. Edna Mae's house was the second one from the corner and distinguished from the rest by the large mesquite tree, whose limbs overtook the front yard and sidewalk. I took advantage of whatever shade the tree offered and parked close to the curb. Like most of the yards in Sun City West, hers was covered with crushed granite. I looked at it carefully as the mail truck moved farther down the block.

I remembered how thrilled my father was when they first moved here and he didn't have to mow a lawn. Their only decision was the color and size of the granite. Apparently homeowners could select rock sizes ranging from four inches to fine particles like pea gravel. My mother's yard was somewhere between a half inch and dust. Now I was about to check out the suspicion I had about Edna's yard.

The mailbox paralleled the edge of the driveway and was just a few feet from the set-in garbage container. Only the container's lid was visible. The can itself was underground, a concept designed by the developers so that Sun City West would look aesthetically pleasing without unsightly garbage cans. Large pinkish rocks covered the area, only to be contained by a brick border that separated Edna's house from her neighbor's. I bent down and picked up one of the rocks. Heavy little sucker. I set it in the palm of my hand and used my fingertips from my free hand to move it. The rock wasn't going anywhere. My mother said Edna had slipped on some of the rocks scattered near the mailbox. Well, unless it was a vulture or an eagle, those chunks of rock weren't scattered there by any bird. Or a rabbit, for that matter.

It wasn't likely the stones were disturbed by a coyote either. I'd seen those animals on the move, and they didn't kick up rocks like bulls or cattle. Maybe my mother wasn't so nuts after all. I was beginning to think Edna Mae Langford slipped on those rocks because someone put them there. I stood for a second or two staring at her yard and wondering what kind of person would scatter stones in a driveway so that an elderly woman might fall. Someone interested in her money? Her property? Or worse yet, one of those disturbed individuals who always seem to make the headlines. *Naked man smashes pottery against house while listening to Italian opera.* I tried to get those images out of my mind as I walked back to the car.

In spite of being set on full blast, the car's air conditioner didn't provide me with much relief from the heat. I all but staggered into my mother's house a few minutes later, only to find she'd invited some friends to join us for lunch. For a would-be detective, I failed to notice the maroon Buick parked a few feet from her mailbox.

"There you are, Phee," my mother shouted from the kitchen. "I want you to meet Shirley Johnson and Lucinda Espinoza from the book club. They're joining us for lunch. Come on.

Sit down. And don't give Streetman any scraps. He's under the table. He has a delicate stomach, so I only feed him grain-free food."

And butter cookie crumbs.

I approached the two women, who looked up from the large platter of cold cuts, rolls, and containers of assorted deli salads my mother had placed on the kitchen table.

Shirley was a tall, impeccably dressed black woman who looked as if she'd be more comfortable dining with heads of state rather than with my mother. Lucinda, on the other hand, was short, stout, and haphazardly put together. Her glasses kept sliding off her round face, and her hair looked as if it were stuck in the eighties.

"Help yourselves, ladies," my mother said. "What can I get you to drink?"

As she poured glasses of juice or soda, I introduced myself and took one of her napkins to wipe off my forehead.

"So," Shirley said, "your mother was telling us you came to look into the book curse. Thank the good Lord I'm still on the waiting list for that damnable thing. Frankly, I'm not in such a hurry to read it."

As she reached for a Coke, I couldn't help but admire her gorgeous manicure. Deep burgundy and red colors showed off her dark skin. Instinctively, I folded my hands so she wouldn't notice the last manicure I had was weeks ago.

Lucinda jumped in before I could say anything. "That's a bunch of poppycock. I'm more than half-way through the book, and I'm still here. You know, it's an interesting story. I'm at the part where the mistress reveals she's really the governess's sister and—"

"I knew it!" I blurted out before I realized what I'd done.

"You're reading that book? That cursed book?" The pitch in my mother's voice could have broken stemware from a hundred feet. She was furious.

"Sophie Vera Kimball, how could you put yourself in this much danger?"

"For goodness sakes, it's not as if I'm jumping headfirst from a plane without a parachute, Mom."

"Bite your tongue. You still have a flight home."

"Honesty. I couldn't very well look into something if I didn't know what it was about. I downloaded the novel on my e-reader."

"And . . . ?" she asked.

"And what? I haven't finished it yet. I mean, it's not as if everyone was given a paper copy and then they all died from some mysterious poison that had been embedded into the ink. The book's available electronically as well as in print."

Lucinda gave Shirley a nudge and reached for the macaroni salad. "You see, Shirley, there's nothing to concern yourself about. Just a bunch of hooey."

I paused. Too long. They could probably read the expression on my face. No wonder I never played poker. "I wouldn't exactly say that. I have a hunch, based on what little I've found out so far, that, um . . . maybe, just maybe . . . some of these deaths, like Minnie Bendelson's from eating the chicken salad, might not have been accidental."

Lucinda's hands covered her mouth as she gasped.

"So much for 'hooey,'" Shirley added as she slowly pushed herself away from the table.

"More salad, anyone?" My mother tried to act nonchalant, but there was no turning back from my remark. The ladies glanced at the food and then at my mother before Lucinda spoke.

"My God, Harriet. We have no idea who prepared these salads, do we? And what about the pound cake?"

My mother didn't say a word but ate two slices, followed by some juice. It must have finally occurred to Lucinda Espinoza that no one was about to die of food poisoning. Not in my mother's kitchen, anyway. As my mother wiped the crumbs from her face, she muttered something about needing to "work it off" with a Jazzercise tape. Then she brought up the subject of Jeanette Tomilson's garage incident.

"Someone *had* to have broken in, taken the key off the wall in the laundry room, and started the car without Jeanette knowing."

I wasn't convinced. "How would they know she kept her keys on the wall in the laundry room, and how could they have broken in when there were no signs of anything being disturbed?"

"That's easy," Shirley said between sips of coffee. "Jeanette keeps a spare key under that plastic cactus of hers by the side door to the garage. It practically screams, 'Welcome, Burglars!' Anyone who knows her, who's worked for her, or has witnessed her locking herself out of the house knows they can get in."

Maybe that's what happened, but I thought it was a long shot. "I don't know, Shirley. That doesn't explain how they knew she kept her ring of keys in the laundry room."

"Maybe they didn't know. Maybe it was just a lucky break. Whoever snuck inside the garage might have been prepared to go snooping around for her handbag or something."

For a brief second, I envisioned Whoopi Goldberg in *Burglar* and stifled a laugh.

"But she would have heard them," I said as Lucinda looked up from her plate before breaking into the conversation.

"Not Jeanette. You don't know her, do you? She's got that stupid BlueRay thing stuck in her ear all the time. She'd never hear a thing until it was too late."

I tried not to laugh. "You mean Bluetooth?"

Lucinda went on. "BlueRay, Bluetooth, whatever. I swear we've all lost the art of conversation with human beings. All everyone does is hook themselves up to devices and gadgets all day long. That's why I enjoy our book club so much. Gives us the chance to talk face-to-face. But now, with everyone dropping off like flies, there'll be no book club left. We can all post a message on that Face page!"

I wasn't sure if Lucinda's short tirade was for my benefit or if she was really serious. Judging from the expression on Shirley's face, she wasn't so sure either.

"What I'd like to know is . . . how Edna Mae tripped over those rocks near the mailbox. She should have seen them."

My mother started to say something, but Lucinda cut her off. "Oh, for heaven's sake, ladies. Edna Mae was blind as a bat without her glasses. And she was always misplacing them. That's why she had all those cheap reading glasses lying around her house. As long as she didn't drive anywhere, the rest of us in Sun City West were safe. She probably walked out of the house without her driving glasses and didn't see the rocks. I kept telling her to get bifocals, but she was so stubborn. Said they made her look old."

It was a no-brainer. Everyone whom Edna Mae came in

contact with knew about her vision problems. Heck, even Gertie and Trudy from The Lillian mentioned it. It wouldn't be too difficult for someone to have swung by Edna Mae's house unnoticed and uproot some rocks near the mailbox. After all, no one saw me there today. My mind clicked into action while Lucinda continued to speak. Those two book clubbers were a veritable goldmine of information, and I had to make the most of it.

"I don't know how you stand this heat"—I turned to Shirley—"but this afternoon I plan to take a swim in one of the pools. Do they all have a problem with bees? I don't want to get stung like that other lady from your group."

"Oh, you mean Thelmalee Kirkson. Lordy, what an awful thing. So unexpected. You know, she always carried one of those EpiPens with her. Guess she couldn't get to it fast enough."

"Do you know which pool that was?"

"I think it was at the large rec center across from the dog park," Shirley continued. "Isn't that what you've heard, Harriet?"

My mother nodded in agreement as she reached for Lucinda's cup. Yep, Harriet Plunkett was known to clear a table while people still had food in their mouths. As a kid, I learned to eat with one hand holding on to the plate and the other refusing to part with whatever utensil I happened to be holding.

Concerned the conversation would end too soon, before I had a chance to ask more questions, I stood and grabbed my mother by the elbow.

"Sit down and relax, Mom. I'll help you with this later."

Unfortunately, my tactic had the opposite result.

Shirley and Lucinda both started to stand. I held out the plate of pound cake so it was eye level with Lucinda.

"Are you sure you don't want to stay for another piece?"

I could tell she was tempted, but it appeared as if the Buick belonged to Shirley and Lucinda would lose her ride home.

"Thank you, but Shirley and I have got to get going. Even though she's a retired milliner, she agreed to design a hat for my neighbor and we're heading over there now. Well, Shirley is. I don't need to be there while Irma fusses over colors and materials. Anyway, it was very nice meeting you. Call me if you find out anything about the book. Your mother has my number. I can't just put the book down and walk away. That would be like leaving my laundry in the washer because I was scared to use the dryer. Curse or no curse."

"Not a curse," I said. "More like an opportunity. Do either of you know how that rumor got around about the book being cursed?"

They all shook their heads. What followed would have made Agatha Christie shudder. Everyone spoke at once as if my mother's kitchen had become the Tower of Babel.

"Louise Munson heard it was cursed from Marianne Grotter."

"No, it was Marianne who heard it from Jeanette in the first place."

"Not Jeanette. She was clueless. I think the librarian thought it was cursed."

"No, it wasn't the librarian. It was that guy who's always doing the crossword puzzles."

"When I found out about Marilyn Scutt, that's when it was mentioned."

"No, they thought it was cursed way before that."

Names, places, and accusations flew around the room like confetti during a New Year's Eve celebration and lingered by the front door as Shirley and Lucinda headed out. I turned to my mother and shrugged. "Like I said before, not a curse, more like an opportunity."

Chapter 7

"So, now what are you going to do?" my mother asked as I watched Shirley execute the most complicated, bizarre K-turn to go down the street.

"I'm going to listen to my own advice and go for a swim. It's like nine hundred degrees here. Lucky my brain hasn't melted. By the way, thanks for getting me the visitor's card."

"Let me guess. You're going to the same pool Thelmalee was at when she got stung."

"You asked me to investigate, so I'm investigating. It's the pool or a visit to the hospital's nutritionist to see if I can get the recipe for their Asian chicken salad."

"You're stopping everything to get a chicken recipe?"

"The lady in the dog park said it was the last thing Minnie Bendelson ate. Maybe she died from a food allergy to one of the ingredients instead of passing away from a heart attack. They didn't perform an autopsy. I don't suppose you'd know if she had any food allergies, would you?" *Since you seem to have everything else on record.*

"Hmm, she might have. I'll call around and see what I can find out."

"Good. Meantime, I'm headed for the pool. Just to be on the safe side, do you have any bug repellent?"

"Check the pantry near the laundry room. And be careful at that pool, especially since—"

"I know. I know. Since I started reading that book. Speaking of which, when did *you* get the idea it might be cursed?"

"When Marilyn Scutt was run down in her golf cart. That book was one of the few recognizable things they found at the scene of the accident."

I didn't wait around for a complete description of the accident scene. I grabbed a towel, my swimsuit, and a few miscellaneous pool items before heading for the door as fast as I could, promising my mother I'd be back by five for dinner. *Lighten up, Harriet Plunkett, even the military makes exceptions when you're out on maneuvers.*

Expecting the pool to be packed by early afternoon, I resigned myself to the fact I'd have to park a good distance from the entrance. I was wrong. There were only a handful of golf carts and eight or nine cars in front of the large stucco structure that was part of the recreation center complex. The other buildings included a fitness center, bowling alley, and social hall. An enormous outdoor area for miniature golf and bocce ball was also included in the complex and bordered one of the golf courses. I nabbed a great parking spot and was relieved I could walk the distance without keeling over in the heat.

As I approached the gate to the pool, a large man in swim trunks that were at least two sizes too small was having a heated discussion with the monitor.

"I'm telling you, you guys need to enforce the rules around here. It says, NO FOOD. NO DRINKS. Well, I've got news for you—sugary snacks and candy are FOOD, and all those kids are dropping crumbs and crap all over the place. No wonder we have so many bees all of a sudden. If you guys were doing your job, that lady might not have gotten stung and wouldn't have died last week."

My ears perked up as soon as he mentioned bees, that lady, and death.

"That must have been awful." I handed the monitor my visitor's card. "Are there lots of bees milling around now?"

"There will be," the heavyset man replied, "if they don't enforce a strict NO FOOD policy."

The monitor turned his attention to me with a look that said, "I can't wait for my shift to end." Then he said, "You don't have to worry. We've sprayed the place. It was an anomaly, all those bees."

I thanked him, nodded to the other man, and walked inside the courtyard in order to find a spot for my bag and towel. The glaring sunlight stung my eyes and there was absolutely no shade, not even an awning. Blue and white lounge chairs surrounded the pool, some with small tables next to them. Even the bank of mesquite trees a few yards from the water didn't seem to be providing any relief from the sun.

I wanted desperately to find out where Thelmalee Kirkson had been sitting on the day of the incident but wasn't sure how to go about it. Finally, I decided to stash my things near a group of women and bring up the topic as subtly as I could. If they didn't know anything, they might know someone who had been there.

"Wow, I thought it would be more crowded on a blistering day like this," I said as I arranged my towel on the lounge chair.

"Actually, the worst of the heat is gone," one of them replied. "Most people usually swim in the morning or walk laps in the evening so they can say they got their exercise. We sunbathers pile on the sunblock and soak it all in during the afternoon. But you've got to be smart about it—wide hats, big sunglasses."

"Yeah," said another lady, "too bad we can't bring our own margaritas."

"You probably could, Peg. No one complains about the passel of kids that arrive with their grand-parents and enough snacks to feed an army," another lady replied.

As tempted as I was to tell them about the conver-sation I overheard at the gate, I decided not to get involved with pool issues and stick to my original plan of trying to find out about the incident with Thelmalee Kirkson.

"I heard you have to watch out for bees around here."

A woman with a wide-brimmed sunhat and a striped towel draped over her looked up from the book she was reading.

"Usually we don't have many bees. They mill around by the bushes behind the pool, but last week, well . . . it was one of those freak things anyway."

"What was?" I tried to sound surprised.

"A woman got stung, had a reaction, and died. Who would have ever imagined that?"

"Yes," the woman named Peg added, "especially since she came here every day at the same time to sunbathe. Like clockwork. Day after day. Year after year. And then, without warning—a bee sting and death. It just goes to show that when your number is up, it's up."

"Was she part of your group? I mean, did she sit with all of you?"

"No," Peg said. "See that spot over there by the far end near the showers? That's where she lounged. The place is wide open like the North Dakota Plains. No one wants to sit there now."

"When the snowbirds arrive next month, her chair and all the other ones will be taken," someone said as I glanced at the corner where Thelmalee spent her final moments. Sure enough, there were lots of bushes behind the fence.

By now I was dripping with sweat and the water looked inviting. Across from where I was standing, a large sign read, BATHERS MUST SHOWER BEFORE ENTERING THE POOL. I muttered something about swimming and then headed for a quick shower and a jump into the water. Thelmalee's chair was across from the showers, with a direct view of the pool entrance. I walked quickly to rinse off, certain everyone was looking at me. Didn't want to break any rules. I glanced back at the ladies and they had all returned to their reading or sunbathing. No need for alarm. No one was the least bit interested in what I was doing, and that was a good thing. I leaned over the fence to see if I could spot anything unusual by the bushes. At first glance I didn't see a thing, but

when I looked closer, I spied a small piece of paper
under the bush. Probably just some litter that blew in
from the wind. I decided to enjoy my swim and then
take a closer look from the outside when I was done.

Move over, Miss Marple!

The water felt tepid but still did a decent job of
cooling me off. It was four-thirty when I changed
back into street clothes and left the gated area. The
group of women had already gone, but new arrivals
were trickling in. I skirted around the back of the
building to the bushes behind Thelmalee's chair,
where I swore I'd seen that piece of paper.

Making myself as inconspicuous as possible, I kept
my head down and stared at the ground. My hunch
was right. There was something unusual going on.
The ground below the bushes had been hollowed
out as if someone poured something into the cavity.
Not your usual method for pesticide. Ant stuff, which
we buy by the gallon in Minnesota, is sprinkled directly on the ground and liquid spray is just that—a
liquid. So, what was this? I bent down to find the
piece of litter that had caught my eye when I was
at the pool. Sure enough, I found it. It was a small
cardboard edge from a box, and I immediately recognized it when I turned it over.

It was granulated sugar and not only that, it was
the same brand I buy with the blue and white cane
sugar logo on the box. This was no snack time treat
for anyone's grandkids. Someone had deliberately
poured the stuff into the shallow hole they made
under the bushes. An invitation for every bee in the
county to stop by.

As I pocketed the evidence, I had my suspicions
about Thelmalee's death. Her daily routine was

known to everyone who frequented the pool. It was
obvious she was reading *The Twelfth Arrondissement*.
The book was right out in the open for every passerby
and swimmer to see. Maybe someone knew about her
bee allergy and decided to scare her into believing
the book was cursed. By pouring that amount of
sugar behind the spot where she lounged, they could
practically guarantee she would be stung multiple
times. The question was, why?

Chapter 8

"So, did you figure anything out yet?" my mother asked as we waited for our pizza to arrive. We were seated in a small Italian restaurant a short distance from her house. Five p.m. sharp, so as not to wreak havoc on her schedule. I practically had to run every yellow light from the pool to my mother's house so we'd get to the restaurant "on time."

"No." I glanced at the tacky red and white vinyl checkered tablecloth. "In fact, I have more questions than answers, and everything seems to have tentacles. I find out one little bit of information, but it leads me in a zillion different directions. I haven't even been here a full day. I'm not Hercule Poirot. Besides, I didn't even begin to look into the golf cart accident."

"The sheriff's posse will have an accident report. And I can get you a copy of the newspaper article. Herb Garrett saves all his papers for the month before he recycles them. It'll be in one of them."

"I'll just do an Internet search. And, by the

way, why does Herb save all those papers? That's absolutely ridiculous."

My mother shrugged and reached for a breadstick. "Why does anyone do anything? People have all sorts of habits. It's what makes you comfortable and that's all there is to it."

The pizza arrived before we could discuss the matter any further. Probably a good thing. The place was filling up fast. The food had to be good. It certainly wasn't the ambience, unless you considered black and white blowup photos of 1950s Italy to be a real boon. I later found out it was "double seniors night." Twenty percent off the menu.

We were literally an arm's length from the nearest patrons. My mother was quick to point out some of them.

"That's Sylvia Watson in the corner."

"Book club member?"

"No, I met her at my dentist's office. Nice lady. Widowed. Children live in Seattle, if I remember correctly."

I glanced in the direction of Sylvia Watson, but my eyes caught a glimpse of someone else. It was Gretchen Morin, the librarian. She was a few tables from us having an animated conversation with a bald, middle-aged man with a wide jet-black mustache. He reminded me of one of those cartoon characters who were always on the wrong side of things. At the same table was another couple, a tall gentleman with salt and pepper hair and a lady who looked familiar, but I couldn't quite place her. I quickly turned away and stared at my plate, pretty certain Gretchen hadn't seen me. My mother and I had finished eating and there was no sense lingering.

Especially if it meant getting into a conversation with the librarian. I tapped the edge of the silver pizza tray.

"So, do you want to finish these last three slices or take them home?"

"We'll take them home with the breadsticks and sauce. It'll be tomorrow's lunch."

"Good idea. I'll go pay the check and meet you in the car while you wait for a takeout box."

Before she could respond, I left a tip and walked over to the register. My back was to Gretchen Morin, so there was little chance she'd see me. It wasn't as if I had anything to hide, but I didn't want her to connect me with my mother. Not yet anyway. I preferred to remain Sophie Kimball and not Harriet Plunkett's daughter while I was delving into any secrets behind *The Twelfth Arrondissement.*

My mother opened the passenger door of my rental car and plopped down on the seat, letting out a long, slow breath.

"What on earth was that all about? I haven't seen you rush out of a place since you were in junior high and didn't want to be seen with the family."

"Sorry about that. It's just the librarian was in there, and I didn't want to get caught up in any long conversations. I'm exhausted."

"Oh, I doubt you'd have a long conversation with her. It hasn't been the same since Barbara Schnell retired. Now there's a lady who could chew your ears off. She decided to move back to Oregon and live with her daughter."

Indeed, Harriet Plunkett, my mother, had become a plethora of information regarding the people who lived in Sun City West or set foot in the place, for that matter. I listened wordlessly as she went on about some of them, letting my mind drift in and out of attentiveness as we got closer to the house.

It wasn't until I pulled into the driveway that I spoke. "I know it's early, but if you don't mind, I'm going to take a cool shower and then see what I can find out about that golf cart accident. Does your computer have a password?"

"Yes, it's my name."

"Geez, Mom. You might as well print it on a sticky note and leave it on the monitor."

"I didn't want a password in the first place, but that computer technician insisted I type one in. So I did. One I wouldn't forget. Besides, it's not as if I'm harboring government secrets on the thing."

"What about your bank accounts?"

"I don't do any banking on the computer. I use it to play solitaire."

Unbelievable. A few-hundred-dollar piece of technology when a deck of cards would have sufficed.

"Okay, then. I'll catch you a bit later. I'll be glued to your computer once I'm done showering."

As I let the cool shower water rush over my body, I began to relax. Then, all of sudden, something hit me and I snapped into overdrive. The lady sitting next to Gretchen Morin in the restaurant was one of the women I'd been talking with at the pool. I didn't recognize her at first, without the large sunhat. Suddenly, the tentacles were getting tangled.

That night, I dreamt I went back to the pool, only there was no one in sight. No monitor. No sunbathers. Nothing. I walked past the courtyard and as soon as I saw the water, a swarm of bees came at me. I woke up thrashing the pillow with one hand and waving my arm with the other. The plantation shutters didn't block out the bright sunlight, and it was as if someone was shining a flashlight in my eyes.

I trudged to the bathroom to splash cold water on my face in an effort to clear my foggy brain and I nearly stepped on Streetman. Apparently he had decided to plant himself between my bedroom door and the bathroom. He immediately scurried away when I bent down to pet him. Turning the doorknob to the bathroom, I heard my mother's voice.

"Are you up, Phee? Are you up, Phee? It's getting late."

Well, I am now. Who needs Westminster Chimes when you've got Harriet Plunkett.

"Yeah, Mom," I shouted. "I'm up."

"Good! It's about time. While you were sleeping, I walked the dog and drove over to that new Dunkin' Donuts. I got us some coffee. They're giving away free cups this week. It's a promotion."

"That's great. Terrific. Really. I'll be right there."

Grabbing the lightest weight shirt I'd brought, I slipped it over my head, put on a pair of shorts, and walked into the kitchen. Sure enough, two large Styrofoam cups were on the table, along with an assortment of donuts. I reached over to grab one when I felt something pawing at my leg.

"Isn't that cute? Streetman wants you to give him a piece of donut. You can give him a little morsel from one of the plain ones."

Really? I have to feed the dog a piece of donut first thing in the morning?

I tore off a tiny tidbit and held it out to him. It was gone in a nanosecond and so was the dog.

"See, Phee? What did I tell you? He's very well behaved for the most part."

"Who wouldn't be? He gets butter cookies and donuts. Anyway, thanks for the coffee and breakfast."

"It sounded like you were going to be on the computer this morning, and I didn't want you to waste any time."

Ah, the real reason for this sugary start to the morning— my mother wanted me to get on with my so-called investigation.

"And by the way, Phee, I called around this morning and guess what I found out?" She didn't stop to take a breath. "I found out Minnie Bendelson was allergic to finned fish. Finned fish. Of all things. You would have thought maybe peanuts since everyone seems to be allergic to that nowadays. Can't even have peanut butter in schools. Anyway, I don't think it was the Asian chicken salad that killed her. I mean, if she was allergic to peanut sauce or soy, that would make sense, but she wouldn't have ordered it with that kind of allergy. And they're very careful at the hospital. They keep records of those sorts of things. A million pieces of paper to fill out every time you see your doctor. I'm telling you, it could be that book curse."

I ignored her last remark and took a quick sip of the coffee.

"Finned fish? Like what? Tuna?"

"Tuna, halibut, I don't know. I guess any kind of a fish with a fin. Why?"

"Because white fish, like halibut and tuna, look

an awful lot like chicken. Maybe someone made a mistake in the hospital."

"I don't know how you'd ever find that out."

"Cindy Dolton might have an idea. Looks like an early dog park morning for me tomorrow. Meanwhile, I'm going to get started on that Internet search for Marilyn Scutt's accident. But before I do, I really should have the sequence of events. I can't believe I haven't already done that. I told you I'm not an investigator. I'm all over the place with this. Anyway, just tell me who died first, and I'll write it all down."

"Marilyn, then Minnie, then Edna, then—"

"Whoa. Slow down, Mom. I've got to write this down. Hold on. I've got a small datebook in my bag. I'll just use those empty pages in the back."

As I fumbled around for a pen, my mother repeated the names out loud as if it was a roll call for Arlington National Cemetery.

"Marilyn Scutt . . . Minnie Bendelson . . . Edna Mae Langford . . . Thelmalee Kirkson . . . Jeanette Tomilson . . ."

Then, as I was writing, she repeated the list again, only this time enunciating the word "deceased" after each of the names except Jeanette's.

"I know. I know. They're dead. Well, all but one."

"Good thing Jeanette's alarm system was working. A similar thing happened a few years ago to an elderly man who lived around the corner. He didn't replace the battery in that carbon monoxide and smoke detector of his, and fell asleep with one of the burners to his stove on. He didn't smell the natural gas and no alarm went off for the carbon monoxide exhaust. It was awful. When he didn't show up for his tee time the next day, someone sent a deputy sheriff to check. Course, by then, it was too late. Carbon monoxide poisoning. Or gas. Maybe both. I don't know why they don't manufacture stoves with alarms if you forget to turn the burner off all the way."

"They can't have alarms for everything. We'd be jumping out of our skin all the time," I said.

"I'd rather jump than be six feet under. And not that you asked, but I had the batteries in my smoke alarms replaced last year with those lithium ones. They're good for the next five years."

"That's wonderful. Now, getting back to your list. Are any of the families holding memorial services? That would be a great place to start an investigation."

"Edna Mae's family was having her body shipped back to Wisconsin, the last I knew. I haven't heard anything about Thelmalee. Minnie Bendelson's nephew had her cremated and buried almost immediately. No service. No celebration of life. No nothing. Just ashes and a quick burial. He was the only surviving relative, so I imagine he did what he could. So sad. So tragic. Unlike Thelmalee's troupe. That family's been all over her place scavenging anything they can get their hands on. Shirley and Lucinda were talking about it before you arrived for lunch yesterday."

"Hmm, I suppose families deal with these things differently. Did Thelmalee have a lot of money or valuables?"

"Not that I'm aware of. None of the book club ladies live extravagantly. They all seem to make ends meet, enjoy some dinners out, travel a bit. . . . Why?"

"Oh, nothing. Just wondering, that's all."

I started to get up from the table when I realized I'd forgotten to ask something important. Something even a novice detective wouldn't have overlooked. *So I won't get hired by Scotland Yard. Accounts receivable in Mankato, Minnesota, is just fine.*

"Mom, I know you gave me that list of the husbands, but all I did was glance at it. Tell me, are any of them still alive?"

"Only that rotten scoundrel of a husband Jeanette used to be married to. He's a snotty little pastry chef in Scottsdale."

"That's not a nice thing to say."

"Well, he's not a very nice man, from what Jeanette has shared with us."

"You don't think he could be responsible for any of this, do you?"

"What? And leave the East Valley? He wouldn't be caught dead this side of I-17!"

"Okay, I'll try to compile this information and get started researching Marilyn Scutt's accident. What are your plans for the day?"

"I have an appointment to get my nails done."

"Fine. I don't expect I'll be too long at the computer. If I'm not here when you get back, it means I've gone over to the bank to cash a check."

The strawberry frosted donut I was eating left me craving for another one. For some reason, once I passed forty it got harder to keep my figure. I was still determined. Last thing I needed was to find myself enrolling in Weight Watchers or TOPS. I looked away from the donuts and stared at the window. A beige SUV was backing out of Jeanette Tomilson's driveway.

"Is that the boyfriend, Mom? The beige car at Jeanette's place?"

My mother sprang from her seat and raced toward the window faster than Teddy Roosevelt charging San Juan Hill.

"I didn't get a good look. The car is down the block. It might have been her boyfriend. I don't know what kind of car he drives. It's awfully early in the morning, if you ask me."

"Her business is her business," I said.

"Then why did you point it out?"

"Strictly for investigative reasons. You concocted that idea about the boyfriend being married and his wife wanting to harm Jeanette. I figured I'd better take note of the car."

"Some note. All you found out was that it's beige."

"That's not all. It was an SUV."

"Aha. Now we're getting somewhere. A big beige car. The kind married men with kids drive around in. It's the boyfriend. It has to be. I'll bet he's married with teenagers. Was there a bicycle rack on the back? Those families are always toting around bikes."

"A bike rack? Where do you come up with this stuff? And once again, we don't know that she has a boyfriend."

"We don't know that she doesn't."

I did know one thing. I had to take a look at real tangible evidence and didn't want to waste time speculating about Jeanette's social life. I took the last sip of my coffee and tossed the Styrofoam cup in the trash.

"I've got to get started on that police report. When are you leaving for the nail salon?"

"In a few minutes. I've got to change my clothes

first. I don't want them to clash with my new nail color. I'm trying to decide between a fall bronze look or something in burnt sienna. Maybe I'll have them match it to the highlights in my hair. Anyway, I'd better get a move on."

"Don't worry about the kitchen. I'll wipe the table and straighten up."

I hadn't finished my sentence when I noticed my mom had already left the room. It wasn't until I was in the middle of reading the accident report when she shouted from the door leading into the garage that she was on her way out.

I yelled back, "Okay. Catch you later. Have fun!" and then turned my eyes back to the Maricopa County police report.

There was absolutely nothing suspicious about Marilyn Scutt's tragic death. She had just moved into the far left-hand lane of RH Johnson Boulevard in her golf cart when she was struck head-on by a car that was perpendicular in the intersection. The driver failed to see the median and instead of turning left into *his* left-hand lane, he turned into her lane. Apparently, the eighty-one-year-old man was from out of state and not familiar with the area. Or familiar with reading signs, for that matter. No alcohol. No drugs. No texting while driving. No book curse. Simple confusion. Simple confusion that resulted in death.

Of course, my mother and her friends would say the man's confusion was caused by the curse and not the fact he should have given up his license years ago. There was no sense pursuing this particular death as far as I was concerned. I had enough on my plate with my suspicions about what was in Minnie

Bendelson's salad. Not to mention what I'd seen at the pool and in Edna Mae Langford's driveway.

I felt as if I were up to my nose in clues and up to my ankles in mud. Mom had already returned from the nail salon by early afternoon. Burnt sienna. At this point, I was getting restless. The only exercise I'd had was moving my rear end back and forth in the computer chair and stretching my neck. Unless you counted shaking your head and muttering, "This is getting me nowhere."

As I glanced at the computer screen, I realized it was the same time yesterday when I had the conversation about Thelmalee with those ladies at the pool. Then, of all things, I saw one of them with the librarian at the Italian restaurant last night. What if they were in cahoots to commit murder? Shouldn't there be a motive?

Yeesh. My mother's bizarre scenario about the possible wife of Jeanette's boyfriend was starting to make more sense. Still, I couldn't dismiss the fact something unnerved me about the librarian. It went beyond the typical stereotype schoolmarm like Marian in *The Music Man*. No, Gretchen Morin was more Mrs. Danvers from Daphne du Murier's *Rebecca* than *Rebecca of Sunnybrook Farm*, blond hair notwithstanding. I had a bad feeling about this and needed to act on it.

"Mom, I'm heading over to the pool for a while. It's hot out, and I could use a swim."

"Now? In the middle of your investigation you're going to stop and go swimming?"

"I didn't want you to make a scene at the restaurant last night, but I didn't leave in a hurry because of the librarian. Not totally, anyway. The librarian was with three other people, and one of them looked familiar. I didn't realize who it was at the time. When I got in the shower before bed, it dawned on me. It was a woman who frequents the pool where Thelma-lee was stung. And that sting was no accident. That woman might know more than she was willing to say yesterday."

My mother's eyes lit up. "Good idea, Phee. Get her to talk. Maybe she's the wife of Jeanette's boyfriend."

"Mother, we don't even know who Jeanette's boy-friend is, let alone the remote possibility that some sunbather from the recreation center pool is his wife. If the guy even has a wife! I just thought the woman might have seen something suspicious around the time of the incident."

My mother draped a dishtowel over the sink and pulled up a chair. "Do you want me to go with you? Maybe we can both get her to talk."

The blood drained from my face. *Get her to talk?* More likely, it would be *get my mother to shut up.* I could just picture it—my mother going on and on about something until the woman in question was forced to dive into the water to get away from us.

"No, I can handle this. Besides, there's something else that I need you to do."

"What? What? Anything."

"Find out who Jeanette's boyfriend is. You once said there are no secrets in Sun City West. So . . . someone is bound to know."

After a brief pause, my mother stood as if she were watching a winning horse cross the finish line. A horse she had bet on.

"Herb Garrett! Her next-door neighbor. If Herb

doesn't know, then no one does. I've got to go look up his number."

I threw my swimsuit into a large tote bag, grabbed a towel, and headed out the door. The minimal traffic on the road didn't translate into a quick drive. I found myself muttering awful phrases under my breath like, "Move it, you ancient fossil" and "The sign says Stop, not Park." I blamed it on the heat. I swore it was affecting my brain and making me irritable and impatient.

Fifteen or so minutes later, I showed my visitor's pass to the monitor. It was a different man from the one on duty yesterday. This one was taller, younger, and incredibly tanned.

"You missed the excitement," he said as I walked inside the pool area.

"Oh no. Not another fatal bee sting."

"Nah, just a senior citizen who had to be escorted out by the sheriff's posse. Screaming something about a book curse. A book curse. Of all things. The guy had to be drunk or suffering from heatstroke. Honestly. What will they come up with next?"

"Yeah, that's something." I smiled to myself. I now had the perfect opener to a conversation I intended to have with the librarian's friend. All I needed to do was spot her wide-brimmed sunhat and go from there.

The group of women from the other day was considerably smaller but still lounging in the same area. I approached them as if I were the newest member of their clique.

"Hi! Nice to see all of you again. I really enjoyed that swim yesterday and came back for more. Heard

I just missed quite the scene a few minutes ago. What was that all about?"

By now I had placed my towel lengthwise on a lounge chair and started to sit down. My rear end barely touched the chair when one of the women explained.

"I only caught the tail end of it, but some guy walked over to a woman who was reading a book by the shallow end and all of sudden started yelling at her and wouldn't stop. The woman's gone now, and I don't blame her. That guy was something else. Waving his arms in the air and screaming about a cursed book. At one point he tried taking her book and throwing it into the water. That's when a few people stopped him and the monitor called for the sheriff."

"Have any of you ever seen that man before?" I asked.

The ladies looked up from their assorted devices, books, and magazines and shook their heads.

The woman kept on talking. "Men that age all look alike. Balding heads, sunglasses, and beer bellies."

"So, um . . . he was bald and not in the best physical shape?"

"That pretty much describes him." She adjusted her floral sunhat. "And do you know what else? I'll tell you what else. As the deputy was escorting that man out of here, the lunatic gave Peg the finger. The finger!"

A buxom woman with a white sunhat removed her dark glasses. "He didn't give me the finger, Joanne, his hands were waving all around."

"Actually," another one of the women said, "it looked more like he was trying to give you a thumbs-up."

Peg seemed to start getting irritated.

"Ladies, please. He didn't give me any fingers or thumbs. Let it go."

I changed the subject quickly and Peg looked relieved. "I don't suppose any of you ladies know what book that person was reading?"

"No, it happened at the other end of the pool," Joanne said. "The guy probably had one too many before he got here. And I still think he was flipping the bird, or whatever you call it, at Peg."

Before Peg had a chance to respond, I continued with my version of Twenty Questions. The woman who was with the librarian at the restaurant wasn't with the sunbathers today, and that was a bummer. Still, I wasn't about to give up. "Gee, I thought your whole crew from yesterday would be here. It's even hotter today."

Peg nodded. "Sandra and her sister, the redheads, had a luncheon somewhere, and I don't know why my sister-in-law, Josie, isn't here. She must have gotten tied up at the office. Too bad. She would have gotten a good laugh out of that guy screaming about the cursed book."

I did it, Mom. I found out who that lady with the librarian is—Josie. Josie something. The one without the red hair. And Peg from the pool is her sister-in-law.

"Oh." I tried to sound as innocent as I could. "I thought I saw a Josie Martindale signed up for the book talk at the library when I was in there. Is that her? Your sister-in-law?"

"No," Peg said. "My sister-in-law's Josie Nolan. She and my brother, Tom, are Nolan and Nolan Realty. And I'm Peg Nolan. Nothing to do with realty."

"Ah," I said. "Nice to meet you, Peg, and everyone

else, too. I'm Phee. Well, I'd better get into the water. Glad *that's* not cursed."

A few of the women chuckled, and I grinned as I made my way to the shallow end, grabbing the metal stairs as I walked down the steps into the water. A man and a woman were standing a few feet from me.

"Hi!" I said, using my cheeriest voice. "Did either of you notice what book that lady was reading when the man started screaming at her?"

"I didn't know she was reading a book," the man said.

The lady with him made some sort of chortling sound and poked him. "You don't notice anything, Harold. She was reading Shakespeare."

"Wow," I said. "That's pretty heavy for summer poolside reading."

"I'm pretty sure it was Shakespeare. I saw part of the title, *The Twelfth* . . . it had to be *The Twelfth Night*."

I felt like jumping up and down. If this were Vegas, I'd bet my entire stash she wasn't reading Shakespeare. No one reads Shakespeare in triple-digit weather at a pool. It had to be *The Twelfth Arrondissement*. The cursed book rumor was spreading faster than head lice in a kindergarten class.

Chapter 9

Still exhausted from the day before, my body reacted to the alarm clock going off by jolting me with one big, muscular spasm. I wanted desperately to turn over and go back to sleep when I remembered I had to be at the dog park by six to find Cindy Dolton again. Why couldn't she walk Bundles at nine like a reasonable person?

I had gotten the routine of stumbling into the bathroom down to a science and was out the door and on my way to the park before my mother and Streetman even got up. Herb Garrett had gone on the all-day bus to one of the casinos yesterday, so my mother couldn't find out about Jeanette's boyfriend from him. Not yet, anyway. She said she was lucky she tracked Herb's whereabouts down from the mailman, who happened to run into Herb the day before. At least it would give my mother something to do this morning while I picked Cindy Dolton's brain for more information about Minnie Bendelson's Asian chicken salad.

The dog park was a veritable hotbed of activity

when I arrived. At least nine or ten small, mostly white dogs were running all over the place and peeing on the fence. Some apparently didn't bother to hold it before getting into the place, and I had to watch for puddles by the concrete entrance.

Cindy Dolton was seated on one of the benches underneath a palm tree. Suddenly, the man she was speaking with made a mad dash to clean up after his dog, and I used the opportunity to take his place.

"Hi! We spoke the other day and—"

"Yes, of course. You're Harriet Plunkett's daughter."

I nodded as I moved myself out of range from a small black dog that was about to use my leg as a fire hydrant. Cindy looked down at her feet, presumably to make sure the dog hadn't gotten to her. Satisfied she wouldn't have to wash her clothing, she continued to speak.

"You know, sweetie, I felt so badly about that poor woman's death. And it must have been quite a shock for her nephew."

"Her nephew?"

Now we're getting somewhere.

"He was the one who brought in her tray with the salad. Always so helpful. He was on his way to visit her when the kitchen delivery staff was making its rounds. Gave them a hand by bringing in her tray since he was going that way anyhow."

I tried to think this through before I spoke. It was crucial. "You mean he walked over to her bed and plunked the tray on her bedside table?"

"Not at first. He put the tray on the dressing table by the door, behind the screen. Came over, gave his aunt a kiss on the cheek, then went to get the tray. Said he only popped in for a minute and had to leave. Work, I imagine. Said he'd be back in the evening to visit and that he hoped she enjoyed her lunch. So sad. She died minutes later. After he had gone."

Cindy let out a long sigh while I absorbed everything she had said. If this nephew of Minnie's had indeed found a way to put a small bit of tuna or other whitefish into her salad, how did he know she'd be eating salad in the first place? I bit my lip as Cindy yelled out something to Bundles about not eating stuff from the ground. Not that Bundles bothered to listen.

"Did the nephew ever tell you his name?"

"Gary. Minnie called him Gary."

"It must be so terrible for him. It sounded like he was there often."

"Why, yes. Yes, he was. In fact, he was the one who filled out her food selection card and put it on the door when he left. He put mine there, too, so the night nurse didn't have to bother with it."

"Food selection card? I thought you ate whatever they prepared."

"Oh, honey. You must not have been in a hospital recently. It's like room service at a hotel. Costs as much, too, if not more."

So that's how he knew what she'd be eating.

Out of nowhere a voice bellowed through the dog park. "HEY, CINDY! Your dog is pooping!"

"ALL RIGHT. ALL RIGHT." She turned to face me.

"I've got to get this before Phil over there has a stroke. It was nice talking with you. Say hi to your mother for me. Lovely lady."

We stood and I thanked her as I headed back to the concrete entrance. The puddles that were left earlier had dried in a matter of minutes. Still, I paid attention to where I stepped until I was safely in the car. As I started the engine, I realized a small piece of the puzzle might be making sense.

Gary, the nephew, knew what his aunt had ordered for lunch. He must also have known she was allergic to finned fish. It wouldn't have been that difficult to sneak a piece of tuna or something in some tinfoil or plastic wrap and then dump it into the chicken salad while the tray sat unseen behind the screen in Minnie's hospital room. I wanted to jump up and down screaming, "I found the murderer. I found the murderer," only I knew it was pure speculation on my part. The only salient point was knowing speculation wasn't the same as imagination. I really believed I was on to something.

Anxious to share my revelation with my mother, I wasted no time getting back to her house. I was about to say something as I stepped into the kitchen, but I never got a chance.

"Herb doesn't know who the boyfriend is," my mother announced as soon as she saw me. "And that beige SUV isn't the boyfriend's."

It took me a second to process what I was hearing before I responded.

"How do you know? I mean, how does Herb know?"

"Because he's never seen the beige SUV before. He has seen a blue Mazda on more than one occasion, and some occasions were longer than others."

"Really?" For a split second the image of that nosy neighbor from *Bewitched* came to mind. I pictured Herb spying through Venetian blinds and bit my lip. "If we see a blue Mazda, we'll take a look and find out who's getting out of it." My God! I was just as bad as Herb and the lady from *Bewitched*.

"Good idea, Phee. And when he leaves, you jump into that rental car of yours and follow him!"

"What? I'm not going to tail some guy like *Hawaii Five-O*."

"Then how are you going to find out who he is? You have to find out who he is so we can find out if he's married."

"Mother, I'm putting this one on the proverbial 'back burner,' so to speak. I've got another lead to follow."

"You do? What? What is it?"

I told her about my conversation with Cindy Dolton and my suspicion about Minnie's nephew.

"No wonder he was in such a hurry to have her cremated and buried. Had to remove all of the evidence."

"I tend to agree, but let's not get ahead of ourselves. It's a suspicion. A good one, but nonetheless, a suspicion. It still doesn't explain the other deaths. I'm going to look over the few notes I've taken and try to make sense of this."

If this were one of the many accounting nightmares I run into, I'd do a quick spreadsheet and work backward, but I wasn't dealing with numbers, just relationships. I was tempted to give Nate a call, but I thought I'd hold off a bit longer.

Making myself comfortable at the kitchen table, I looked at the notes from my date planner, as well as my mother's notes and other information I'd jotted down on scraps of paper. It was a hodgepodge of names, occupations, and causes of death with nothing that linked any of the people together. What I really needed was one of those large whiteboards that every crime show touted from *Castle* to *Criminal Minds*. For a minute, I seriously considered making a quick trip to Office Max but changed my mind. I was only here for a week or so, not a change in careers. Besides, this one didn't come with a salary or benefits.

I did the next best thing. I took six pieces of white computer paper and taped them together to form one big poster. Then I set up all the names in columns with their information written underneath. *Minnie Bendelson, one surviving relative—nephew Gary, at hospital the night before her death, brought food tray next day, had her cremated—fast.* My fourth-grade teacher would have been proud. The only thing I was missing was the timeline. Detectives always had a timeline. I needed five, if you counted Jeanette Tomilson.

More white computer paper. More tape. I stood and walked to the drawer where my mother kept that stuff and glanced out the window. The beige SUV was backing out of Jeanette's driveway. I hurried over to get a closer look. The license plate was too small to read, but the white sign on the rearview window was as clear as could be: WEST VALLEY HOME MORTGAGE SOLUTIONS. If it said MARY KAY COSMETICS or SCENTSY, I wouldn't have given it another thought. But mortgage solutions? It was the first thing I wrote down when I started the timeline.

The SUV could belong to a friend of Jeanette's, but what if she was in serious mortgage trouble and had to find a way out. Still, that wouldn't explain the recent waves of unexpected deaths.

After forty-five minutes, I was no better off than when I started. At least I had a nice, well-organized chart to stare at. And that's exactly what I did for another five minutes until my mother interrupted me when she headed out the door.

"I've got to run a few errands, Phee. Well, actually, they're having a sale at Sher's Women's Clothing. If you didn't insist on dressing like a lumberjack in jeans all the time, I'd offer to buy you one of those cute, frilly tops and a nice pair of polyester pants. You have a decent figure, you know."

"Lumberjack? Polyester? What??? Oh, never mind. Polyester is the last thing I'd wear, and for your information my jeans happen to be fashionable."

"Sure, if you're Paul Bunyan. I was only offering some input."

Input my you-know-what. It was the same conversation that had been going on between us since my puberty. Yeah, maybe I did prefer sweatshirts to fancy tops, but so what? I was never going to dress with the same panache as my mother. At least I never nagged my daughter about her clothing choices, unless they were way too extreme. I tried putting this out of my head and concentrating on the work I had to do. Work that was taking me way too long.

Paint drying on a humid day was faster. I wasn't going to get any further without more information, and unlike Streetman, who was in his dog bed snoring away, I didn't feel like sitting around waiting for Harriet Plunkett to get back.

If there was something more to these deaths, I needed to delve deeper, because the last thing I believed was they were caused by a book curse. A book curse! Oh my gosh! I realized immediately that I needed to find the man who created the disturbance at the pool to see what he knew about a curse.

Quickly, I gathered up the papers from the table, put them in a neat pile on the dresser in the guest bedroom, and headed over to the sheriff's posse station, hoping that by the time I got there, I would have concocted a solid enough story to learn the name of the man at the pool.

I've never been great at lying. Couldn't even fib as a kid without breaking into a sweat. At least out here in triple-digit weather I had an excuse for any beads of perspiration dripping down my cheeks. Luckily, I didn't have to stray from the truth.

The posse office was a three-minute drive from my mother's house, if you were lucky enough to make all the lights. It was actually part of a larger complex that featured a philanthropic foundation and a resale shop. The entire structure looked like some sort of beige arcade, and I felt as if I was about to try my luck at one of the booths. At least I had my story straight as I approached the woman seated at the posse's reception desk. She wore a small name tag that read, DONNA, POSSE VOLUNTEER. I prayed she wouldn't ask too many questions and greeted her as cheerfully as I could.

"Hi! I'm hoping you can help me with something."

"I'll try," the woman replied, brushing a few curls from her forehead. She appeared to be in her late fifties or early sixties and had one of those no-nonsense looks about her. She'd make a great partner for Gretchen Morin.

"I was at the main recreation center pool yesterday when a man was escorted out for creating a disturbance. Well, I came here to tell you that it really wasn't much of a disturbance and that I hope he doesn't get into any trouble with the sheriff's department."

So far so good. I'm sticking to the truth.

"Yesterday? At what time?"

"Um, early afternoon. Around two."

The volunteer officer typed something into the computer on her desk and waited. I wasn't sure if I should make small talk or not and decided to keep my mouth shut. *"Anything you say can and will be held against you."* In this case, I didn't want to offer up any more information than I had to. I learned that from years of watching my cousin Kirk. The kid wasn't satisfied digging himself into a hole where my aunt Ina was concerned; instead, he managed to trench out an entire abyss.

"I'm going over to Joey's to play."

"Be back by five for dinner."

"We're going to be in his yard playing with lawn darts."

"With what?"

"Lawn darts. They're called Jarts."

"Who's going to be watching you?"

"No one. His mom's out shopping."

"You're not going. You can stay right here and play something safe in the house."

Yep, if nothing else, my cousin taught me to respect that old adage, "Loose lips sink ships." I smiled and kept still. Donna, the posse volunteer, tapped her fingers against the desk and stared at the screen.

"Oh yes, here it is. No, no charges were filed. The man wasn't intoxicated or under the influence, so the matter was referred to the recreation center. It's up to them if they decide to penalize him."

"Penalize him? Like a fine?"

"No, they don't do that. They might ban someone from using the pool or whatever area was in question for a while. Could be for a week, two weeks, sometimes as much as six months, depending upon the situation."

I wonder if Streetman got the maximum penalty. . . .

"Oh, I'd hate to see that poor man banished for six months over something so minor."

"Well, as I said, it's up to the rec department and—"

Suddenly, the doors swung open as two officers tried to assist a very, very elderly woman inside. One of the officers shouted out, "Donna, can you bring a chair over here?"

"Of course." The volunteer officer stood and turned to me. "Excuse me for a second."

As Donna raced to get a chair, I sidestepped the desk and positioned myself so that I could get a good view of her computer screen. I only had a matter of seconds. I leaned slightly forward and scanned the page. Lots of details. Lots of writing. The name? Where the heck was the name?

I could hear Donna and the officers speaking as they tried to assist the lady. *Please don't watch me. Just help that lady.* I literally had zero time to get the information I needed. Any second and Donna would be back at her desk. Damn! Where the heck was that name? I looked closer. She had scrolled down for the write-up. I edged in, prayed she wouldn't turn around, and moved her mouse until it touched the side arrow to the right of the screen. Then I moved it up.

Why are they always able to find this stuff right away on TV? Someone shoves in a flash drive and unloads

government secrets while the rest of us wait for that
stupid buffering circle to quit spinning.

I scrolled up farther and held my breath. Bingo!

Jerry White

Jerry White. I repeated the name to myself, along
with the other information I had managed to see—
the name of his street and the number.

"Gosh, I hope that woman will be all right." I took
a few steps toward Donna so she wouldn't notice I'd
been snooping on her computer.

"She's just confused. Not sure where she lives.
They'll get it straightened out. Anyway, as I was saying,
there are no charges made against that gentleman."

"I'm so relieved. Thank you again for your trouble
and have a good day."

"Same to you."

The minute I got into my car, I wrote down the
name and address of the man who was sputtering
about a cursed book. Then I programmed what I had
into the rental car's GPS and waited. Voilà! He lived
in Sun City West and only a few miles from my current location. Now all I needed to do was come up
with a reason to pay him a visit.

Chapter 10

Whispering Oaks was a long, lovely street off the main drag. I had no idea why they named it Whispering Oaks since there wasn't a single oak tree within miles. I guess the developers didn't think Whispering Palms had the same ring to it.

Jerry White's house was six or seven houses down on the right. It had a huge date palm tree in front, surrounded by a circle of smaller palms. Everything looked immaculately groomed, including the house—freshly painted with bright coral trim. Whoever this man was, he certainly took care of his home.

In the five or six minutes it had taken me to get here, I hadn't come up with a reason to talk to him. I couldn't pretend to be selling anything, and it would look awfully strange if I walked up to his door to ask for directions. Then again, this was a senior community and maybe it wasn't so unusual for people to get lost. I couldn't very well sit there arguing with myself. What if Jerry was looking out his window, same as Herb Garrett. No, I had to make a move.

I got out of the car, leaned in to grab my notepad and pen, and started for his front door. Just then, the garage door opened and a small white dog came running out. Behind him was a man screaming his lungs out.

"Izzy! Get back here! Come on, boy. Get back!"

The dog was headed straight toward me and didn't appear to be very threatening, so I ran over and got ahold of him by the collar. The man was only a few feet away and out of breath.

"Thanks so much! I thought I'd closed the door that leads to the garage when, all of a sudden, the dog escaped. I was on my way to the post office. Good thing you were in the neighborhood. I hate to think what could have happened. We have so many coyotes around here and Izzy is defenseless."

The white dog looked at me as if to acknowledge what his owner had said. As he picked the little guy up, I got a good look at the man's face and gasped. It was the middle-aged man with the jet-black mustache who was dining with Gretchen Morin that night in the Italian restaurant. First, Josie from the pool, now him. Maybe luck was on my side.

"Are you all right?" he asked.

"Yes, yeah . . . I'm fine. I was taken back when you mentioned coyotes. I'm not from this area. In fact, I was trying to find, um, er . . ." I frantically tried to visualize the names of the other streets from the GPS and muttered "Foxfire Drive" before regaining my composure. "I was looking for Foxfire Drive and really blew it."

"Oh, that's just one street over. Go back to one

hundred thirtieth, make your first right, and it will be there."

"Thanks. I appreciate it. By the way—"

Before I could finish, he cut in. "Say, haven't I seen you at . . ."

I held my breath. What if he'd seen me in the restaurant? *Well, so what? He doesn't know who I am. It's not as if he was going to pick up a phone and call the librarian.*

"The dog park! That's where I've seen you. I'm there first thing in the morning with Izzy and then again around seven at night. Like clockwork. Anyway, it was you. Talking with Cindy Dolton. Didn't see your dog, though. What kind is it? Izzy is a Coton de Tulear. People always mistake him for a bichon and get on my case for not having him groomed properly. Can you believe it? So, which dog is yours? I might have seen it."

Oh, you've seen him all right, but he's not mine and I make no claim to him.

"I don't own a dog. I was in the park for another reason. I was talking to Cindy Dolton about my mother's friend who passed away recently. It's so sad. Really. Cindy shared a hospital room with the woman."

"Oh, I'm sorry to hear about your loss."

Take a breath. This may work. This may actually work. Go for it!

"Yes, it was so sudden. So unexpected. And if that wasn't enough, one of the woman's dear friends told me about this book curse. You see, poor Minnie was reading some book from her book club, and I guess she wasn't the only one in that club to pass away unexpectedly. Some of the ladies in that club believe it had something to do with the book."

The man beamed as if I'd just told him the Publishers Clearing House van was on its way.

"Now, I'm not one to believe in all that hocus-pocus either," he said. "But from what I've heard, that book should be avoided at all costs. Get it out of the library! I've heard firsthand that whoever reads it will have a pretty dark cloud following them. Maybe a death cloud."

"A death cloud?" This guy obviously watched too many Star Wars *movies. Even George Lucas wouldn't be saying that.*

"You said you heard it firsthand?"

"Not directly, no. But firsthand. I overheard the librarian talking about it to someone when I went to check out some books. That person wanted her to take the book off the shelf, and she refused. Policy and all that nonsense."

I felt like screaming, "Liar! Liar! You know the librarian. You had dinner with her the other night!" But I acted nonplussed. "A book curse, huh?"

"You never know about these things. Bad juju and all of that."

"Bad juju?" Who is he kidding? He's beginning to sound like he just picked up the script for some old 1940s movie.

"Well, I really don't go in for all that stuff."

"You can't be too careful. Frankly, I'm warning anyone I see with that book. In fact, I was thinking of shooting off an e-mail to the local paper about it."

I could understand why my mother would fall victim to this nonsense, but this guy struck me as someone who was manipulating the situation for his own good.

The question remained, "Is he manipulating it to commit murder, and if so, why?"

I thanked him for his directions and took off for Mom's. If nothing else, I'd be able to connect some dots to the names on my prized chart. The car's air conditioner was set on maximum, but I was still uncomfortable. How do these people live here year-round? I ignored the speed limit and hoped I wouldn't get caught. Slamming the car door shut, I raced to the front door as soon as I arrived.

A thin layer of perspiration clung to my body like Saran Wrap. I threw my bag on the couch the minute I walked into the house and headed straight for the shower. In three days, I'd gone through more shirts and undergarments than I did in a week back home. The shower was quick and I was just slipping on a clean top and shorts when Mom pulled in. With laundry in hand, I opened the door to the garage as she stepped out of the car.

"Whoa! Now that's what I call service."

"Hi! I thought I'd throw a load of wash in. I'm down to my last pair of—"

"Leave it there. Wait till after seven. That's when the rates go down."

I wasn't about to argue over electricity rates with so much other stuff clogging up my brain. I put the laundry on top of the machine and walked back inside.

My mother wasted no time beginning her own interrogation. "So, did you get anywhere? What did you find out?"

"Sharpie markers work better than the other kind."

"What?"

"I didn't find out much. Remember I told you

about a guy who made a huge disturbance at the pool yesterday because he was yelling about the book curse? Well, I tracked him down and spoke to him and you'll never guess—"

"Tracked him down? You didn't go into his house, did you? He could be dangerous."

"No, I didn't go into his house. Anyway, Mom, he was the guy at the restaurant. The one sitting at the table with the librarian."

"Aha! So what did you find out?"

"Either he's the biggest nutcase in your community, or he's really dangerous after all. He could be using this book curse thing to cover up something worse."

"How do you know that? Stay away from him."

"I don't know anything. I just have a funny feeling, that's all. And I'm exhausted. Absolutely exhausted."

"It's a good thing it's Thursday night. We can relax at the movies."

"Movies? What movies?"

"Every Thursday night at the Stardust Theater they show a movie. It's close. A few blocks from here, across from the sheriff's posse station. Big beige stucco building."

"Everything around here is stucco and beige. Did the developer find a sale on paint colors?"

"Don't be silly. The specs for the complex stated that buildings must blend into the original desert landscape."

"Fortunately you didn't buy ocean-view property."

My mother chose to ignore my last comment and continued on about the movie.

"It's only two dollars. Tonight is *Show Boat*. We'll

have an early bite to eat and go. You can throw in your wash when we get home."

"*Show Boat*? That movie was made before I was born."

"Good. Something new for you to see. I'm going to get comfortable and then we'll sit down and go over everything we've found out since you decided to start this investigation."

"Decided? You mean got roped into, coerced, nagged . . ."

"Doesn't matter. This book curse isn't going away by itself."

After what seemed like hours of comparing notes with my mother, I was actually glad to be going to a movie. Even if the heartthrob had been dead for decades.

The Stardust Theater reminded me of the old auditorium in my high school—upright no-nonsense seats and a strict no food or drink policy. No wonder it was only $2.00. Still, it gave my mother a short respite from all the anxiety she was feeling over the recent events.

We took our seats in the back by the aisle. I could slip out easily if I became too uncomfortable or too bored. Lucky for us we arrived early, because the place was filling up quickly. *Show Boat* apparently had quite the following. I was barely getting settled when my mother stood and whispered that she saw a friend of hers across the rows and wanted to say hello before the movie started.

I got up, let her out, and sat back down. The lights had started to dim, but they hadn't opened the curtain yet to reveal the screen. Soft music was playing and people were still talking to one another. Surprisingly, there were a number of cell phones in use, too. Technology had reached this generation as well.

Figuring it was okay, I took out my iPhone to check my e-mail. I was busily scanning messages when I overheard the conversation behind me. Women's voices. Seniors maybe, but far from elderly.

"No one expected her to break a hip and then die in the hospital. Who would think—"

"We were only trying to help. Nothing else was working. For goodness sakes, she even refused to wear one of those alert things in case of a fall. And she refused to have safety bars put in the shower. Said they were for old people!"

"We really should tell the sheriff's department. What if someone saw us there?"

"SHH . . . no one saw us. Besides, people are pointing to that book curse and you're pretty well covered."

Moving my shoulders back, I tried to feign some sort of a stretch so I could turn my neck and see who was talking, but the minute I leaned back, my mother poked me in the arm. She had returned to her seat and I jumped. I figured it was a great opportunity to see who was behind us. It wasn't. One of the ladies dropped something and the two of them bent down to look. My mother was oblivious to all of this.

"Good thing I managed to find you, Phee. It's getting even darker in here. You'll have to meet Gloria Wong. She used to live in the house behind me but moved in with her daughter. We had a lovely chat."

Before I could say anything, the theater went

pitch-black and an announcement was made to turn off all cell phones. *Great. Really easy to turn it off in the dark.* I fumbled around until I was satisfied my ring-tone wasn't going to ruin the overture.

Unfortunately, I never got a look at the ladies seated in back of us. And while Magnolia and Gaylord were singing love songs, I was repeating the dialogue I overheard, pausing every now and then to linger on the words "We were only trying to help."

For a long movie, it wasn't as agonizing as I thought it would be. It seemed to fly by in no time with rich melodic songs, some terrific dance routines, and a heartbreaking romance to boot. I swore I could hear people sniffling at the end. Too bad I couldn't hear those women behind me.

The minute the houselights came on, I stood and turned around. It was too late. Whoever was sitting in back of me had already blended into the crowd headed for the exit.

"Phee"—my mother pulled on my arm—"don't you want to stay and watch the credits?"

At this point, it didn't matter, so I sat back down and stared at the screen. We were the last few people to leave the theater, and I quickly found out why my mother didn't race out the doors like everyone else.

"The parking lot is a madhouse and half these people can't drive. No sense rushing so someone can put a dent in your car."

"I see your point. The rental company would charge me a fortune."

We took our time getting to the car. Then we waited while a lineup of vehicles pulled onto the street. It was slow going as we drove the two miles to her place. Apparently everyone living in the vicinity of my mother's house had decided to see that movie.

"Mom," I said as we waited at a red light, "you're not going to believe the conversation that was going on behind me when you went to talk to your friend Gloria."

I then proceeded to tell her what I had overheard. "What if it was Jeanette sitting behind us? I suspected she was up to something that first night with the carbon monoxide leak. It seemed too contrived. As if she wanted to make herself appear like a victim, too. If it *was* her in back of us, she all but admitted to killing Edna Mae."

"Anyone can admit to anything sitting in a dark theater. Too bad you didn't turn around to get a better look."

I forced myself to keep my mouth shut.

The light finally turned green and we moved along. There were two SUVs in front of us, each competing for the slowest speed on record. By the time we turned onto my mother's street, we were still following one of them. It slowed down when it got near to our house, and I kept a good distance behind.

"Mom! Look! That's the beige SUV we keep seeing in front of Jeanette's house. At least I think it looks beige."

"See who's getting out!"

It was Jeanette. She got out and walked in front of the vehicle just as her garage door opened.

"She must have taken the garage door clicker with her," my mother said.

"Uh-huh." As Jeanette entered the garage, the driver of the SUV started down the street. I hit the high beams to get a better look at that car. Sure enough,

WEST VALLEY HOME MORTGAGE SOLUTIONS was as visible
as could be.

"Do you want me to follow that car, Mom?"

"Are you nuts? It will look too obvious. People are
always calling the sheriff's station to report someone
is following them. Especially at night. Lucinda once
called, but it turned out to be the newspaper guy
on his delivery route. Of course, that was daylight.
No, you'll think of something else."

Yeah, sure I will.

I lowered my headlights and took my time pulling
into the driveway. I could have kicked myself for listening to my mother. Now I was left with a nagging
question—Who was driving the beige SUV?

Chapter 11

That thought plagued me for at least twenty minutes as I tried to get some sleep. What if it was a woman in that beige SUV and she and Jeanette were the two voices I heard behind me at the theater? Jeanette certainly knew Edna Mae from the book club, but what reason would she have for harming her? Then again, the voice did say, "We were only trying to help. Nothing else was working." Did Edna Mae need help? And if so, why would it be Jeanette's concern?

Jeanette. Jeanette. Jeanette. That woman was ruining my sleep. First the wackadoodle story my mother came up with about the wife of Jeanette's boyfriend (and we don't even know if she has one) and now an entirely different Jeanette—perpetrator instead of victim. Was there a way real investigators figured this out? Maybe if I had paid more attention in my Intro to Psych class in college . . .

I slowly let Jeanette slip out of my mind and wafted into a wonderful oblivion. Wonderful until the obnoxious ringtone from my cell phone sent a shock through my body like lightning striking a golfer. I never should have turned it back on after the movie. I jumped up and reached across the nightstand for the phone.

It was the middle of the night. Or at least it seemed that way. Everything was still dark. *Who the heck could be calling me?*

I expected my voice to be clear and audible, not the foggy jumble of syllables I sputtered out. "Hullo. Who's this . . . what's-the-matter?"

"Phee! Did I wake you? Phee! It's me. Nate. Nothing's the matter. Sorry. I thought you'd be up by now."

It was starting to sink in. Nate. Nate calling me at some obscene hour.

"Up by now? It's still dark."

"There's only a one-hour time difference."

"Tell that to the sun."

"Sorry kiddo. Listen, I got the info back from Rolo. The book's as clean as a whistle. No cyphers. No secret messages. No nothing. Believe me, he gave it the once-over. But there *is* one thing."

"What?"

My mind was starting to clear, and I knew this was probably important.

"That book isn't off the grid. It's so far off it would take light-years to even reach the grid!"

"What are you saying?"

"I'm saying no one's ever heard of it. Or the author, for that matter. Who the heck is Lily Margot Gerald? No info there either. Nope, this gal is totally, and I do mean *totally*, off the radar."

"Huh?"

"You know, Phee. When something is that un-known, it almost becomes suspicious for that very reason."

"Like the book was planted or something?"

"Something. But what? I don't know. Anyway, the sales information for *The Twelfth Arrondissement* is pretty dismal. Given the Amazon rankings and the info Rolo was able to get from other distributors, the book only sold a handful of copies, and I'll wager those were the ones your mother's book club is read-ing. How many women are in that club?"

"It varies. Usually twelve to seventeen, but they share books and take them out of the library, too. Why?"

"Well, according to the information Rolo dug up, and don't ask where, even the worst-performing self-published book usually sells seventy-five copies. It would appear yours didn't even reach twenty percent of that."

"How did he find out that information?"

"Let's just say Rolo's skills aren't limited to cyphers and codes. His real expertise is computer hacking. And let me tell you, I'm on thin ice here. Seems the book curse piqued Rolo's interest and once that happened, there was no stopping him."

"Oh my God. You're not going to get into any trouble, are you?"

"Let's hope not. Working on cyphers is one thing, computer hacking is a whole different animal. How-ever, since Rolo is acting 'solo' on this, I'm going to look the other way for the time being."

"That's a relief, but I'm not getting anywhere here. I fly back next week, and it can't be soon enough.

I'm no investigator. All I'm doing is spinning my wheels. Everything I touch seems to have tentacles, and in order to get information, I'm fudging the truth at times. Is that what you have to do in order to pull information from would-be suspects?"

"Yeah, sometimes. I prefer to think of it as a strategic tactic. So, what did you find out?"

For the next ten minutes I told Nate everything about everyone. From my suspicion about Minnie Bendelson's death to my mother's obsession about a jealous wife. I didn't leave anything out. The dog park, the pool, the theater, and my conversation with Jerry White. By the time I was finished, Nate knew more about Sun City West than most of its residents.

"Keep at it, kiddo. If there's something to connect all of this, you'll find it. Meanwhile, I'm sure Rolo will keep me posted on the book end of things. It's still pretty darn strange that this particular novel would be selected for your mother's book club."

"Thanks, Nate. I appreciate it. Hey, before you hang up, who's handling accounts receivable while I'm gone? I dread the thought of walking back into a mess."

"Not to worry. They dragged in Moira Donahoe."

"That's wonderful! How did they manage that? When she retired she swore she'd never set foot in that office again."

"Moira likes you. Said you were the only competent clerk in a . . . what did she call that? Oh yeah, 'in a kennel full of tail-chasing dogs.'"

I giggled. "Thank her for me. And you, too. Catch you later."

"Okay, kiddo. Hey, you do know you can call me if

you have any questions or if you just want to talk over stuff. Right?"

"Absolutely. And get an App with a time zone map!"

I tapped the End button and glanced at the window. The sun was just coming up, and I was wide awake. No possibility of getting back to sleep now. I threw on my shorts and a top and walked into the kitchen to put on a pot of coffee. I figured that while it was brewing, I could watch the local early-morning news from the small TV on the counter, inches away from the table. I made sure the sound was low, hoping Nate's phone call hadn't disturbed my mother or Streetman and that they were still enjoying some sleep.

A commercial for high-speed Internet ended and the anchor came back on the air. I was halfway listening to her when I heard the words "interesting story coming out of Sun City West, following our Breaking News."

I turned the volume up a notch and listened to the "Breaking News" about a foiled carjacking in North Phoenix. Then another series of commercials. I waited patiently for the "news" out of Sun City West, expecting some story about a coyote or golf tournament. What I heard instead hit me harder and faster than the brew sitting in the coffeepot.

"That's right, Sean," one of the two news anchors went on. "Apparently there's a book circulating around Sun City West that some people claim puts a curse on its readers."

The banter continued as I took my first sip of coffee.

"Is this a popular book that most of us would

have sitting on our shelves or downloaded on our e-readers?"

"Not at all. And until this story came out of Sun City West, no one had heard of it."

At that moment, the female anchor held a copy of the book up high and read the title out loud. *"The Twelfth Arrondissement."*

"The Twelfth Arrondissement? I've never heard of it, Carla. So, tell me, what's the book about, and what's this curse?"

"I haven't had a chance to read the book, Sean, but from what I can tell, it's some sort of gothic romance-mystery."

"And the curse?"

"Well, that's just it. A book club in Sun City West, Booked 4 Murder, got a little more than it bargained for when four of its fifteen or so members died unexpectedly and a fifth member had a near encounter with death. They were all engrossed in reading that book. We'll expect to have more on that story on the evening news when their librarian joins us."

"I'll be holding my breath for this one, Carla, but I'm not so sure I'll be putting the book on my reading list anytime soon."

As both anchors chuckled and moved on to the next story, I held back the urge to run into my mother's bedroom and shake her awake. Instead, I popped a bagel into the toaster and went to get my notes. I couldn't imagine how that story got to the news media. Jerry White? He mentioned sending an e-mail to the local paper. Did he decide to contact Channel Five instead?

All of those local news stations have a "Push This Icon" button on their Web sites for the locals to share anything they deem newsworthy. Heck, Mankato had that, too. Did Jerry decide to forgo the letter and just push a button? Whatever the deal was, I planned to be glued to the TV for the evening news, even if it meant sitting through a zillion commercials.

I was halfway through my second cup of coffee when my mother walked into the kitchen. She barely had time to say good morning when I told her what I had just seen on the news.

"Goodness, Phee. It had to be one of the women from the club. Or . . . wait a second. You said the librarian was going to be on the news tonight? Maybe it was her. Trying to get some attention."

"The librarian didn't strike me as someone who wanted attention. But the man she was having dinner with the other night sure did. Our very own Mr. White. The one who made a spectacle of himself at the pool. He told me yesterday he planned to send an e-mail to the local paper about the book. Remember? I mentioned it to you last night, after the movie."

"Yes, of course I remember. It was only a few hours ago. Hand me my coffee cup from the strainer, will you? And grab me one of those Corelle dinnerware plates. Streetman likes to eat off of them. Refuses to use a bowl."

"You mean we're eating off of the same plates as the dog?"

"The dishwasher sanitizes everything."

I shuddered as I reached behind me for the cup and plate. My mother walked over to the small cubby area in her kitchen that doubled for an office or "catchall," depending upon the day, and rummaged through a stack of papers.

"There's one way to find out, Phee. Here's the list

of all the members in Booked 4 Murder. Seventeen names, but only fifteen are regulars. We can't be wasting time. You're flying back, when? Oh, I remember. This coming Thursday. That gives us less than a week."

"Wasting time? Less than a week for what? I'm knocking myself out here chasing down rumors and starting up conversations with anyone remotely connected to that book."

"Yes, yes. Nick and Nora Charles would be proud of you, but sometimes you have to take a more direct route, and I'm going to help with the driving."

"What? What are you talking about?"

"I am going to call everyone on that list and ask them two questions."

"Only two?"

"Stop being funny, Phee. I'm going to come right out and ask them, 'Did you contact the TV station?' and 'Were you the person who recommended that book in the first place?'"

I raised my eyebrows.

"And you think they're going to tell you the truth?"

"Let's put it this way, if someone in the club made that call or pushed that button, or whatever it is that they had to do, it will be common knowledge by lunchtime."

"What about suggesting the book in the first place?"

"I don't think anyone is going to admit to that. I know I wouldn't. But if anyone knows anything, they might be tempted to rat out the culprit."

"Nice club, Mom."

"It *is* a nice club. And a cursed book doesn't belong there."

I started to pour myself another cup of coffee and then thought twice. I'd be way too jittery to accomplish anything. I set down the cup and took a quick breath.

"Mom, when we were at the Italian place that night, Jerry White was having dinner with the librarian and another couple. I recognized the lady from the pool—Josie Nolan. I found out her last name by snooping around. She and her husband own a realty company. And . . . she was at the pool the same time Thelmalee got stung. Could be she's the one getting this rumor circulated about a cursed book."

"Why would she do that?"

"I have no idea, but my gut feeling is that someone in the library is behind all of this."

"Now you're thinking like Columbo. Go! Go find this Josie Nolan and nag her to death!"

"Mom, you've been watching way too many crime shows. And that one's been off the air for over a decade."

"But you're going to do that, aren't you? Find that Nolan woman, I mean."

I let out a long, exaggerated breath. "Yeah, I suppose I am. I'm going to rinse off and head over to Nolan and Nolan Realty. Time for me to look into a nice retirement place in Sun City West."

My mother almost jumped from her chair and, for a minute, I wasn't sure if she was ecstatic at the thought of my eventually living here or overjoyed because I was checking out a "viable lead" in this bizarre investigation of hers.

"Josie Nolan may think she's showing me property, but my motives have nothing to do with real estate.

Have fun making your phone calls. Maybe we can make more sense of this when I get back."

I rinsed off my coffee cup as my mother turned up the sound to the TV. I could hear the commercials all the way to the shower.

Chapter 12

Nolan and Nolan Realty had a large office on the main drag, perpendicular to a pharmacy and bank. When my parents first started looking at retirement communities, they visited Florida. It wasn't the humidity or bugs that swayed them away from the ocean. It was the fact that every corner seemed to have a bank, a florist, and a funeral home. That's when my mother insisted on Arizona. In no uncertain terms.

"You can forget Florida all together. It's like they're saying 'Give us your money and drop dead!'"

At least in Sun City West the funeral homes were tucked away. As for the banks, heck, they all wanted our money. I laughed to myself when I thought of my mother's commentary. I think I was still smiling when I walked into Nolan and Nolan.

The reception area was tastefully decorated in a Southwestern theme with a fancy oval table featuring information about the community. Off to the left was a side table with a large Keurig coffeemaker and all the fixings. The receptionist had a spot on the right and there were smaller, private offices on both sides.

I walked into the room just as the thirty-something behind the desk got off the phone.

"Hi! Can I help you?"

"Yes, I'm here to see Josie Nolan."

"Oh"—she glanced at her computer—"do you have an appointment? I don't see anything listed, but Josie sometimes makes appointments and forgets to tell me."

"No, I didn't make an appointment. I was hoping to catch her since it's so early."

"Hang on a second. I'll get her."

Just then, a tall, middle-aged man strode into the office, and the minute he removed his sunglasses, I knew exactly who he was—the other half of Nolan and Nolan. I recognized him from that night in the Italian restaurant. Tall, salt and pepper hair. I took a seat quickly and pretended to busy myself with some of the brochures as he spoke to the receptionist.

"Non-shedding bichon-poodle, or whatever you call it, my ass! Just look at all the white hairs on my trousers! And the dog drooled on me. Happens every time I go over there to do business. That gutter mutt costs me a fortune in dry cleaning. Any messages for me, Chelsea?"

"I left them on your desk, Mr. Nolan. And before I forget, your sister stopped by and wanted you to call her. Something about your broker. I told her you'd be back soon, but she didn't want to wait. She was with a girlfriend. Same one who comes in all the time for the coffee."

"Okay. Okay. I'll get to it. Darn this dog hair. It's all over me. I'd better not have any showings until

I can run home and change. I don't want people thinking I work for a kennel."

With that, Tom Nolan disappeared into his office and, seconds later, Josie Nolan emerged from hers. Without her wide sunhat and dark glasses, I was able to get a good look at her face. Highlighted hair. Young fifties, maybe. Tasteful makeup. Perhaps even a session or two with Juvéderm. She reached out her hand and greeted me as if we were old friends.

"Hey there, I recognize you. You were at the pool the other day. Visiting from out of state. I hope you're here to tell me you've decided to buy property in Sun City West."

I opened my mouth, but nothing came out. *I'd better come up with something.*

I cleared my throat and smiled. Too wide. Too toothy. *I better not overdo this.*

"Yeah, uh, I really enjoyed the pool. It's a great community. I'm far from retiring, but I was thinking of getting a small vacation place that I could rent out. I'm from Minnesota and it would be a good investment. No snow emergencies to deal with here."

Real estate's always a solid investment. Look at Donald Trump. I could really do this.

"That's for sure, Miss . . . ? Miss . . . ?"

"Kimball. Call me Phee."

"Okay, Phee. Why don't you take a seat in the waiting area, and if you don't mind, fill out one of our short questionnaires describing what you're looking for and your price range. It's much easier that way and will save us time. I'll be happy to go over some of the listings with you when you're done. Chelsea will give you the form and a pen. And help yourself to coffee and those little cupcakes. They're terrific. Local baker."

"Sure. Great. Talk to you in a few minutes."

Josie said something to Chelsea as I eyeballed the cupcakes. I wasn't really in the mood for more coffee, but a tempting treat made by a local baker was too much to resist. I got up and walked over to the table. A small plastic server held packets of artificial sweeteners and Half & Half cups, while the real sugar was in a glass bowl with a spoon. Nice touch.

Suddenly, my mind flashed to that piece of litter I found on the ground where someone had sprinkled enough sugar to attract an entire hive of bees. It was a long shot, but something told me I was staring at evidence.

As I reached to help myself to a cupcake, I studied the table. It wasn't so much a side table as a credenza. It had cabinets on the bottom. Probably where they stored the cups, plates, napkins, and sweeteners. Chelsea, the receptionist, was busy on her computer, and Josie had gone back inside her office. The coast was clear.

I leaned in and opened one of the cabinets slightly. Just enough for me to glance down. Phooey. Piles of stuff from the Chamber of Commerce. I moved farther to the center and tried again. Getting closer—paper plates and cups. *Only one more cabinet to go, Sherlock!*

My neck made a weird creaking sound as I turned my head to scan the room again. This time voices drifted from another office. Someone was finishing up a conversation and would be in here at any minute. I pulled the cabinet door open and sure enough I saw the familiar blue and white box of cane sugar. *So what? It's the most popular brand on the market.*

Acting as if I knew what I was doing, I picked up the box and started to pour a bit of sugar into the bowl. Innocent enough if anyone caught me. Part of the cardboard edge of the box had been pulled off in order to pour the sugar in the first place. Was I staring at the actual box that someone used to lure the bees to the pool? Without comparing it to the paper edge I pocketed that day, there was no way of knowing.

Then I had a thought. I'd tear the edge off farther to see if it matched the one I had back at the house. My heart started pounding as if I was about to break into a safe. Still, no one was looking as I leaned across the table. I tore the cardboard slowly so as not to make a sugar mess. It was just about off the box when the voices grew behind me. They were a few feet from me. A man and a woman. *Stay focused. Tear the rest of that sucker off!*

With a quick snap, I had freed the paper and grasped it in my hand. Then I slowly bent down and put the sugar back before stuffing the cupcake into my mouth and taking a seat near the coffee table.

Were they looking at me? Had they noticed what I was doing? I hadn't been that self-conscious since junior high. No one was looking at me. The man and woman were having their own conversation, and it was a doozy. Apparently I wasn't the only one to catch the morning news.

"Oh, for God sakes, Valerie! You know how the media blows things out of proportion. There's no curse on Sun City West. People have accidents. People die all the time," the man said.

"But you heard that TV woman, George. She said there's no such thing as a coincidence."

"Never mind what she said. She just wanted to get viewers. Now come on, Val. Are we going to see this place or not?"

They were out the door before I could hear the rest of their conversation. One thing stuck, however. "There's no curse on Sun City West." Was this rumor expanding to the point of a city-wide curse instead of a book-club curse? I walked over to Chelsea.

"Please tell Josie I'm sorry. I just remembered I have to take my mother to an appointment. I'll take this form home and drop it off later. Thanks so much."

"Sure. No problem."

I was out the door, cardboard edge tucked safely in my bag. I couldn't wait to put that little puzzle together. Again, I hurried to Mom's and prayed no one noticed how fast I was going.

No sooner had I pulled into the driveway when I saw my mother standing at the front door.

"Get back in the car! Hurry up!" she yelled.

"What? What's going on?"

"That blue sporty car that's always at Jeanette's house just turned right at the corner. Follow it! Follow it and find out who it is!"

"Mom, I was about to—"

"Whatever you were about to do can wait. Get going! We need to know who the boyfriend is."

My mother blocked the door like a goalie in the NHL. I shrugged and started toward the car.

"Wait! Phee! Wait! Maybe you should take a can of something with you, just in case."

"A can of something? You have pepper spray?"

"Pepper spray? No, that stuff's dangerous. I have Lysol."

"Oh, geez. Never mind. He's probably gone by now."

"Not if you hurry. The speed limit is twenty-five, and he didn't appear to be speeding. You can catch up."

Sure. I'll just pretend I'm Steve McQueen in Bullitt. *Then again, that didn't end too well for the guy in the Charger.*

I backed out of the driveway and turned right at the corner. Sure enough, the blue car was still visible down the long block. Picking up speed, I managed to situate myself three or four car lengths behind him. The blue Mazda made a left-hand turn onto U.S. Route 60, or Grand Avenue, as it was known to the locals. We were heading south, into the city of Surprise. Good thing, too, because the other direction would have taken me to Wickenburg and eventually Las Vegas. Grand Avenue was the only diagonal street that ran across Phoenix's rigid grid design. I read somewhere it was built to create a gateway to California in the late 1920s.

Someone from the middle lane made a quick move, and I was now one car removed from the Mazda. Still, I could see where it was headed. Straight down Bell Road, the busiest and most highly trafficked road in that city. I watched carefully, expecting the guy to turn into one of the malls or shopping centers. Instead, he kept on going until he finally turned into a development.

A left. A right. A long circle. A twisting street. Another circle. *Who the heck designed this community, and how much were they drinking before they penciled in the streets?* The blue Mazda pulled into a driveway of a two-story beige house on a cul-de-sac, and I was only a few yards behind, praying he hadn't noticed me. I pulled up past the driveway and circled quickly around until I was in front of the house directly across from him. I expected his garage door to open, but instead, he got out of the car and walked to the front door.

Meanwhile, I reached down to the catchall between the two front seats of my rental car and pulled out a pen I'd stashed there. Using the back of a receipt from the gas station, I wrote down two numbers—the house and his license plate, all the while glancing at the man and waiting for him to take out his key.

Instead, the door opened and a tall, young blond woman motioned for him to come inside. Very formal. Very deliberate. *Nice going. This isn't his house. More like a house call.* I didn't stick around to wait. Whatever business this guy was up to, it was none of mine.

After circling around that development a few times, I finally found my way out and headed back to Mom's. My hands were itching to take out that piece of cardboard from Nolan and Nolan to see if it was a match to the one I found under the bush at the pool.

I was relieved when I finally pulled into her driveway. As I walked to the front door, I glanced across the street to see if there were any other questionable cars in front of Jeanette's house. The last thing I felt like doing was chasing another one down. Thankfully the street was quiet and vacant. No cars in driveways and none on the street. No sooner had I turned the spare key in the door lock and pushed open the door than my mother appeared a few feet away.

"Lock the door behind you. I have to show you something. It was a threat. Someone put it on our security door—see for yourself."

She shoved a letter-size piece of white paper at me. "So? What do you think? It's a threat, huh? We're next on the book curse list."

"Slow down and give me a second."

The paper had two sentences in big bold print: *"Bug Off!"* and *"OR ELSE!"*

"I'm right, Phee. Aren't I? Whoever taped that paper to our door must know we're on to them."

I stared at the paper again and started to laugh.

"You think it's funny?" my mother said. "Marilyn, Minnie, Edna, and Thelmalee didn't think so."

"Mom, take a closer look. This paper is printed. Printed. No one wrote you a note and if anyone did, I doubt they'd take the time to have it professionally printed. It's got to be part of something else. Maybe something came loose and we didn't see it."

Before my mother had a chance to say anything, I stepped outside and looked around. Sure enough, wedged into one of the small cacti was another piece of paper. The sticky tape that was supposed to secure it to the other sheet had come loose.

"See for yourself, Mom. It's not a threat."

The second sheet looked just like the first one, only it had more information.

BUG OFF!
Welcome to the West Valley's
newest exterminating services!

OR ELSE!
Run the risk of unwanted
scorpions, spiders, and pests!

**THIS COUPON GOOD FOR
$25 OFF YOUR FIRST VISIT!**

A phone number and address appeared at the bottom of the page.

My mother was furious.

"They shouldn't advertise like that. Someone could have a heart attack."

"It's just an attention-getting gimmick. And most people wouldn't overreact."

"Most people aren't dealing with unexplained deaths from a book curse."

I ignored her last comment and headed for the couch.

"Don't make yourself comfortable, Phee. We're meeting Lucinda, Shirley, and Louise from the book club at Bagels 'N More for lunch. You didn't meet Louise. Louise Munson. Very nice lady. Taught home economics before they just handed you a microwave and told you to push a button. Anyway, when I started to make my calls, Lucinda was at Louise's house, and both of them thought we should talk about this. She was going to call Shirley to tell her. So, what did you find out from the blue Mazda? Who is he? Is he married?"

I paused for a moment, letting everything she had

just said sink in. I kept my response brief. "You'll be pleased to know I engaged in a very specific police tactic."

My mother's eyes got wide.

"It even has a technical name."

By now, she was practically salivating. "What name?"

I responded slowly and deliberately. "Wild. Goose. Chase."

Chapter 13

Bagels 'N More was about two miles from my mother's house. It was a stand-alone restaurant flanked by a discount tire shop and a taco place. Judging from its parking lot, it appeared most of its customers were getting their tires taken care of. Same could be said for the taco joint. The nice thing about Bagels 'N More was its large patio with green and orange umbrellas shading the round tables like lily pads. As the name suggested, it featured all kinds of bagels and fixings, plus breads, muffins, and cakes.

When we got there, Shirley, Lucinda, and the lady who I presumed to be Louise were all gathered around a large table in the rear. As my mother and I sat, Shirley announced Myrna would be joining us.

I cleared my throat while reaching for the menu. "Myrna? Who's that?"

Shirley immediately responded. "Myrna Mittleson. She's in the book club, too."

Then, in a grand gesture, my mother sighed and leaned into the table. "I guess I'll have to hold off on what I was about to say until she gets here. I hate repeating things."

For a second, I was almost caught off guard. *She hates repeating things? She LIVES to repeat things. Over and over again.* Growing up, I could have sworn she invented the word "nagging." I tried not to laugh and buried my face in the menu.

"There's Myrna now. Over here, Myrna!" someone shouted.

I looked up from the menu to see a tall brunette with bedazzled glasses approach us. She and my mother apparently shared the same flair for style.

After some quick introductions and some not-so-quick orders *(My God, if I were that waitress I'd commit hari-kari with the bagel slicer!)*, my mother finally got to the real reason we were here.

"The book curse, *our* book curse, was all over Channel Five this morning. Someone in our group had to have called that TV station and I, for one, would like to know who."

Lucinda was practically indignant. "You don't think any of us would call, do you, Harriet?"

Before my mother could respond, Louise stated that "maybe someone would do such a thing if they wanted attention," but Shirley would have no part of it.

"Good Lord! It makes us look like we stepped out of the Middle Ages." Myrna, who was otherwise pre-occupied trying to find a coffee cup, suddenly joined the conversation. "I'll tell you what it does! It gets everyone going in the wrong direction so if one of those women was really murdered, it would be blamed on the curse."

Lucinda made a *tsk tsk* sound, shook her head, and looked directly at Myrna.

"That curse is a bunch of hooey. But do you think someone was really murdered? Who? Not Marilyn. The sheriff's department ruled that out. And Minnie had a bad heart. And Thelmalee, an allergy. And Edna Mae—"

"We know, Lucinda, we know," my mother said. "We don't have to go over the entire list. So, once and for all, did anyone here call the TV station?"

Silence. Dead silence. Everyone looked at one another, and I looked at all of them. I'd seen enough crime shows to look for the signs—someone looking down, someone fidgeting, someone biting a lip . . . Nothing. They were all waiting for someone to confess, only no confession came. The only thing that came was our food, and I'd never seen bagels so welcomed in all my life.

"Okay." I tried to keep them focused. "If no one here called, who do you think might have alerted the news?"

Accusations were hurled around the table like ripe fruit at a carnival clown, but as soon as one name was mentioned, all other names ceased. Gretchen Morin, the librarian.

"It would only make sense," Shirley went on to explain. "She'd get so much attention for that library, it would mean more funding. And while I'm at it, maybe she did more than notify the TV station."

An audible series of gasps ricocheted around the room.

"You're not saying she had something directly to do with these deaths, are you?" I asked.

Shirley shook her head and cleared her throat.

"All I'm saying is, the library is always struggling for funding and she could lose her full-time job. Lordy, we all know desperate people do desperate things. Besides, you know what she's like, don't you? She's cold, deliberate, and disconnected. The only time I saw her really animated was when she was talking about type fonts, of all things."

Lucinda pushed her plate toward the center of the table. "Maybe she's not Miss Personality, but that doesn't make her a killer."

Shirley's voice started to rise. "I'm NOT accusing her of killing anyone. At least not intentionally."

I had a similar thought brewing and couldn't keep still. "You mean, maybe she tried to scare people in the club and things got out of control?"

"Exactly," Shirley said.

"Then why would she call even more attention to it by going to the news media?"

"Because," Shirley continued, "the last person anyone would suspect would be a quiet, bookish librarian."

"Which brings me to my next question"—my mother leaned back and raised her head—"did anyone at this table recommend that book?"

As if it were choreographed, all heads were shaking no.

"I'd never even heard of it," Myrna said. "Usually we read books where someone has heard of the author."

Louise laughed. "The author? I didn't even know what an *arrondissement* was. I had to look it up."

My mother was persistent. "So again, ladies, none of you recommended *The Twelfth Arrondissement?*"

Again, the heads shook.

All but Shirley, who said, "Of course, that leaves the other club members. The ones who aren't here. The snowbirds. And the ones who are dead. That's about two thirds of our club."

My mother nodded in agreement. "I'll be phoning the ones who can still pick up. We really need to figure out how that book got on our list and who called the TV station. I don't know about anyone else, but I plan to be glued to the nightly news."

The ladies all seemed to talk at once.

"I already have it on my DVR."

"Me too."

"It's on my Hopper."

"You have DISH?"

"Yes, I hate cable."

"I cancelled my Bridge night so I could watch it live."

My mother acknowledged each speaker with a quick nod as if she were the CEO of a Fortune 500 Company. "Good. We need to get an answer before next week's book club meeting. Some of us are too unnerved to read that novel, and those who did read it are probably beefing up their life insurance."

Her comment was followed by nervous laughter and a waitress who couldn't get us out of the restaurant fast enough. Unfortunately, she put the bill on one check. After what seemed like hours straightening it out and reaffirming everyone's commitment to the evening news, my mother and I got back in the car and headed to her house.

I pounced on her before she even put the keys into the ignition. "You didn't tell me there was a book club meeting next week to discuss *The Twelfth Arrondissement*. When? What time?"

"It must have slipped my mind, Phee. It's Wednesday at ten. We meet and then go out to lunch. The good news is you'll still be here. I just hope I can say the same about the other members of the club. We need to find out who's behind this, and we need to do so before next Wednesday."

"I think we can safely eliminate the crew that was here today. Who's left?"

"Cecilia, Lydia, Constance, Marianne, Ada, and Riva. Some of them are snowbirds and aren't back yet. Still, I'm calling all of them when we get home. And Jeanette, too."

"Mom, do you think the librarian is behind all of this?"

"I'm beginning to think so. Librarians do a lot of research. Enough to ferret out a cursed book and present it to a group of unsuspecting senior citizens as if it were a fancy partridge on Christmas Day—platter and all."

Other than that bizarre little scheme my mother had rolling around in her head about a vindictive wife who tried to kill the husband's girlfriend, aka Jeanette, and my well-thought-out and quite feasible scenario involving Minnie Bendelson's ingestion of finned fish, we really had nothing. Nothing until this moment.

It seemed, with absolute clarity, that Gretchen Morin possessed the only real motive for murder. Well, maybe not murder, but certainly for fabricating a book curse and stirring up a lot of people. Not to mention her possible role in some rather suspicious deaths. And, she had help. Josie Nolan, for one. They sure looked like bosom buddies at the restaurant.

I was certain Josie was the one who put the sugar

under the bush to ensure Thelmalee would get stung. I wasn't so sure she intended for Thelmalee to bite the dust. I planned to find out as soon as we got back.

"I have a clue I'm working on, Mom, and if it fits, we may know exactly *who* has been doing *what*."

"What clue? What clue?"

So I told my mother about what I discovered under the bush by the pool and, more importantly, about the two pieces of cardboard from the cane sugar box I was going to piece together. She immediately stepped on the gas and ignored the twenty-five-mile-per-hour speed limit once we turned into Sun City West. We reached the front door in record time, and I took off to grab my precious clue.

My hands tremored slightly as I placed the recently torn piece of cardboard from today's venture next to the one I'd stashed in a dresser the other day.

"Damn! Not even close."

I was practically wailing. "And I was so sure it was her. I would have bet money if it was a horse race and Josie was running. Damn!"

"That still doesn't mean she didn't do it," my mother said. "Was that the only box of sugar in the credenza at the realty office?"

"Yeah, and believe me, I was petrified I was going to spill the stuff all over when I went to tear off the edge. It was pretty much filled to the top."

"And you said they had a sugar bowl sitting on the countertop?" my mother asked.

"Yes. Yes, a full bowl of sugar. Sugar that had nothing to do with Thelmalee's bees."

"Phee, if that sugar bowl was full and the box you were holding was nearly full, then *that* box couldn't have been the one someone used to pour sugar under a bush. You were holding a new box. The one in question is probably in their trash."

"Oh my God, Mom. I've got to get back over there before they take out the garbage. They probably have a trash basket sitting right next to the coffeemaker. I can't believe I didn't look. What made you realize that? Seems you're the one with the detective skills."

"When your cousin Kirk was little, he tried to sneak sugar out of the boxes all the time. Not to mention cereal. Your aunt Ina got to the point where she actually used a marker to indicate where she left off."

"Wow. Remind me to thank her next time she calls."

My mother gave me a questionable look, and I quickly added, "And you, too."

I was nearly out the front door when something dawned on me and I turned back. My mother had made herself comfortable on the couch next to Streetman. She already had the phone in her hand to contact the rest of the book club.

"Don't start dialing yet. We need a plan. A diversion. I can't go rooting through their trash unnoticed."

"What did you have in mind? I'm not going to make a disturbance in there. I have to live here, you know."

"You won't even have to go there, Mother. Listen, all you need to do is to call the receptionist and keep her on the phone. I've got your number on speed dial. I'll let it ring once and stop. That will be your signal to call Nolan and Nolan. I'm banking on the fact Josie won't even be in the office. It's her sunbathing time at the pool. If I'm lucky, it will be a slow afternoon and no one will see me."

"So if you find an empty sugar container you're just going to carry it out of there?"

"Uh, I hadn't thought about that. My bag is way too small to stick it inside."

"Hold on. I have pocketbooks for every occasion. I never throw them out."

Within seconds I was outfitted with an enormous Vera Bradley bag that most likely had the first pattern she ever designed. It was large, loud, and perfect for the job.

"Don't call anyone until you hear from me. I'll phone you the minute I'm back in the car. Last thing I need is a busy signal," I said.

"Okay. Okay. I've got it, Miss Marple."

There was nothing Miss Marple about me. Well, the bag maybe. Miss Marple was shrewd and deliberate, not to mention a heck of a lot older. Unlike her, I was operating by the seat of my pants and hoping I wouldn't get kicked in that very spot. No one would dare kick Miss Marple. I clutched the Vera Bradley bag and went out the door for the second time.

I tried not to think about what the fines were for speeding tickets in Arizona as I hit the gas pedal. So far I'd been lucky not getting caught. At least in this state. I rationalized that if I did get stopped for speeding, it wouldn't go on my Minnesota license. I'd already succeeded in garnering a few points back home for running a red light because I'd forgotten to set the DVR and didn't want to miss the finale of *The Good Wife*. What would my excuse be this time? A pressing need to pull something out of an office trash container?

Less than a mile to the real estate office and the traffic slowed down. Really slowed down. Two cars ahead of me a golf cart was practically at a crawl. And next to it, one lane over, another golf cart was moving at a snail's pace. *Dear God, can't they pull over and let the normal traffic go by?* I knew golf carts weren't allowed to go over thirty miles an hour, but these guys were doing half that speed. The two cars in front of me made left-hand turns at the next intersection. More likely out of frustration than anything else. I plodded along behind a golf cart that had a flag from The Ohio State University hoisted on its roof and a large sticker that said, GO BUCKEYES. I made a mental note to never, under any circumstance, root for the Buckeyes. Two intersections later, the golf cart signaled right and made a left-hand turn. I shuddered. At least there were no fender benders, and I could see the Nolan and Nolan Realty office across the street.

There was only one car in their parking lot when I arrived. It was a Ford Fusion parked off to the side. Probably Chelsea's, the receptionist. It looked like something she would drive. I was about to go inside when I realized I needed a reason to be there. Luckily, I had one—the realty form. It was stashed in my bag—only the bag was at Mom's since I was now sporting the giant Vera Bradley.

Just walk in and tell her you lost the form. So what if she thinks you're a bumble-head. One excuse is as good as the next.

I opened the car door and started to get out, when all of sudden someone screamed from the other end of the parking lot. It was a woman's voice. Turning around, a lady started running toward me, arms flailing in the air. It was Cindy Dolton, yelling at the top of her lungs.

"Bundles! Bundles escaped from the dog park! He's headed down the block!"

Before I could say anything, she ran past my car toward a series of smaller establishments. Her voice pierced the air like an ice pick. If I was Bundles, I'd keep on running, too. But I wasn't her dog and I felt as if I should do something. I got back in my car and drove down the street slowly, searching for the small white dog.

A streak of white tore through the intersection and headed straight for The Presidential Arms, a large senior citizen complex. I executed the fastest left-hand turn on record and watched as the little bugger stopped to leave his mark on the beautifully manicured oleanders.

Cindy Dolton was a good two blocks away, closer to a coronary than she was to her dog. I pulled up in front of the bushes, leaned over, opened the passenger door, and shouted, "Here, boy! Want to go for a ride? Go for a ride?"

Bundles immediately turned his attention to me and leapt into the car as if he'd been waiting for a chauffeur all morning. I coaxed him onto my lap, leaned over again, and closed the door. "Gotcha, little buddy!" I waited for Cindy Dolton to round the corner. She came into view, panting and huffing her way down the street. Bundles moved from my lap to the passenger's seat and proceeded to lie down. Cindy was gasping for air, pausing every few seconds to yell for her dog. I know she was trying to say "Bundles. Bundles," but it sounded more like "Undles. Undles."

Now it was my voice that jarred the neighborhood

as I rolled my window down. "It's okay! I've got him. Get inside."

Cindy opened the side door and Bundles jumped all over her, licking her face as if none of this was his fault. I was positive the woman didn't even register who I was. She was totally focused on her dog.

"Oh my God! I can't thank you enough. He could have been killed! Some half-wit at the dog park went out the side gate and Bundles ran through it. That gate is only supposed to be used for the maintenance people. The front gate has double entry for safety. Oh my God! My poor little Bundles!"

The dog was about as nonplussed as an animal could be. He finished licking Cindy's face and started to clean his front paws.

She turned her attention back to me. "Oh my goodness. You're Harriet's daughter. What a coincidence that you were in front of the realty office. Thank you so much for saving Bundles's life."

"No problem. I'll drive you back to the dog park. You must be exhausted from all that running."

"Out of breath, but not exhausted," Cindy said. "Usually I just take Bundles to the park early in the morning, but I had some free time today and thought he'd enjoy another outing. Believe me, when I see that nincompoop who left the door open, I'll certainly have words with him."

"Uh-huh."

"I know it's none of my business, but since I saw you in front of Nolan and Nolan, are you buying property?"

Not if I can help it, but the thought did cross my mind. And exited out of there as fast as possible.

"Um, er, no. I mean, I don't know. I just pulled in

their lot to get something out of my eye. The dust is terrible here."

No sooner did I say that when I realized I would be heading back to that office. What if Cindy drove past on her way home and saw me? I had to think fast.

"Of course, I may wind up going back there. They have free maps of the area and I could sure use one."

"I know what you mean. I've lived here for seven years and sometimes I get lost. And who's got time to start fiddling around with one of those GPS systems? Oh, here we are at the dog park already. You can just drop me off at the gate. I'm going to plop myself on the benches and relax before I take Bundles home."

There were a few small dogs milling around and three or four ladies sitting on the benches. I envisioned Cindy telling those ladies about "the nincompoop who left the gate open." She thanked me again and carried Bundles straight into the park. I immediately turned the car around and headed back to Nolan and Nolan.

In the ten or fifteen minutes that it had taken me to rescue the dog and return him and his owner to the park, the lot in front of the realty office had filled up. Damn! I couldn't very well go inside and be seen by people as I rooted through the trash. Aggravated, I continued down the street and turned at the intersection that led to my mother's house. *Great work, Miss Marple.*

Chapter 14

"You're back!" my mother shouted. "I never got your call. Did you try to call me? I wasn't on the phone with anyone. What happened? Did you get the empty box?"

"No, no, and no. I didn't call. I didn't get the box. I didn't go in."

My mother looked at me dumbfounded. I couldn't tell if she was perplexed or annoyed because she didn't get a chance to start calling the ladies from the book club.

"Had to rescue a dog. Never got out of the car. Give me a minute and I'll explain."

At that point, I walked into the kitchen and took a bottle of water from the fridge. Then I proceeded to tell her exactly what had happened and why I couldn't go back inside. "So I guess that's one clue we'll never find."

"Of course you'll find it. You'll find it once they close."

"Huh?"

"It's a realty office. And a big one at that. They're not going to leave their trash basket filled till the next day. Someone is going to take it out to their Dumpster behind the building. All of those buildings have Dumpsters. After five you'll go back and check the Dumpster."

"WHAT? Are you nuts?"

"Phee, I've seen detectives do this all the time—*Cagney and Lacey*, that crew from *Castle, Rizzoli and Isles.* . . ."

"MOM!" My voice all but exploded. "Number one, I'm not a detective. And number two, more importantly, neither are they!!! They're actors! Actors, for heaven's sake."

"Well, I'm sure that's what detectives do."

"I'll tell you what they don't do. They don't tamper with evidence. You should know that. You watch enough of those shows."

"You'll wear gloves. That way you won't be tampering with evidence, you'll be finding it."

"Honestly. You'll justify anything to suit yourself."

"You need to do this, Phee. What other choice do you have?"

"Aaagh."

She had a point. I hated the thought of digging through someone's trash, but then again, if I could link that empty box of cane sugar to Thelmalee's death, I'd have part of the book curse figured out. After all, it wasn't as if someone was going to confess to all of this nonsense.

"Fine. Fine. I'll go after dinner. That'll give me enough time to get back for the evening news. Did they say what time the librarian would be on?"

"At six. So, let's eat a bit earlier. At four-thirty. That'll give you an hour. It shouldn't take that long."

"You're not coming?"

"No, I have to stay here. What if one of the book club women calls? Or Streetman needs to go out? You'll be fine, honey. It won't get dark until seven or so. You'll be back way before then. In time to see what that Gretchen Morin has to say."

I shrugged as I tossed the empty water bottle into the recycling basket by the laundry room.

"It's almost four now, Mom. I'm going to answer some e-mails and then review my wardrobe."

"Your wardrobe?"

"Yep, for the finest garbage-rooting, trash-sifting outfit I can find."

At precisely 5:36, I pulled into the parking lot of Nolan and Nolan. It was totally empty. There were no lights on in the office. I followed the side driveway to the rear of the building and, sure enough, I found myself looking straight at two small white and red Dumpsters.

I got out of the car quickly and put on a long pair of obnoxious yellow rubber gloves my mother had been saving for "something major that needs to be cleaned." I walked over to the first Dumpster and lifted the lid—recycling. Nothing but bottles, cans, and lots of cardboard boxes. If I'd bothered to take a closer look, I would have seen the recycling emblem on the side of the Dumpster. Yet another reason why I wasn't cut out for investigative work.

"The Treasure of the Sierra Madre" was waiting for me one Dumpster over. At least I prayed it was. I lifted the lid and peered inside. A few heavy black plastic bags and a bountiful supply of white kitchen-size trash bags. *It has to be the kitchen size. Go for it.*

Opening a sealed plastic trash bag while wearing heavy rubber gloves was impossible. I did the next best thing. I ripped a small hole on the top and moved all sorts of paper products around. Used coffee cups, wooden stir sticks, napkins, plates, and a few paper containers from a Chinese restaurant. No sugar cane box. On to the next bag. Same story, only this time it was two small pizza boxes. I had barely punched a hole into the third bag when I was blinded by blue and red headlights. The sheriff's posse!

If my daughter could have seen me leaning head-first into a Dumpster, yellow rubber gloves up to my elbows and police car flashers on my rear end, she'd be doubled over in hysterics. I couldn't believe my own mother, her grandmother, had put me up to this; and I, for one, wasn't laughing.

A deputy in his late fifties or early sixties got out of the car and walked toward me. Not a volunteer posse member, but a sheriff's deputy. I could read the large yellow lettering on his vehicle. MCSO. Maricopa County Sheriff's Office. The volunteer posse cars looked the same but didn't have those letters. I knew the posse handled routine matters like conducting welfare checks and responding to nuisance calls. Serious matters were relegated to the deputies. Terrific. They sent the big guns after me.

"Excuse me, ma'am, but you're not supposed to go through the Dumpsters. Got a call from dispatch. The people living in the complex behind you got suspicious. Thought you might be planting something dangerous."

Ma'am? When did I become a ma'am? Must be these garbage-rooting clothes.

"Oh, I'm so sorry. I know. I know. But I have no

choice. You see, I was at the realty office today and I made myself a cup of coffee. When I was done, I threw the stirrer and some napkins in the trash. And I think my gold bracelet came undone and went in there with it. By the time I realized, the office had closed. I really, really need to find that bracelet. It was a gift from my mother and she would be, um . . . let's just say it wouldn't go over well."

I wiped moisture from my eyes, hoping the deputy would mistake it for sentiment and not what it really was—sweat.

He took a breath and looked at his watch. "Okay. You can have a few more minutes."

"Thank you so much. I know I'll find it."

"I'd stay to give you a hand, but I've got another stop to make. Don't take all night. I'll be swinging back by here."

"Oh, that's fine. I understand. I appreciate it. And please tell the residents behind us they have nothing to worry about."

"Shall do."

The deputy got back in his car and I turned around to look at the apartments, trying to suppress the urge I had to give them an old-fashioned Bronx salute. Instead, I made a grunting sound and went back to the plastic bag with the recently punched hole in it. No dice there either. More plates, cups, and crumpled pieces of paper. There had to be a week's worth of office litter inside the Dumpster, and I was getting annoyed. After all, the bag I wanted should have been on the top. I decided to take another approach and reach for a bag that was off to the side, figuring that maybe it started off on top of the bigger bags and rolled over.

I tore into that one full force, only to have liquid shoot up into my face. Damn! Full cups of coffee. Who threw away full cups of coffee? By now I was really getting exasperated. I was certain the people living in The Presidential Arms complex were watching my sideshow intently. Who wouldn't? It was probably the best reality show on TV that evening.

Mumbling a few choice words, I tossed the coffee-filled bag back into the Dumpster and grabbed the bag that was on the other side. I had to make it quick for fear the deputy sheriff would be circling back any minute. Like a desperate gambler, I muttered, "Come on, baby, Mama needs a new pair of shoes," and ripped the side seam of the bag wide open. PAY DIRT! The sugar cane box was inches from my hand. I unzipped the Vera Bradley and stuffed the cardboard box inside, grinning like a toothless baboon who'd just been given a bowl of mashed bananas.

YAHOO! I was absolutely ecstatic as I flung the Vera Bradley over my shoulder and tossed the white plastic bag back into the Dumpster along with the yellow gloves. *That's right, Mom. I'm throwing them away. I'll buy you a new pair. I'm not going to wash these out!* I was about to walk back to my car when I realized a piece of trash had fallen on the ground. It was an e-mail message someone had printed out. Part of it was missing, including the address, but the sentence I saw was enough to convince me there was more to the sugar cane box.

Listen, it's getting out of control. I'm afraid
someone is really going to be murdered.
And put a muzzle on your—

A muzzle on your what? Your wife? Your husband? Not a dog. Who? Too bad the paper was torn so I couldn't see the rest of the message.

I jumped into the car and headed right out of the parking lot. *Good night, Presidential Arms, because the real reality show is about to begin.*

Chapter 15

"Mom!" I shouted, shoving the front door wide open. "I found it! I found it! And that's not all!"

"SHH! That news segment is coming on. What took you so long? Never mind. You didn't miss anything. Quick. Sit down. The empty box isn't going anywhere."

"Turn the sound up. I need to wash my hands. I was rooting through a Dumpster. A Dumpster!" I was practically screaming.

"Shh. Tell me after the show. And whatever you do, don't try to move Streetman from the floral chair. He's likely to snap off your fingers. He doesn't like to be disturbed when he rests."

"I thought you said he didn't bite."

"He doesn't. Unless you disturb him. Then he snaps. Snaps, mind you, not bites."

"Yeesh. I'll take the armchair."

Plunking myself down, I stared at the TV screen and watched as the feature was introduced. Typical studio setting for an interview. Gretchen Morin stood out as soon as the segment began. Her long blond hair framed her shoulders and hung gracefully over her sleeveless blue dress. She was seated on a stool facing Nina Alvarez, the evening anchor. Both women were holding copies of *The Twelfth Arrondissement*.

"I've DVR'd this," my mother whispered. "In case we need to review it."

I was about to say something when Nina Alvarez spoke.

"This evening we're pleased to welcome Gretchen Morin, the librarian at Sun City West Library, for what's turning out to be quite the book stir. I'm holding a copy of a little-known gothic romance-mystery that some of its readers believe put a curse on them. Gretchen, can you tell us more?"

"Certainly, Nina, and thank you for inviting me. The book, *The Twelfth Arrondissement*, is just that— a gothic romance-mystery by an upcoming author, Lily Margot Gerald."

At that point, Gretchen held the book in the air as if it were a royal baby being put on display for the realm. She cleared her throat softly. "Having read the book, I can tell you it has a moving plotline, well-developed characters, and some interesting twists and turns."

"What about the curse, Gretchen?" Nina broke in. "Can you tell us about that?"

Gretchen looked a bit put off. "The novel was selected as a book of the month by the Sun City West Booked 4 Murder book club."

At which point my mother pointed a finger at the screen and yelled, "Liar!"

"Shh. I want to hear this."

Gretchen went on. "Unfortunately, shortly after the

club members started to read the book, four of them died unexpectedly and a fifth had a close encounter with death."

"Here it comes, Mom. Here it comes. Nina is going to push her for more information."

"Shh. Now you're the one who's interrupting. Listen."

The TV banter continued. "Oh my goodness, Gretchen. No wonder it got the reputation of being cursed. When you say these club members died unexpectedly, can you expound on that for our viewers?"

"I don't have police or hospital reports, but I do know one of them died in a car crash, two died in the hospital, and one succumbed from a bee sting. Oh, yes. Another was almost poisoned by carbon monoxide."

"Whoa. That's enough for me to select another book for my fall reading. Seriously, do you think people are overreacting about this alleged book curse?"

"I most certainly do. As I mentioned before, it's a quality book that deserves a large readership."

"If that's the case, how come no one has heard about the book?"

"That's not unusual. It takes up-and-coming authors quite a while to get noticed. Even the famous ones, whose names are bandied about, were unknowns at one juncture in time."

"True. True. But none of them had books associated with such a high number of deaths. What percent of the book club passed away since they began reading the book?"

"About thirty percent."

"So approximately one-third. I would venture that number is more than an anomaly. And that number doesn't include the person who nearly died. Correct?"

Gretchen stared into the camera. "Yes."

"You said earlier you thought this was a well-written book. Did you notice anything unusual about the book? Hidden messages? Spells?"

"No, nothing of the sort."

Nina Alvarez leaned closer to Gretchen. "Let me be quite frank. Do you believe the book is cursed in any way?"

"Absolutely not."

"Well, it's certainly getting that reputation. I wouldn't be surprised if people purchase it to send to their enemies."

Like a well-planned paid advertisement, Gretchen held up the book again. "Books cannot be cursed. And if people do buy the book for nefarious purposes, all they'll find is an interesting novel, well worth reading. Again, no book curse. This is the twenty-first century."

"And there you have it, viewers. No curse. Still, I'd put a warning on the jacket—Read at Your Own Risk. Thank you, Gretchen, for joining us this evening. Oh, and by the way, when will the book club be discussing this novel?"

"At their meeting this Wednesday in the library."

"Can anyone attend?"

"Absolutely. We have a large room and lots of chairs."

"Get out your event calendars, folks. This may be one meeting you might enjoy attending. I know our news crew will plan to be there. And now, over to you, Kimberly, for the weather."

The screen changed abruptly and a tall, slender woman with short dark hair approached the weather map and began to talk. My mother clicked the Mute button just as the phone rang. I leaned back and watched the visual as I listened to my mother's end of the conversation.

"Yes, we just finished watching it. . . . Uh-huh. Uh-huh . . . I thought so, too. That witch wants everyone to read the book. Uh-huh. Uh-huh . . . No, no, I don't think you need to bring your priest to the book club meeting. It's a book club, not an exorcism. Uh-huh. Okay. Sure. Talk to you tomorrow. Uh-huh. Bye."

"That was Cecilia Flanagan from the club. You haven't met her. If you join me tomorrow at the food bank, you'll get to meet her and her sister."

"The food bank?" *Now what?*

"Oh, I forgot to mention it. I volunteer at the food bank a few Saturdays a month."

"That's great, but if you don't mind, I think I'll use that time to track down some more leads. And speaking of which, I've got to check that sugar cane box and show you what I found in the Dumpster."

I took the sugar cane box from the Vera Bradley bag and went into the guest room to grab the cardboard tab I found under the bush by the pool.

"This better match. After all I went through tonight, it better match," I muttered.

I held the sugar cane box with one hand and the tab with the other. Like a kid whose science experiment just yielded a frothy volcano, I couldn't control the exhilaration I felt.

"It's a perfect fit! A perfect fit! Like Cinderella's shoe for a murderer. Oh my God, Mom, it's a match! This proves Josie Nolan was responsible for Thelmalee's death. And I found another bit of evidence that proves Josie wasn't working alone. Look!"

At that point I handed my mother the ripped e-mail I found behind the realty company. "Don't you see? Josie Nolan's probably in this deeper than mud in Missouri. I knew it the minute I saw her with the librarian that night."

For a brief second, I felt like Miss Marple, Hercule Poirot, and Sherlock Holmes all rolled into one package. I could hardly contain myself. "I did it, Mom. I did it. No book curse. Just murder."

My mother put the note on the table and muttered two words that instantly deflated my growing ego. "Circumstantial evidence."

"Huh? Do you even know what that means, or are you simply saying that because you've heard it on TV?"

"Of course I know what it means, and that's what we have here—circumstantial evidence. And here's another word for you—motive. Motive. What motive would Josie or any of those pool women have to kill Thelmalee? Don't give me that look. You did a great job. A wonderful job. . . ."

At that point, my mother walked over and gave me a hug. "It's just that it's such a small piece in this entire book curse, honey."

"Do you think we should call the sheriff's posse station and let them know what we've discovered?"

"NO! Absolutely not. They'll just put this stuff in a

box somewhere and ignore the whole thing. And for all I know, they could arrest you for tampering with evidence."

"Tampering with evidence? Now it's tampering with evidence? When you wanted me to look for it, it was just *finding* evidence."

"Don't you need a search warrant or something?" my mother asked.

"To go through garbage? Which, by the way, was your idea. My God, Mom. You're driving me crazy."

"Look, Phee. Let's put this evidence in a plastic bin and hold on to it while you continue your investigation."

"You make it sound as if I know what I'm doing. I'm not so sure."

"Well, I am. Something in that police department back in Minnesota must have rubbed off on you."

Chapter 16

My mother had already walked the dog and left for the food bank by the time I had gotten out of bed, showered, and dressed. Sitting at the kitchen table, I couldn't help but mull over the fact she volunteered in her community. And by mull over, what I really meant was, feel guilty. Truth of the matter was, I hadn't "given back" to my community since my daughter started college.

In the flurry of years between my daughter's elementary school and high school graduation, I had participated in countless bake sales, bowl-a-thons, dance marathons, car washes, raffles, and anything else that raised funds for the needy, the sick, and the four-legged. But with my daughter on her own as a first-year teacher in St. Cloud, I centered on work and work only. I didn't want to admit it, but I had become much more insulated. That was, until I signed on for my new role as de facto investigator for cursed books. Crazy as the situation was, I was beginning to think of it as some sort of community service. After all, I wasn't getting paid, and I certainly wasn't getting a promotion.

The cream blended into my coffee as I thought about a possible motive for Josie and the sunbathers, but none of it made sense. Could it have been a real-estate deal gone bad? I'd read about those things and even saw versions of them on *48 Hours*. Still, it wasn't adding up. Not yet, anyway. No sooner had I lifted the cup to my mouth when I saw the familiar red and blue flashers out the window. The sheriff's posse? Now what?

Taking a quick gulp, I walked over to the window for a closer look. Not the posse. It was the fire truck and they had stopped in front of Jeanette's house again. My first thought was that someone had succeeded in murdering her. *Make that 35%, Gretchen.*

I grabbed my set of keys and made sure the door locked behind me. No sense inviting trouble if indeed some nutcase was making the rounds of the neighborhood. Besides, Streetman didn't strike me as much of a watchdog. I headed straight across our terra-cotta path to the sidewalk and hurried across the street. Amazing. Herb Garrett was already standing in front of the fire truck and waved his hand to acknowledge me. He appeared to be holding in his stomach. I was afraid he'd lose his breath any moment.

"Hey there, cutie. Don't worry. It can't be anything life-threatening or an ambulance would be here as well as someone from the sheriff's department. They'd either send a deputy or a posse volunteer."

Jeanette's beige and tan house with coral trim appeared to be fine as I approached Herb. No flames, no smoke, no nothing. Not even a branch out of place on her oleander and lantana bushes.

I walked toward him and took a closer look. Nothing. The fire department often changed smoke detector batteries for residents, but I seriously doubted they would arrive flashers and all. I was about to say something to that effect to Herb when Jeanette literally came racing out of her front door, her long blond hair flying all over the place and her arms flailing in the air.

"SNAKE! SNAKE! There's a huge snake in my house! OH MY GOD! SNAKE!"

Seconds later, four firemen came out of the house. One was carrying a five-gallon bucket and another one was holding a long, pronged rod. The man with the bucket walked over toward Jeanette and spoke.

"It's okay, ma'am. We've got him. Appears to be a king snake or a coral snake. They're both pretty similar. The coral is venomous, but the king is harmless. We'll release it in the desert."

"Can you drive to Tucson and release it there? I don't understand how something like this could have happened. This is a residential area. A residential area, for crying out loud!"

Jeanette was beside herself, and I could tell the fireman had all he could do to keep himself from laughing.

He bit his lip and tried to answer her. "Snakes can slip under a garage door, under a security door, or even get inside a tote bag that someone may have put on the ground for a few minutes. I wouldn't worry about it. Chances are it's a king snake. Anyway, you're all set. Have a good morning."

He immediately got inside the truck, snake in the

bucket and all. The vehicle headed down the street, this time with its lights off.

Jeanette walked over to where Herb and I were standing. She was still visibly shaken. "I had just walked into the bathroom to put on my lipstick and there it was! All coiled up by the door to the clothes closet. I could have had a coronary. I swear, nothing like this has ever happened before. I feel as if that stupid book cursed all of us! And that librarian. Did either of you see her on TV last night? She practically took out an ad for the entire world to read that thing."

I let out a breath and took a step closer to Jeanette. "Yeah, I saw the segment. And yeah, it did seem like she really was promoting the book. And the club, too. She invited everyone to attend on Wednesday."

Herb let out some sort of grunt and mumbled, "That should be a real sideshow. Maybe I ought to mark it on my calendar." He looked at both of us and added, "I was only kidding. That's the last place I'd go. Anyway, glad you're okay, Jeanette, and nice seeing you again, Phee. I'm going home for my morning breakfast. Have a good day, ladies."

We stood silently as Herb made a beeline for his house, but I swore he gave me a wink just before heading to his front door. Jeanette, on the other hand, was flustered.

I gave her a pat on the arm. "Yikes. I imagine that really was scary, finding a snake like that."

"Scary? That's an understatement. I'm a complete wreck. Now I'm going to be looking under the beds, inside the closets, and in all the corners for the next month!"

"I'm sure you don't have to worry. Snakes don't travel in packs. They're kind of loners, from what little I know."

Of course, I did know that snakes got really weird around mating season, but I had no idea when that season was in Arizona. Spring? Summer? It was still late summer. I decided to change the subject and revisit the Stardust Theater's movie of the week.

"Um, by the way, was that you sitting behind my mother and me at the Stardust Theater the other night? My mother adores those old musicals."

"I didn't see your mother or I would have said hello. I was sitting up front with a friend. We got there too late for any of the good seats and had to leave as soon as it was over. Didn't even stay for the credits."

For a second, I felt as if someone had let the air out of my tires. So much for pinning Edna Mae's death on Jeanette. Then again, she could be lying. How on earth would I know? I decided to pry a bit more.

"I'm amazed you can still keep your sanity. I mean, with the carbon monoxide incident and now the snake. You can't really believe that has to do with *The Twelfth Arrondissement*, do you?"

"Up until that book landed on our club reading list, my life was pretty ordinary. I don't know what to think."

I tried to focus on what I was going to say next, knowing I'd probably never get another chance. "I don't mean to be nosy . . . I mean, it's none of my business . . . but, oh gee, this is what they always ask on those police shows . . . Jeanette, do you have any enemies? You know, like, say a jealous ex-wife or . . ."

Her eyes nearly popped out of her head and, for a minute, I wasn't sure if she was going to tell me to "go and pound salt" or break down in a hysterical cry. "Jealous ex-wife? I have an ex-husband, but, believe me, no one would want to marry him. I can't believe I ever did. And enemies? Whoa. That's such a strong word. No, I don't think so. But I did let go of my cleaning lady because her rates got too high and her work got too sloppy. We didn't part on the best of terms. Although, I did say I'd give her decent references. And I once had a major disagreement with Shirley Johnson over who should be cast to play Christian Grey when *Fifty Shades of Grey* became a movie. Can you believe that woman told me I had absolutely no "film sense," whatever that's supposed to mean. But enemies? The kind of enemies who would try to kill me? Absolutely not. That's why it all comes back to the book. That stupid cursed book."

"You don't really believe that, do you?"

"Like I said, everything around here was perfectly fine until that thing appeared on our reading list. Look, I'd love to stand and chat with you, but I've got to get going. Tell your mom I said hi."

"Um, sure thing. Have a good day."

Jeanette walked back to her front door; then I crossed the street and unlocked our door. I made a point of looking down to be sure there weren't any snakes waiting to slither inside. Then I made another point of going right to the kitchen to see if the blue Mazda was going to pick her up.

Chapter 17

Forty minutes later, a second cup of coffee and no blue Mazda. I did, however, see Jeanette's garage door open and her car backing out onto the street. It was a white KIA Sportage and looked as if it had just come out of the showroom. I had test-driven that same model earlier this year when I considered trading in my car but then decided against purchasing a new car. Didn't need any more payments. I had enough bills on my desk to start a mini Leaning Tower of Pisa. Maybe Jeanette's finances were better than mine. Maybe West Valley Home Mortgage Solutions was personal, not professional.

I looked at my mother's kitchen clock. It was already past ten. I couldn't afford to let the rest of the morning waste away. I was hell-bent on finding out if any toxicology tests were done on Minnie Bendelson since my "finned fish" theory was still in play, and I had to do a little more digging into Thelmalee's unfortunate demise. I wanted to rule out any involvement with members of Thelmalee's family. My mother had been quite emphatic about the fact Thelmalee's relatives were "scavenging the house like seagulls tearing off barnacles from a ship."

Since I wasn't sure how to begin with acquiring a toxicology report, I figured I'd call Nate later in the day to ask him. That left me with Thelmalee. I had already checked the phonebook and had written down where she lived. Less than a mile from my mother's place. I thought I'd drive over there, introduce myself as a friend, and offer my condolences to the family.

Grabbing my bag, I headed for the door, making sure there were no snakes in the vicinity before closing and locking it. My mother would never forgive me if Streetman had an encounter with a snake. As I started toward Thelmalee's, something dawned on me. It would be very rude to arrive without bringing something. Flowers wouldn't make sense at this point, but food was always appropriate. A quick stop at the supermarket and I had a large bakery box of assorted cookies in tow.

The immediate area surrounding Thelmalee's beige and blue ranch home looked like Costco's parking lot. Cars everywhere. California plates. Arizona plates. Colorado plates. One vehicle, a black Dodge Ram pickup, was sitting in her driveway, its bed filled with furniture and boxes. Apparently my mother was right. The family was doing some picking.

I parked across the street to avoid getting blocked in on the off chance more relatives would be on their way. With my bag flung over my shoulder and the box of cookies under one arm, I made my way to the front door and rang the bell. My first impression of the family was ingrained in my head before I even laid eyes on anyone.

"Will someone get the damn door?" a voice screamed.

"What?" It was another screamer.

"Someone's at the door! Can't one of you idiots open the door?" Still another screaming voice.

"I'm in the middle of something! Maisy-Jayne, open the door for your mother!"

With an armful of cookies getting heavier each minute, I was beginning to have second thoughts.

"Maisy-Jayne! Did you hear me? Get the door!"

I pictured a sweet little girl with blond curls approaching the door and letting me inside. Instead, I found myself face-to-face with a girl about thirteen or fourteen who could have easily passed for a member of *The Munsters* or *The Addams Family*. Except, those kids didn't have pierced eyebrows or a silver pin sticking through their lip. I don't know what I would have done if my daughter had gone through the Goth stage. The sheer cost of makeup would have put me in the poorhouse.

The girl looked at me, turned away, and yelled, "I opened the stupid door. Now what?" I started to say something when she shrugged her shoulders, glared at me again, and walked out of the room.

Unsure of what to do, I closed the door behind me and took a step inside. It was a madhouse. An absolute madhouse. The TV was on, but no one was watching it. Two smaller children, a boy and a girl, were jumping on the couch and poking each other. A middle-aged woman was sitting on a cushion in front of a large cabinet, going through all of the contents.

"What about the mattresses, Carleen? Take 'em

or leave 'em?" someone shouted from one of the bedrooms.

"If they're gross, leave them alone. Otherwise, we'll take them back with us," came another voice from a different room.

The woman who was sifting through the cabinet started to walk toward the bedrooms when she saw me standing in the middle of the room.

"Are you the lady from the estate sale?" she asked.

I shifted my weight from one foot to the next as I looked around the room. The kids on the couch were using a large table lamp as a shield while they continued to poke at each other. At the rate these people were going, I doubted there'd be anything left intact for a sale.

"No, no, sorry, I'm not. I'm a . . . I mean, I came here to give my condolences to the family. Thelma-lee was in the Booked 4 Murder book club."

"That figures," the mother said. "Look, we're kind of busy right now. Got to get this place cleaned out and on the market. So—"

"UNBELIEVABLE! FREAKING UN-BELIEVABLE!"

The woman stopped and turned her attention to a middle-aged man whose stomach had seen one beer too many and whose razor was probably still in mint condition. The man went on ranting as if I wasn't in the room.

"UNBELIEVABLE! Those worthless morons at the hospital sent us the wrong report. Good thing we got the right death certificate, or we'd never straighten this mess out. But look at this! Would you look at this?"

He shoved a legal-size paper at the woman who

was about to throw me out of the place and stood back while she took a good look.

"Who the hell is Minnie Bendelson?" she screamed.

My jaw dropped open as if I were a pelican about to store a week's worth of fish. It was all I could do to keep from saying anything.

"How am I supposed to know?" the man yelled back. "But they sent us her damn toxicology report. I don't give a ripe tomato how she died, but the lawyers are itching to find out if it really was a swarm of bees that killed your mother."

"Of course it was a swarm of bees, Lenny," the woman said. "Everyone at the pool saw what happened."

At that point, the two kids who were quickly wreaking havoc with the furniture noticed the big box of cookies I was holding. "Cookies! I want to eat them now!"

"Yeah, me too!"

The woman turned to me, pointed to the kitchen, and said, "You can just put them on the table. The kids will help themselves."

As I walked to the table, she handed me the report and said, "Do you mind? Just throw it in the garbage since you're going in there."

"Hey, Lenny and Almalynn!" someone bellowed from the other side of the house. "Carleen and I need some help with these mattresses!"

"Can't you get Maisy-Jayne or Frankie to do it?"

"Frankie's sitting on the pot, and I don't know where my niece has gone off to!"

"All right! All right! We're coming!"

"I'm calling the damn hospital first," the man whom

I assumed was Lenny shouted out. "Then I'll be back to deal with mattresses."

In the midst of what I could best describe as a *Jerry Springer* episode waiting to happen, I quickly folded the report and shoved it into my bag. By now, the two kids had dumped most of the bakery cookies on the table and floor, and I was itching to get out of there.

"Um, well, sorry for your loss," I mumbled. "Good luck with the, uh, mattresses and your report. Nice meeting you."

I was out the door and crossing the street toward my car when a slender woman who looked to be about my age walked over to me. She was wearing a long, loose-flowing peach tunic and all I could picture was one of those kids tugging at it asking her if she brought them any candy.

"Hi! Are you with the Kirkson family? I'm Sherry Fairchild from Sherry and Jenny's Fare Estate Sales."

She waved her hand in the direction of a light blue minivan that had an estate sale sign on its door, and I acknowledged it.

"Sorry. No, I, um, er . . . I was just dropping off some cookies for the family. They're all inside."

"Oh, you must have been a friend of the deceased. My partner, Jenny, was the one who set this up. I've never met the family, but Jenny said she didn't want to deal with them."

Gee. Big surprise there. I took a quick breath and didn't say anything.

"That's so unlike my partner. Frankly, I'm a bit skeptical of what I'm about to encounter. Any ideas?"

"I never met Thelmalee Kirkson's family until today, but I think they're going to be a handful."

"I just hope they don't have an overinflated idea of what items are worth. Sometimes people put outrageous price tags on all sorts of things for sentimental reasons," Sherry said.

"The family didn't strike me as having a whole lot of sentimentality, but then again, I was only with them for a few minutes."

"From what my partner described, I feel as if I'm walking into a den of pickpockets and scavengers."

I wanted to add the word "rude" to the description, but simply muttered, "Uh-huh."

"Jenny even told me one of the sons-in-law was furious his mother-in-law died because she had been giving them a portion of her social security each month and, according to him, 'some stupid bee ended the gravy train,' whatever that was supposed to mean."

"Um, Thelmalee Kirkson died of an allergic reaction to a bee sting."

"Oh dear. So her death was really unexpected. How sad. And you know what else? The other son-in-law complained that now no one was going to be making the payments on his new truck. Good grief. I dread going in there. Anyway, here's my card in case you ever want to hold an estate sale."

I took the card, put it in my bag, and thanked her. She hadn't realized it, but Sherry Fairchild had just eliminated the extended Kirkson family as suspects. The "pickpockets and scavengers" didn't want Mama's "gravy train" to make its last stop.

That left me with my original suspects and some tangible evidence. All I needed to do was find a motive that would link them to Thelmalee's murder. I also needed to rule out the possible murder of

Minnie Bendelson. Thanks to the Kirksons, and a blunder at the hospital, the answer to that question was safely stowed in my bag. I couldn't wait to read what it said, and the perfect place was just a few minutes away at Bagels 'N More.

I arrived as the lunch crew was starting to trickle in. There was a great corner table by the window, so I made a beeline for it and plunked myself down. As the aroma of hot garlic and cheese filled the air, I realized how absolutely famished I was. Much too ravenous to read a report without food in my stomach. Thankfully the service was fast. Wiping the last crumb from my onion and cream cheese bagel, I reached for the document. Within seconds, I was lost. Why couldn't I be tracking down someone's accounting nightmare and not a medical one?

Obtaining a toxicology report and being able to understand it, as I quickly learned, were two different things. I read it over and over again between sips of coffee, each time understanding less and less. The same could be said for my smartphone. If I had any idea how to snap a picture of the report and send it to Nate, I would have done so immediately. Learning how to use that phone was "on my list," but, like so many other technological things, it stayed there indefinitely until the device was rendered "outdated."

Therefore, I was forced to drive to the nearest UPS store to fax the thing. Luckily the place was close by in a small shopping center right in the middle of Sun City West. I left Nate a brief voicemail explaining I was sending him a toxicology report and that he needed to call me in the evening.

It took me all of five minutes to have the sheet of paper faxed to Nate, care of the Mankato Police

Department. I folded the original back into my bag and started toward the door when a man who'd been using the copy machine spoke.

"So, are you enjoying your stay at Sun City West? The heat's starting to dissipate finally. We're back to the high nineties and low hundreds."

I gave him a funny look, as if to say, "How did you know I was visiting?"

"You don't recognize me, do you? I'm one of the monitors from the rec center pool. I was there the day you asked about the bees."

"Oh, I'm sorry. I'm terrible with names and not so great with faces either, apparently."

"Well, you're seeing me out of context. If I were back at the pool, you'd remember."

"The only thing I remember was worrying about getting stung."

"That incident was such a fluke. Poor woman. There's been nothing like that ever since. No bee activity at all. In fact, the spot she used to occupy has now been commandeered by the group of women who used to sit closer to the entrance."

"The, uh . . . sunbathers?"

"Yeah, that cluster of five or six of them, depending on the day. Well, now they can just spread out at the other end and watch the comings and goings at the pool. They've got the perfect ringside seats," the monitor added.

I thought back to the bush and the small hole. There was no sugar in there, just the piece of cardboard. It was highly doubtful that whoever poured the stuff came back to scoop it up or they would have taken the evidence with them. No, more than likely, every bee in the vicinity helped himself to that poolside treat. And that was how Thelmalee got stung.

"Do you know the women from that group? They seemed friendly when I was there."

"No, not really. I did recognize the one as Josie Nolan from the realty company since her picture is plastered all over the community, but as far as the others go, no. We get so many people through the gates and, even though I check their rec cards, I don't memorize their names. I'd be on information overload. Well, anyway, I hope you have a great visit. Maybe I'll catch you at the pool one of these days."

"Maybe. It was nice talking to you."

The man went back to his project at the copy machine and I had one more stop to make before heading back—Edna Mae Langford's street. She lived in the "combo zone," as my mother liked to call it. Since the developers couldn't make up their minds about the landscaping, the houses on her block wound up with gravel lawns, Palo Verde and mesquite trees, chunky bismuth palms, and more boulders than the backdrop for a John Wayne movie. I should know. My cousin Kirk and I watched a zillion of those westerns as kids.

I really didn't expect anyone to be on the street at this part of the day. It was too hot to be walking a dog, too miserable for yard work, and too "iffy" for catching anyone at their mailbox. Still, I wanted to revisit the so-called scene of the crime again.

Just as I expected. No one in sight. Only the UPS truck stopping to make a delivery across the street from Edna Mae's. The driver was already pulling away from the curb by the time I got there. I was about to keep on going when the door to the house opened and an elderly woman stepped outside to check the delivery. It was a large box.

I immediately sprang into action. *You've got nothing on me, Miss Marple.*

I rolled my window down and shouted, "Do you need some help with that?" Before she could answer, I was out of the car and across the street, taking the woman completely by surprise.

"Why, thank you," the lady said. "It's wonderful to have such good neighbors. Especially when you're getting on in years. Things aren't as easy anymore. You know, I thought about moving to one of those senior living complexes where they serve you all the meals and do your housework, but I'm not ready for that yet. Maybe in a year or two, when I turn ninety. Then it will be a choice between The Lillian and The Monte Carlo. Or maybe I'll take one of those cruises around the world. Those ships have excellent health care, you know."

"Uh-huh," I mumbled as I started to hoist the box. It was large and cumbersome, but not too heavy. My bag kept interfering with my maneuverability, but I still managed to get inside and put the box on her kitchen counter.

"Thank you so much. It's a new queen-size water-proof mattress cover. They got the order wrong the last time and had to resend it. Of course, the last time the delivery came, there was no one to help me. I had to kick and drag the box inside. And when I was finally done and about to shut the door, do you know what I saw?"

I shook my head.

"I looked up and saw poor Edna Mae Langford

lying facedown in her driveway. Thought she'd had a heart attack. I called nine-one-one right away."

"Ohhh . . . so you were the first person to see what happened?"

"Not what happened. Just Edna Mae facedown. I was so preoccupied getting that box inside that I didn't see what was going on across the street."

The woman paused to take a good look at me. "How do you know Edna Mae?"

The words stumbled out of my mouth. "I, er, um . . . Edna Mae Langford was in the Booked 4 Murder book club."

"Oh yes. Yes, indeed. She loved those meetings. Loved talking about mysteries. Poor woman. Imagine falling in her driveway and then dying from pneumonia in the hospital. She once told me her family wanted her to wear one of those medical alert necklaces, but she said they were for old people. Didn't want any help around the house either, and didn't want to move into assisted living. Let me tell you, that place was a hairsbreadth away from disaster. I went in there about a month ago because her mail was delivered to me accidently, and do you know what I saw? It made my hair stand on end. Edna Mae had all of her newspapers and letters piled up on the burners. Good thing there wasn't a frying pan in sight. Surprising that something in her house didn't kill her. I mean, the way she lived and all. Poor Edna Mae. I feel so badly that such a nice woman died from falling in her driveway. How does such a thing happen?"

"I really don't know," I said. "It was fortunate that you were able to call nine-one-one so she didn't have to lie there too long in pain."

"You know, if it wasn't for that UPS delivery, she might have been there for hours. People stay inside during this heat. That's why I was so surprised to see a woman pacing in front of Edna's driveway a few days after that accident. It just so happened I was dusting my blinds and looked out the window. Saw that shiny white car and thought it must be a realtor. They snap up these houses like crocodiles and they're the only ones who can afford new cars."

Unless it was the person responsible for the accident. They always return to the scene of the crime. And my hunch all along might be right if that shiny new car turns out to be a KIA.

"Uh, yeah. I imagine you're right. Well, I'd better get on my way." I turned to face the door. Then I had what best could be described as an epiphany. A real epiphany!

"Can you tell me, I mean . . . do you know . . . does the UPS truck arrive in this neighborhood around the same time every day?"

"You must not get many deliveries. It comes like clockwork. Usually to the Dennersons or the McCaffertys. They get their prescriptions from Canada. Too much paperwork if you ask me. And they get their dental work done in Mexico. Right over the border by Yuma. Too much driving for me. Those are two things I can do without. Paperwork and driving. Oh, and waiting for deliveries. That would make three. Three things I can do without. Don't you think so?"

In that split second, she had unwittingly provided me with a key piece of information that would help me put this book curse to rest.

"Yes, I suppose. Anyway, I should be going. Hope your new mattress cover works out for you."

"Oh, it will. It will. By the way, I'm Beverly Mortenson. You can call me Bev."

"Nice to meet you, Bev. I'm Phee, and it was nice chatting with you. Have a great afternoon."

"Oh, I will. You know, you can stop by anytime to visit. Anytime at all."

I wanted to tell her not to wait until she was ninety to move into The Lillian or to board a cruise ship, but I didn't want to be intrusive. Instead, I reiterated what a pleasure it was to meet her and headed out the door.

As I walked to my car I thought about Sherry Fairchild and the encounter she was having with the Kirksons. I pictured her running for her life, the lovely peach tunic torn to shreds and Maisy-Jayne screaming in the background. Maybe even some broken lamps or pottery to complete the scene. If ever a company had a reason to tear up a contract, Sherry and Jenny's Fare Estate Sales didn't have to look any further than Thelmalee's front living room.

Chapter 18

It was five and still no call from Nate. My mother and I were sitting in her living room finishing up a frozen pizza. It must have dawned on her I needed to eat because she'd stocked up the freezer with enough frozen dinners to keep Stouffer's in business for the next decade.

"I'm telling you, Mom, whoever scattered that granite gravel around Edna Mae's driveway made sure it was after the mail delivery and around the time of the UPS truck delivery so Edna Mae wouldn't lie injured in her driveway for very long. They wanted her to be found quickly."

"Well, isn't that thoughtful of them." She took another bite of her pizza.

"Actually, it was. I think whoever did this to Edna Mae didn't expect her to die. And I think it was one of those women sitting behind us at the Stardust Theater Thursday night. Remember? I told you one of them said something like 'we were only trying to help,' and the other one was scared they might have been seen. Seen doing what? They were talking about someone who broke a hip. It *had* to be Edna Mae."

My mother stopped chewing and motioned for me to continue.

"Do you think it could've been Jeanette and her friend? The one with the beige SUV? They were at the theater that night. They might have been the ones sitting behind us. No offense, Mom, but the voices I heard sounded a whole lot younger than that geriatric sea-of-gray crowd in there. Besides, Jeanette's fairly young in comparison with the rest of the population here."

"Sea of gray? Now you know why I color my hair. Look, your hunch may be right. Who knows?"

"I talked to her this morning after the fire department removed the snake from her house."

"You didn't tell me you talked to Jeanette this morning. You just said something about a snake. What did she say?"

"I outright asked her if she was sitting behind us at the theater and she said no. That she and a friend had arrived late and had to sit down in front."

"Do you think someone planted that snake at Jeanette's house?"

"I really don't know what kind of person would go that far. Even a jealous wife. Who might in this case turn out to be an imaginary jealous wife since we don't even know if Jeanette has a boyfriend. For all we know, the blue Mazda could belong to her accountant."

"I still think it's quite possible someone put the snake in her house."

"Well, I don't. I happen to agree with the fire department. This is the desert and the native habitat for snakes. You know what I think? I think you'd rather believe someone snuck into Jeanette's house and put a snake there because you don't want to think about the possibility a snake could get into your own home."

"That's ridiculous. Pass the pizza. And remind me to get batteries for the flashlight. From now on, no one walks around here in the dark without a flashlight. And I think I'll put some night-lights on the floor outlets. For Streetman."

I chuckled to myself as I took another slice.

"I can't eat another piece," my mother said. "Do you want any more, or should I put the rest in the fridge?"

"Definitely in the fridge. I'm stuffed."

No sooner did I wipe the last bit of sauce from my lips when my phone began to ring. Nate! Finally! It had to be him calling me about the toxicology report.

"My phone's ringing. I've got to take it."

I got up, grabbed the phone from my bag, and quickly slid the arrow. "Hello?"

"Hey, I'm impressed, Phee. Toxicology reports and all. You're becoming a regular crime scene investigator."

"Very funny. The only thing I'm becoming is more and more frustrated each minute. At least detectives get to solve one case at a time. I'm looking at a jumbled mess of things that may or may not be connected. Anyway, can you please help me out with that report? I don't understand any of it."

"What is it you're trying to determine?"

"Did Minnie Bendelson die from an allergic reaction to fish?"

"Nope, not at all. No sign of histamine in her blood."

"Then I suppose she really did die from her heart condition or natural causes."

"Yep, afraid so, Phee. The report listed her age as eighty-seven. Not a spring chicken."

"You know what this means, don't you? Everyone will say it's because of the book curse. Nate, I was certain her nephew tainted her chicken salad with fish so she'd have an allergic reaction and die. The guy had the means and the opportunity. Aren't those the things the police are always trying to determine?"

"Yeah, *that* and motive. What about motive?"

"He was her only surviving relative. He'd get everything. Her house, her money . . ."

"Her bills . . . Sorry to disappoint you, kiddo, but I think this lady just died. Plain and simple. So, what else have you found out from snooping around?"

I walked past the kitchen into the guest bedroom, sat on my bed, and told Nate everything that had happened so far. Including the sugar cane evidence I found and the most recent snake incident.

"Hey, for someone who's supposedly getting nowhere, you're doing a phenomenal job. Look what you've already discovered—someone wanted to harm or scare Thelmalee, and someone else wanted to do the same with the gravel lady in the driveway."

"Edna Mae," I said.

"Yeah, Edna Mae. You've already ruled out the golf cart accident as legit, and now you can cross off this one. No poisoning. What about the lady with the snake in her house?"

I told him all the details from Jeanette's snake incident as well as what happened the night I arrived when the fire department responded to a carbon monoxide call.

"My mother thinks Jeanette has a married boyfriend whose jealous wife is behind these incidents."

"Were you able to verify any of that?"

"Not in the least. The boyfriend is about as real as Santa Claus, but my mother is still sticking to her theory."

"Whoa. Who said Santa Claus wasn't real?" He chuckled. "Listen, Phee, like I said before, I think you're doing a bang-up job with this. You've got a combination of hype and rumor going on, but you've also uncovered some real solid evidence that points to foul play. Now you just have to connect the dots."

"What if they don't connect?"

"Too many coincidences. There's got to be a link. Oh, and I almost forgot. I was going to call you myself with this little tidbit of information that came to my attention."

"What? Moira Donahoe is enjoying her old job so much she wants it back?"

"No, nothing like that. Although she's doing a pretty decent job of it and says to tell you hi."

"Well, what then? What's the tidbit?"

"Rolo called to let me know that the book spiked."

"Spiked? What's that mean?"

"It means sales went up dramatically. At least in

Arizona. Suddenly *The Twelfth Arrondissement* is getting noticed."

"Oh my gosh. I bet it has something to do with that TV segment from Friday night. I didn't mention that, did I?"

"No, what segment?"

Nate listened intently as I told him all about Gretchen Morin and the news anchor, Nina Alvarez, who practically told the whole world that if they wanted to get even with someone, all they'd need to do was buy this so-called cursed book and send it as a gift.

"Oh brother. Talk about marketing tactics. Anyway, Phee, I've got to get going. Give me a call if anything more comes up."

"Same with you. And thanks, Nate. I need all the support I can get."

"You're doing fine. But I agree with your mother. Take a flashlight if you're walking around at night."

He clicked off the phone and I automatically looked at the floor. All clear. It was safe to go back into the other room.

"I hope you don't mind, Phee," my mother said as I walked into the living room, "but I told Lucinda and Cecilia we'd go to Bingo tomorrow afternoon at their church. They're both working the concession."

"BINGO? We're going to a Bingo game?"

"Not just *a* Bingo game, it's a HUGE one. Half of the community will be there. I guarantee it. We need to get there early to get a good seat."

"A good seat? It's not like the movies."

"Worse. Everyone wants to be near the concession stand, and so do I. I don't want to walk a mile and a half to get a snack. Besides, you'll pick up lots of gossip by being that close to the refreshments. Trust me. And some of it might pay off. Probably better than our Bingo cards."

My mother paused for a second. "Oh, and whatever you do, don't take the table directly in front of the concessions. Take the one to the left or the right. In case I get stuck talking to someone on our way in, you need to hustle over to a table. Just not the one right in front."

"Why? Does that one have a curse on it?" I tried to not laugh.

"Very funny, but, in a sense, yes. Yes, it does. The curse of Roberta Young, Paula Darren, and that miserable Miranda Lee something-or-other. They think they own that table and refuse to let anyone sit there. I swear, the three of them all but mark their scent on the table."

"You'd think management would do something about it."

"The management is too busy running the game than to deal with that kind of nonsense, so those women just get away with it."

"How do you know them? Are they in the book club, too?"

"Oh, heavens no! Who'd put up with them? The only reason I know who they are is from what Lucinda and Cecilia tell me."

"Uh-huh. Well, maybe someone will cast a Bingo curse."

"That's not funny, Phee."

I stifled a giggle and continued to watch television until I was too tired to pay attention. "I'm off to bed,

Mom. By the way, what are we doing for breakfast? Cereal or something here, or did you want to go out?"

"It's Sunday. We'll go out to brunch somewhere."

"Sounds good. Good night."

"Good night, Phee. And check behind the doors before you go to sleep. I heard snakes travel in pairs."

"Then there'd be another snake at Jeanette's place, not ours. Good night!"

Chapter 19

St. Stephen's Church sat on the northwest corner of a major intersection with a parking lot that rivaled the Mall of America. I took my daughter to that mall once when she was eight or nine, and I swore I'd never do that again. I forgot which entrance we used and it took us hours to find the car. At least my mom and I knew which entrance we were using for Bingo.

The lot was filling up quickly. My mother was pitching a fit we might not get the table she wanted. I couldn't imagine why on earth she had to sit in front of the concession stand when I was absolutely stuffed from breakfast. We had just left a Sunday buffet at one of the continuous care communities not far from her house. My mother insisted upon going there because "they serve every meal as if it's about to be your last." I wasn't all that thrilled and told her as much when she suggested it.

"Sounds depressing," I said.

"It's not. Trust me. Myrna and Louise eat there all the time. They serve gourmet food and the atmosphere is absolutely delightful. Floral displays, ice sculptures, even fancy cheeses with names you can't pronounce. And it's less than twelve dollars. It's like being on a cruise without getting seasick. And it's open to the public."

"Sure it is. They want to lure unsuspecting people into their continuous care web. I know how that goes—independent living, assisted living, skilled nursing, and then what?"

"I'll tell you what. Prime rib. Roast turkey. Spiral ham. Personalized omelets. You can't find that at a Denny's."

She had a point and off we went to The Grand Colonial. Now, sitting in front of St. Stephen's Church, I felt like the blueberry balloon girl out of *Willy Wonka and the Chocolate Factory*. It would be hours before I'd even dare to put a morsel of food into my mouth.

"I'm dropping you off in front, Phee. Go in and get us the card packets and good seats. I'll find a parking spot."

"You sure you don't want to switch places? I don't mind driving around for a spot."

"No, go on in. I'll see you in a minute."

A steady line was beginning to form by the entrance to the social hall and I hurried over. Once inside I could see four large tables with Bingo cards and markers in assorted colors. I purchased two sets of cards (ten games) and two markers—a green one and a red one. Then I sprinted past the doorway to locate the concession stand and my mother's table of choice.

As I headed for the table to the left of the concessions, someone tapped me on the shoulder. It was none other than Jerry White, book alarmist, dog owner, and dinner companion to one Gretchen Morin.

"I thought I recognized you. You're the lady who grabbed Izzy before he took off. So, were my directions okay?"

Directions. That's right. I asked him for directions. I had to stop and think for a minute. *Where did I say I was going? What street? As long as he doesn't ask, I'll be fine.*

"Yes. Great. Thanks. Um, by the way, looks like you might need to have a chat with the local librarian regarding that book you were so concerned about. Did you see the news on TV Friday night? After that segment, everyone's going to be beating down the door to get their hands on a copy. I don't think the readers are too worried about . . . what did you call it? Oh yeah, bad juju."

"Well, they should be worried and so should that librarian."

I glanced toward the doorway, expecting my mother to burst on the scene at any minute, but instead, who should come charging toward us but Gretchen Morin herself. A nanosecond after he uttered the word "librarian." Speak of the devil. I could hardly contain myself. Jerry White turned bright red and froze as she approached. I knew she was about to say something to him when I literally spared him the embarrassment of a bold-faced lie.

"Miss Morin! Nice to see you again. You remember me from the library? I was the one who had the questions about the book club."

Gretchen stood perfectly still, trying not to make

eye contact with Jerry. Like a seasoned poker player, she remained stone-faced.

"Anyway, this is . . . oh, how embarrassing. This gentleman helped me out with directions the other day."

Jerry White immediately stepped in as if this was the first time they were being introduced. He held out his hand and said, "Jerry White, nice to meet you."

"Likewise," Gretchen replied.

"Miss Morin is the director of the library. I'm sure you'll have lots to talk about. Mr. White has some interesting opinions about books."

Both of them stood there dumbfounded.

"Well, anyway, nice seeing you two. I'd better get a table before my mother walks in."

Turning quickly from them, I started toward the table I was supposed to grab. Then I literally swung my body around before either of them could make a move.

"Oh, I almost forgot"—I stared directly at Gretchen—"I plan to attend that book club meeting on Wednesday. Imagine the local book club selecting a book that might be cursed. I wonder who'll own up to *that*. Anyway, I'll be sure to have something interesting to tell my friends back home."

Before either of them could say anything, I raced over to the table on the left of the concession stand, tossed the Bingo cards and markers on top of it, and sat down as if I was taking the last spot in musical chairs.

Seconds later, my mother had seated herself next to me. "Don't be obvious, but look at the table to your right," she whispered. "I'm surprised they haven't staked a territorial flag in the middle."

I turned my head and tried not to giggle. A large plastic troll with orange hair sat in the middle of the table, surrounded by three or four smaller trolls with green and red hair. Some sort of unicorn was a few inches away near a bottle of Fiji water. And that wasn't all. The table sported a lineup of card dabbers and rabbits' feet in assorted colors. And if that wasn't the end-all, someone had actually brought their own tablecloth. And not your run-of-the-mill kind either. This one was white with green shamrocks and leprechauns.

"I see what you mean," I whispered as my mother tore off the first sheet in her card packet.

"I told you, Phee. Listen, I spoke to Cecilia and Lucinda on my way in and told them that if they noticed anything suspicious, they are to let me know."

"Suspicious? Like what? Someone swiping a Bingo card? They'd get crucified in here, no disrespect intended."

"No, suspicious as in the conversations they over-hear. You'd be surprised at what they can find out in two hours."

"Well, I found out something as soon as I came inside the door. Remember that first night when we were eating at the Italian restaurant? Well—"

Just then the announcer introduced the game and my mother shushed me.

"You can tell me later. The first game goes quick. It's just a straight line."

I only knew of two kinds of Bingo games—the straight line and covering the entire card. I was out of my league in the first ten minutes as the announcer

introduced the "Roving L" and the "Postage Stamp."
It went on from there, with all sorts of variations
and no winners from anyone at our end of the room,
including the "lucky table" next to us.

"Intermission is going to be at the end of this
game," my mother said. "I'll cover your card. Go and
get us some popcorn. It doesn't have many calories.
And diet soda. You'll never get the chance once they
call intermission. Hurry up."

She was right. No sooner had I arrived back to our
table when a veritable stampede of people headed
straight for the concession stand.

"This makes a school cafeteria seem like a Victorian
tearoom."

My mother simply muttered "uh-huh" and swallowed some of her soft drink.

"Did Lucinda or Cecilia say anything to you?" she
asked.

"No, not really. Well, Lucinda said it was nice to
see me again and she introduced me to Cecilia. But
if you're referring to anything about the book or
unexplained deaths, then no. They didn't mention
anything. By the way, Mom, was Cecilia ever a nun?"

"A nun? Whatever gave you that idea?"

"Oh, I don't know. Maybe the fact everyone here
is dressed real casual in floral tops and pants and
she's wearing a white blouse, a long black skirt, a
black sweater, and believe it or not, black hose. And
her hair is pulled back into a bun that couldn't be
any tighter."

"Cecilia doesn't like to stand out. Besides, she says
it gets cold in here because someone keeps turning
the air-conditioning down."

I didn't want to get into the irony of what my

mother just said, so I sort of acknowledged her and looked around. It was impossible to see the concession stand. The crowd had engulfed it completely as my mother continued to chomp on her popcorn.

"Don't worry. If they hear anything out of the ordinary, they'll let me know."

She continued snacking while I looked through the other cards, wondering what bizarre pattern the announcer would call next. Shoving a handful of popcorn into my mouth, I continued to stare at the crowd. It was starting to dissipate.

"FIVE MINUTES UNTIL THE NEXT GAME. IF YOU NEED TO USE THE RESTROOM, NOW WOULD BE THE TIME."

Unbelievable. They actually had to tell people when to use the restroom.

"If I had to go to the ladies' room, I'd just go."

"And leave your game card? You don't know who you can trust."

"It's just a game, Mom."

"Tell *them* that," my mother said, her arm making a wide sweep across the room. Just then, Cecilia gestured back, waving frantically at my mother.

"Keep an eye on my cards in case the game starts. I've got to see what she wants."

My mother got up, walked to the other side of our table, and took two or three steps toward the concession stand. She was too far away for me to hear anything, but it didn't matter. I knew she'd repeat everything Cecilia told her verbatim. In fact, I was counting on it.

The room got suddenly quiet as my mother returned to her seat. Her voice was low, but I heard every word.

"The librarian had an argument with some man.

Bald. Dark mustache. Cecilia overheard everything because the two of them, the librarian and the man, were standing right next to her, off to the side."

"Did Cecilia say what they were arguing about?"

"Only that Gretchen said, 'You're making things worse.' And then the man called her a name Cecilia refused to repeat. But Cecilia heard the man say he was the one who arranged for the TV interview with Nina Alvarez."

"Was that all she heard?"

"Yes. Shh . . . it's starting."

I didn't say anything as the announcer kept calling out numbers. Four more Bingo games were played and still no winners from our side of the room. I turned slightly to see how the table next to us was reacting. One of the women picked up an orange-haired troll, smoothed its hair, and re-positioned it while another lady sprinkled some of the Fiji water on the table. And here we were, worried about a book curse.

"NEXT GAME UP AND GRAND FINALE—CRAZY LARGE KITE!"

Every number came up except ours. I had to resist the urge to poke my mother and tell her that we should go shopping for plastic trolls.

"N–forty-two! THAT'S N–forty-two!"

"BINGO!"

The voice came from clear across the room. "BINGO!"

"Phooey," my mother muttered. "We didn't win the game."

"What Cecilia overheard is better than us winning."

Mom's eyebrows seemed to furl, and I knew she was weighing what I had just said.

"I suppose you're right. Come on, we'll take the

small exit door by the quilt display. We won't have to elbow our way through the crowd."

She was right about the exit, but not the parking lot. In a matter of seconds, we joined an endless throng of people walking toward their cars. Everyone except the two people I wanted to spot. I knew Gretchen and Jerry were up to something, but hunches, premonitions, and bad feelings don't solve mysteries. They just widen the web.

"I know those two are guilty, Mom. Bad juju my you-know-what. Where did you park your car?"

"Off to the left, by the corner of the lot."

I looked around and the parking lot was worse than the one at the Stardust Theater a few nights ago.

"Why don't we just grab a seat on one of those benches by the memorial garden and wait a few minutes for this place to clear out. These drivers are making me nervous. I don't know how you can stand it."

"Make sure your insurance is paid up. Look, there's a shady spot over there." My mother pointed to a low-hanging mesquite tree with a long concrete bench in front.

I sat and watched the "near misses" in the parking lot. "I can't believe Cecilia remembered everything they said. You were right, Mom. Verbatim. How'd she acquire that kind of skill?"

"She's a retired school secretary. You'd be surprised at the skills she has."

"I'm telling you, I think Gretchen Morin is orchestrating this. It's a great way to cover up a murder by leading people on to believe all those women died from a book curse."

"But Gretchen didn't seem to believe there was

a curse. Remember what she said during that TV segment?"

"Oh, I remember all right. She played it downright cool. Too cool. Even when Nina Alvarez mentioned giving the book as a gift to your enemies."

"None of this makes sense. And why would Gretchen hide the fact she knew that man. What was his name? Oh yes, Jerry White. Why would they act as if they didn't know each other?" she asked.

"Darned if I know. Like I told you before, I'm not very good at this."

The parking lot started to clear out and we made our way to my mother's car. I was still holding up hope I'd catch a glimpse of Gretchen with Jerry as the Bingo game let out. It turned out to be impossible with that huge crowd and the number of exit doors, even though I kept a good lookout from our spot on the bench. Now the only people trickling out of the doors seemed to be the staff.

My mother got unusually quiet and I knew what that meant. She was hatching a plan for me to snoop around in another unlikely place. What would Nate do? I figured I was sleuthing as best I could with information garnered from Cindy in the dog park, Gretchen at the library, the sugar cane box from the realty office, and the bizarre ramblings from Jerry White. Not to mention the Kirksons and Edna Mae's neighbor. I get extra credit for the Kirksons. If it was a paying job, I'd demand time and a half. I was trying to get the unpleasant thought of the Kirksons out of my mind when my mother tapped my elbow with hers.

"I have a thought, Phee, and before you say anything, hear me out."

"Like I have a choice."

"Very funny. I think you need to do some more surveillance at the library."

"Surveillance? This isn't the Pentagon."

"And good thing, too, the way they conduct business. Look, honey, all you need to do is some discreet snooping around. You probably won't even run into the librarian. She'll probably be sitting at her desk. So, I suggest, and it's just a suggestion, that you mill around the stacks and listen to people's conversations. The people who patronize the library are there all the time and you're bound to uncover something. Oh. Try to listen in on the conversations from the library clerks. If any of them are part of this, they won't be able to keep their mouths shut."

"Unbelievable. Absolutely unbelievable. You really *do* want me to spy on people."

"Not spy. Nose around. There's a difference."

If there was a difference, it had to be as subtle as hell. I'd never hear the end of it, so I agreed to add the library to my unending list of places I had no intention of frequenting ever again. I spent the rest of the day reviewing my notes, thinking up aliases I could use, in case all else failed, and rewriting my information chart. By the time I closed my eyes, I was exhausted.

At precisely 2:34 a.m., according to my iPhone, I bolted out of a deep sleep, wide awake. Not the groggy, sleepy wakefulness that came with morning, but a full-blown I'm-on-my-feet-and-raring-to-go that would not allow me to get back to sleep. Rather than toss and turn, I decided to get up, take my papers out again, and give them another look-over.

If this was what insomnia was like, just shoot me now.

Tiptoeing into the kitchen, I used the dimmer switch to give me just enough overhead light above the kitchen table. The last thing I wanted to do was wake my mother or, heaven forbid, the dog. *He gets grouchy when you wake him.* I spread the papers and my carefully crafted chart in front of me and started to look them over when headlights shone down the street.

Who'd be coming home at this hour? There wasn't a heck of a lot of nightlife in Sun City West. I walked over to the kitchen windows, making sure the plantation shutters were only partially opened, enough for me to get a good look. It was a sheriff's car, and it was stopping right in front of Herb Garrett's house. I dimmed the light above the table to get a better peek.

Herb Garrett's garage door was wide open, and the sheriff's posse was now knocking on his front door. I stood like a mannequin, trying to process what was going on. Herb came out a few seconds later and walked over to the garage. Then he and the posse volunteer went inside the garage. Then the posse volunteer left, the garage door went down, and the house lights went out.

Herb didn't strike me as the kind of person who would be so forgetful as to leave his garage door open all night. It was certainly closed when my mother and I got back from Bingo, but that was in the late afternoon. Then again, Jeanette didn't seem like the kind of person who would be careless either. As least no one had started Herb's car.

I turned the overhead light back on and studied my carefully written chart, this time focusing on the miscellaneous information I'd gleaned in the past

three days. I wasn't really looking forward to playing
I Spy at the library in a matter of hours, but I wasn't
about to argue with my mother.

One thing troubled me as I reviewed my notes,
and it was the conversation I overheard behind me at
the Stardust Theater. I was certain it was Jeanette.
And then, like a thunderbolt, it hit me—Jeanette said
she and her friend arrived late and had to sit in
front, but when my mother and I got there, all of the
front seats were taken, and we didn't arrive late. We
were on time. So Jeanette had lied! It *was* her admit-
ting to some sort of involvement regarding Edna
Mae Langford's death, but was she the person who
was afraid that someone had seen them, or was she
the other one? The woman who said not to worry
about it.

A slow surge of adrenaline was making its way
through my body as I tiptoed back to my bedroom to
grab my iPhone for a Safari search. The library
would have to wait until later in the day. I intended
to find some very, very needed mortgage advice from
the West Valley Home Mortgage Solutions.

Chapter 20

At four-thirty, I crept back into bed and managed to doze lightly until seven. That was when a call from Nate interrupted any further chance I had of sleeping.

"I didn't wake you again, did I, Phee? The sun's been up for hours in Arizona."

Yeah, the sun may be up, but not from the inside of my eyelids.

"No, it's fine, Nate. Really. I should be up. I was. I mean, I was up really late last night and then went back to bed."

"Oh, that explains why you sound so tired. Listen, I won't keep you, but I wasn't sure if you saw the article in yesterday's *USA Today*."

"Article? *USA Today*? No, I didn't."

"It's just a short release from the Associated Press, but it's about Sun City West's book curse."

"WHAT?" Now I was wide awake.

"Yep, seems they picked up the story almost overnight from that local TV station. The article pretty much says what everyone already knows—four unexpected deaths, a possible attempt at murder, and everyone thinking they've got some sort of cursed book on their hands."

"That's incredible."

"Not really. Rolo did a little more data tracking on *The Twelfth Arrondissement* and guess what?"

He answered before I formed a syllable.

"Book sales are going up, up, up!"

"I didn't think people had that many enemies."

"Listen, kiddo, someone is using this publicity to sell their book. The question remains, are they merely opportunistic or is there something more sinister taking place?"

"You mean you think people would actually kill someone just so their book would become a best-seller?"

"It sounds like every cliché you've ever heard, but yes, I've seen people kill for less. So, did you dredge up any new information since we last spoke on Friday?"

"Not really. Went to a Bingo game yesterday, where my mother's friend overheard a very telling conversation between the librarian and the guy who went berserk at the pool. I got to hear it thirdhand, but it substantiated part of the theory I'm working on."

"Which is . . . ?"

"That Gretchen Morin is behind all of this. Do you think Rolo can check her out?"

For a moment the line went quiet and then Nate said, "Not only can he, but he's already on it. The guy reminds me of one of those spinning tops. Let's pray he doesn't run out of energy. Go back to sleep. I'll catch you later."

Going back to sleep wasn't an option. I threw on

some clothes, left my mother a quick note, and drove to the nearby convenience store to get coffee and a copy of yesterday's *USA Today*.

I was back in less than twenty minutes with two cups of coffee and the paper. My mother had just stepped out of her bedroom, every hair on her head perfectly in place, when I walked in. I couldn't seem to remember if I'd bothered to run a comb through mine when I left the house. It didn't matter.

"Goodness, Phee. Don't you use mousse or anything on that head of yours? You didn't go out in public like that, did you?"

"I, um, yeah, I did. I got you some coffee and yesterday's *USA Today*. The cashier at the convenience store didn't seem to notice my hair."

"Thin, elderly man with frizzy eyebrows?"

"Yeah."

"That's Martin Chomwitzer, and it wouldn't be your hair he'd be staring at."

"Eeew. That's unsettling. Next time I'll go to the drive-through at a fast-food chain. Anyway, here's *USA Today* from yesterday."

"Huh? I don't read that paper. And why would I read yesterday's news? I watch CNN, the networks, and the local news. And I read the local paper."

"Well, the local paper didn't print the Associated Press article about *The Twelfth Arrondissement* like *USA Today* did yesterday."

"What?"

"Nate called me a little while ago to tell me, and I drove to the convenience store to get a copy. I knew they'd have some left. Those stores always do."

"Let me see the article. What does it say?"

"Nothing we don't already know, but now the whole world does. Imagine that."

The article was brief and to the point, but it left lots of room for interpretation. "Are you thinking what I am, Mom? That all these deaths were somehow connected to making that book popular?"

"I knew it. It's that miserable librarian. I bet she wrote the book in the first place and used a penname. This never would have happened if Barbara Schnell was still running the library."

"Look, we don't know if Gretchen actually orchestrated some of these unexpected deaths, or if she wrote the book under the name of Lily Margot Gerald, but one thing's for sure, she wanted that book to get read. And more than that, she wanted it to get popular real fast. If Cecilia Flanagan overheard that conversation right, then Gretchen used Jerry White as her "stool pigeon" to create a stir on local TV. Anyway, I've got one more lead to check out this morning before I go to the library."

"Where? Who? What lead?"

"The only person we haven't yet identified—the driver of the beige SUV. I'm going to check out the West Valley Home Mortgage Solutions to see what I can find out."

My mother shook her head and bit her lip at the same time. "Other than that sign on the SUV, I've never heard of them. They could be anywhere in the West Valley. Anywhere. Make sure you fill up that rental car with plenty of gas."

I couldn't tell if she was disappointed the address was one piece of information she couldn't provide me with, or if she was really worried I'd wind up lost in the desert somewhere.

"It's okay. I know where they are, thanks to the search engine on my iPhone. They've got an office, or at least an address, in Peoria on Happy Valley Road. That's not too far from here."

The relief on my mother's face was obvious. "What are you going to say when you get there?"

"I'm not sure. I'll think of something on the drive over there. I'm sure it will rival my prior performances."

"You're really starting to enjoy this, aren't you, Phee?"

I shrugged.

"You know, I'm really glad you came out here, and I think you're doing a yeoman's job of figuring out this book curse. The truth of the matter is that all of us in the book club were getting rattled. I mean, which one of us was going to be next? You don't think that there's going to be another death just so that book gets on the best-seller list, do you?"

"Uh, gee. I hadn't considered that. But guess what?"

"What?"

"You're starting to take the logical approach and not buy in to the cursed book hysteria. If nothing else, that was worth a flight out here. And by the way, who says 'yeoman's job'?"

Before she could answer, the doorbell rang and my mother immediately headed to the bedroom. Streetman was already under the couch.

"Get that, will you, Phee. I'm not dressed. But don't open the security door. Just the regular door."

"Shouldn't the dog bark when someone comes to the door?"

"The dog should do a lot of things, but I don't want to pressure him."

No, no. Just pressure the rest of us.

I opened the front door and was staring directly at Herb Garrett.

"Hey, good-looking, sorry to bother you so early, but I wanted to let your mother know someone is driving around the neighborhood with one of those devices that automatically opens your garage door unless you push on the garage door Lock feature when you go inside the house. It happened to me late last night. Sheriff's posse woke me up from a dead sleep."

Good-looking? The guy is trying to make a pass at me.
I ignored the remark and acted as if this was the first I'd heard of the incident, even though I had a bird's-eye view last night.

"Gee, that's awful. Burglars?"

"Yep, that's what the sheriff's posse seemed to think. Burglars scoping things out. They apparently open your garage door, drive around, and come back. If it's still open, they go in and help themselves."

"So maybe that's what happened to Jeanette?"

"I don't know. Why would they start her car and leave? Especially if they had to hotwire it. I mean, if they were going to steal it, they'd steal it. Not leave it running with the garage door shut. And if they were going to break in, they would have done so. Nah, I think that was something entirely different. Anyway, tell your mother to push the garage door Lock button at night. And you can always call me in an emergency."

Yeah, right. After I call the coroner and the U.S. Marshals.
"I will. Thanks, Herb. Glad they didn't steal anything."

"Yeah, me too."

Herb went back across the street, only he didn't stop at his house. He went to his other next-door neighbors' and knocked on their door. I figured he was alerting the neighborhood and we were first on the list."

"It was Herb Garrett, Mom," I shouted. "I'll tell you about it when you get dressed."

"Tell me now. I threw on some clothes as soon as I heard someone at the door."

I stood in the hallway by her bedroom and proceeded to tell her about Herb's open garage door and his subsequent visit from the sheriff's posse. "Herb didn't think it was related to Jeanette's incident with the carbon monoxide. Her garage door was shut and the car was running."

Oddly enough, my mother didn't seem too concerned about the garage door.

"So what did he think?"

"Herb and the posse volunteer believe it might have been burglars. With a garage door opener that can circumvent the codes."

"Oh brother. That tops the cake. Want to know what I'm thinking?"

"Um, sure."

"I'll bet Herb was sleepwalking and opened his own garage door. I watch the commercials about those prescription drugs for insomnia. They make people do all sorts of ridiculous things. In fact, only a month ago when I was at the dentist's office, I met a lady who told me about her neighbor who took one of those sleep aides. Do you know what the neighbor lady did?"

I don't know. I don't care. I don't care to know.

"What? What did she do?"

"She got up in the middle of the night, opened her freezer, and took out two pork chops. Then she put them in the toaster and pushed the button down."

"Yikes."

"Next, the woman went into her garage and sat in her car. Fell asleep and didn't wake up until the next morning."

"What about the pork chops?"

"Oh. She never bothered to plug in the toaster."

"That's a really strange story, Mom. I'm on Herb's side with this one. Maybe from now on you should push the Lock button when you go to sleep."

"I always push the Lock button. And I use the deadbolt for the side door into the kitchen. Plus, now I have Streetman."

I looked at the dog. He was sitting under the kitchen table, head bent down, trying to clean his belly. At least I thought it was his belly.

"Yeah, uh, that's a relief."

An hour later, I was sitting once again behind the wheel of my car, this time trying to find out who was driving the beige SUV. I took the highway to Happy Valley Road, avoiding the stop-and-go traffic on Bell Road. The scenario for my unscheduled meeting at West Valley Home Mortgage Solutions was well played out in my mind. Information gathering. That's all I would be doing. Nothing wrong with that. Everyone wants to know about mortgages. And mortgage solutions.

The GPS brought me directly to the spot. There was a Home Depot across the street and a glut of chain restaurants as well. On the "mortgage solutions" side of the road, a number of small businesses shared the long, rectangular building. West Valley Home Mortgage Solutions was the farthest from me as I pulled into the lot.

The place was dotted with cars, but no sign of the beige SUV. Drat. I hated the thought of a wasted trip. Still, I could always go inside and find out who the driver of the car was. Luckily, I didn't have to. As I approached the corner of the lot, a few cars lined up on the other side came into view. The beige SUV was one of them.

I was miles from Sun City West, making it easier to assume a different persona without having it come back to bite me. *Yep, a regular Meryl Streep.* I opened the door slowly, allowing myself a few seconds to study the office. It wasn't too far removed from Nolan and Nolan Realty, with one exception. There was no receptionist. Four separate desk/office areas, two on each side, filled the room. In front was a small credenza with water, fruit, and a coffeemaker. At least I didn't have to go rooting through the trash.

Two agents were at their desks, one on the phone, and the other had just ended a call as I took a few steps farther inside. She appeared to be in her fifties with short highlighted blond hair and a medium build.

"Hi! Can I help you? Leslie Sackler."

"Hi! I'm Sophie, and maybe you can."

"Come on over and have a seat. Can I get you anything? Water? Coffee?"

"No, I'm fine. But thank you."

"So, how can West Valley Home Mortgage Solutions help you?"

Good question, since I don't own a home in Arizona and my current mortgage back in Minnesota is as stable as they get.

"Um . . . er . . . actually, I saw your SUV driving around my neighborhood *(please, dear God, let it be her SUV)*, and that's when I noticed the sign on the back of it. I looked up the address on the Internet."

"Which neighborhood was that? I drive through so many."

Take a deep breath. At least I got the right person. "In Sun City West."

"Ohh."

There was a slight change in her voice, as if I'd said something inappropriate.

"Is there something wrong? I mean, that was your SUV in Sun City West."

"No, no, nothing. It's just that Sun City West isn't really an area I deal with. I just happen to have a good friend who lives there. But that doesn't mean anything. West Valley Home Mortgage Solutions can work with anyone in the valley. Or Arizona, for that matter. We're fully licensed."

"So you must be from Arizona, I imagine."

"I'm originally from Wisconsin," she said. "Most of my family still lives there, but when I found out snow was optional, I moved out here."

My mind didn't process anything more than the word "Wisconsin." The last time I heard it was when my mother was relaying funeral arrangements for the recently deceased members of the Booked 4 Murder book club.

"Edna Mae's family was having her body shipped back to Wisconsin, the last I knew. I haven't heard anything about Thelmalee. . . ."

Wisconsin. Granted, lots of people were from Wisconsin, but when you narrowed it down to how many of them were associated with that book club, the numbers dropped significantly. *Connect the dots.* Jeanette and Leslie were good friends. Leslie was from Wisconsin. Edna Mae was from Wisconsin. Oh my gosh, this sounded like one of those god-awful math logic problems I hated to death. Death. That was the other thing . . .

"Are you all right? You look shocked I chose to move here," Leslie said.

"Oh no, not at all. I was just thinking about all that snow and, uh . . . why wouldn't anyone want to move here?"

"Exactly. So, how can we help you? Are you looking to refinance?"

"Well, I might be. Can you give me some information? Rates and all. And the process. The process for refinancing . . ."

I babbled on and on. It was as if each of my words was sinking me deeper and deeper into some pit where I'd never be able to get out. I had to think fast. I jumped in with a Grand Canyon leap that would either bring me one step closer to what I needed or one step closer to the door. *Don't let it hit me on the way out.*

"An information packet that I could look over would be great and then I could get back to you. I'm one of those people who really needs to study things over. You know, like the people from Missouri, the 'Show Me' state. Does Wisconsin have a slogan, too?

Oh, come to think of it, one of the ladies I know from the library book club is from Wisconsin— Jeanette Tomilson. You wouldn't know her, would you? Of course, that's so silly, there are a million people out here from Wisconsin."

Then, Leslie Sackler made a move I never expected. She leaned over her desk as if to reach for something and knocked over a framed picture. Whatever I said seemed to make her particularly jumpy.

"Sorry about that," she said, avoiding my question. "I've been meaning to get these papers better organized. Hold on, what you need is in the file."

She walked over to a wall in the back of the office that housed a large file cabinet. Quickly, I leaned over and stood the framed photo upright. It was two girls, college aged, standing under a sign that said, GO LAWRENCE UNIVERSITY VIKINGS. Their faces shot out at me as if someone had fired a flare gun. Mystery solved. The driver of the beige SUV was Leslie Sackler, and she was Jeanette's college friend. But why wouldn't she acknowledge it?

By now Leslie was on her way back to the desk, and I took my chance with another bold move.

"I straightened up your picture." I looked closer at the banner above the girls. The line underneath the slogan read, CLASS OF 1982. Then I changed the subject completely, hoping she would dismiss the entire incident.

"So, will I find the directions pretty understandable on these documents?"

"Detailed, but clear enough. Why don't you look them over and give me a call. My numbers are on the top—office and cell phone. Maybe we can set an appointment in a few days to see how our office can help you."

"Sounds wonderful." I stood and took the packet. "I really appreciate your time. Especially without notice. I mean, I'm sure you must be inundated with work and family and all."

"Work maybe, but I'm single. Never married. Just me and my four-legged buddies."

"Well, I'm sure they keep you busy enough. Thanks so much, Leslie. I'll be in touch. Have a great day!"

"You as well."

I sprinted to the doorway like a spaniel on its way to the park, turning my head as I grabbed the door-knob. Leslie was already back at her desk and on the phone. Too bad this wasn't the lottery. I would have placed a bet she was dialing Jeanette Tomilson.

Chapter 21

I had to get to a computer and I had to do it quickly. My mother's relic of a system would take forever, and I certainly didn't want anyone from the Sun City West Library to see what I was doing, so that meant finding a library in Sun City, a short distance from West Valley Home Mortgage Solutions. What the heck did people do before iPhones and GPS? A quick little Safari search and I was on my way. As it turned out, I was pretty close to that city's main library on Ninety-ninth Avenue.

I headed south on Pleasant Valley Road and located the building in less than a half hour. If desert beige was the palette of choice in my mother's community, white was the favorite in this one. The library, along with the other buildings in an enormous recreation center, was gleaming white with a sign that could be seen from the International Space Station. I grabbed the closest parking space and headed inside. With the exception of two women who were checking out books and a few people milling about, the place was practically empty. If it wasn't for the fact that the library was carpeted, I swore I'd be able to hear my own footsteps. It was like being back in school. Only this place didn't have signs that said, "No gum" and "Keep hands, feet and objects to yourself."

Immediately, I found an empty computer and logged on to the free library Internet service. Then, fumbling for my credit card, I purchased a $4.95 monthly subscription to a specialized data site in order to check a source. A few quick clicks and I was all set. Except for one small detail. The information needed to be printed. I noticed the librarian standing a few feet away and motioned for her to approach. I was too afraid to leave the computer for even a split second for fear the program would turn itself off.

The small gray-haired lady with a round face and sweet smile told me it would cost a dollar for the printing. I couldn't hand her the money quickly enough. I was so ecstatic I would have given her ten dollars. With the paper in my hand, I logged off of the computer, walked back to the car, and drove to my mother's house. I had barely set foot in the door when her voice sounded from the other side of the house.

"So, what did you find out at the library?"

"I didn't go there yet." *Well, not the* Sun City West *one.* "I had to check out something else, and you'll never guess what I found out. I even have pictures."

"Pictures? As in photos of people having affairs or doing something scandalous? Who? Which one of the ladies?"

"Oh, for heaven's sake, Mother, nothing like that. I have a yearbook photo, well, actually more than one, of Jeanette and the owner of the beige SUV.

The woman's name is Leslie Sackler, and you'll never guess what."

"Enough with the guessing. Just tell me."

"Leslie Sackler is from Wisconsin. And not only that, but she and your neighbor Jeanette were college roommates and I think . . ."

"Phee, you can tell me all of this later, but you need to get over to the library. Our library. Now. If you wait any longer, most of the people will be gone. The place is like a tomb after three, so hurry up. Jeanette and her roommate can wait."

I threw my hands up in the air, muttered something I'd rather not repeat, turned around, and went back to the car. A tsunami had nothing on my mother.

True to her word, the Sun City West Library was packed. Not like its counterpart in Sun City, where I had used the computer. I slipped into my mother's library unnoticed and headed straight for the fiction aisles. An elderly couple was arguing whether or not they had read one of the Tom Clancy novels, with the man finally saying, "Well, if you can't remember, Bernice, then what's the harm of reading it again?"

I moved to another aisle where a similar conversation was taking place. Only this time it was over a Thomas Perry novel. Then, out of the corner of my eye, I saw a crowd of people in the reference section. And by crowd, I mean at least fifteen or more. Two clerks were trying desperately to offer assistance. I elbowed my way into the mess and shouted, "What's going on?"

One of the clerks looked up. "Everyone wants information about curses, jinxes, and evil eyes."

I didn't have to ask why. I already knew. However,

just to cover my tracks and provide the "official answer" to my mother, I asked why all of a sudden everyone was interested in curses.

The clerk looked at me as if I'd been living under a rock. "Haven't you heard? Rumor has it that there's a cursed book floating around, and it's got everyone on edge. From now on, I only plan to read books written by well-known authors. No sense taking any chances."

I leaned in closer to get a look at the woman's name tag, when all of a sudden a woman's voice shouted, "YOU'RE HARRIET PLUNKETT'S DAUGHTER! HARRIET PLUNKETT'S DAUGHTER. YOU LOOK JUST LIKE HER! I HEARD YOU CAME HERE TO INVESTIGATE THE CURSE."

The voice bellowed through the library like a subway car grinding its way to a full stop five stories below the ground. In that instance, I wanted to be ground into the dirt five stories below, too. And I looked just like my mother? I didn't think I looked anything like her at all. I always thought I favored my father's side of the family.

The woman screamed again, "HARRIET PLUN-KETT'S DAUGHTER!"

I had to get out of there. To make matters worse, I didn't want to run into the librarian. I had to think fast. I couldn't very well walk all the way back to the entrance because that was where the counters and reference desks were, not to mention, her office. My only option was to head for the small door straight ahead and pray it didn't open into a storeroom.

Horrors. It opened into a semidarkened media room where a PowerPoint presentation was about to begin. The screen read, *Wealth Management from*

Saving to Sudden Windfalls. Before I could grasp the implication of the program, I heard a familiar voice and cringed. It was Herb Garrett.

"Hey, pretty lady! Hurry up and grab a seat. I got here early so I wouldn't miss anything the speaker had to say. Is your mother coming?"

"I, uh . . . I mean, no. She's not coming. And I walked in here by mistake. I was looking for the restroom."

"Oh." He sounded disappointed. "It's shorter to go out through those double doors in front of the room and into the computer section. There's a restroom there. Sure you don't want to stay for the program? According to the promo I got in the mail, it's supposed to be pretty good."

"I'm sure. I don't have any wealth to manage."

"Hey, hey. You never know when you'll hit the jackpot."

"Trust me. I won't be hitting it anytime soon. Catch you later."

Wasting no time, I shot out of the room and walked past the aisles of computers until I saw a door that led to the outside parking lot. A door that didn't have an alarm. I imagined that this was one of the last libraries that hadn't caught up to the rest of the world regarding security.

So much for picking up library chatter. All I heard were the discussions about whether they'd read a book and bits of advice straight out of the thirteenth century, thanks to the crowd in the reference section.

"Carry a red ribbon with you to avoid the evil eye."

"Put a mirror faceup under your bed if you plan on having children; facedown if you don't."

"Place pepper and garlic on your doorstep to prevent intruders."

I turned the AC up in the car and tried to digest the implications of a rumor spreading faster than a grease fire. By the time I walked into the house, I was exhausted.

It felt great to plop down on my mother's couch and stretch out my legs. But it wasn't as if I could actually relax. My mother was hovering over me, waiting to hear what I had gleaned.

"The library was a complete bust, unless you consider running into Herb Garrett some sort of prize. Boy does he think he's a regular ladies' man."

"It's all bravado, Phee. If it makes him feel younger, what's the harm? And what was he doing at the library? That's the last place I'd expect him."

"Attending a program on wealth management."

"I'll be darned. I didn't think Herb had that much money. Then again, he's probably trying to figure out how to manage what he has. Never mind about Herb. Did you find out anything else?"

"No, only the facts we already have. The indisputable facts." I made sure to emphasize the word "indisputable." "Josie Nolan planted the sugar so Thelmalee would get stung, and I'm pretty sure Jeanette and her former college roommate, Leslie, are responsible for Edna Mae's death. But motives? Shouldn't I have found at least one motive?"

"I'll give you a motive, if you want one. Make that two—jealousy and revenge. Would you like to hear my theory?"

Whether I wanted to hear my mother's theory or not, I was going to, so I just nodded.

"I'll bet you anything Thelmalee was having an

affair with Josie's husband and she figured out a way to get Thelmalee out of the picture."

"That's preposterous. All this time you've been after me to come up with evidence. Evidence. Evidence. Evidence. Like a broken record. And here you go, coming up with some theory that reads like a Danielle Steel novel."

"I'm entitled to my theories. And you wouldn't knock it if you saw Thelmalee."

"What do you mean?"

"Let's just say, if Helen of Troy was 'the face that launched a thousand ships,' then Thelmalee was the body that brought them all back!"

My jaw dropped wide open, and I was speechless. Luckily the phone rang and we didn't have to continue the conversation. I flipped through the channels and re-ran the events over in my mind while my mother was otherwise engaged with who-knows-who.

"Phee, were you listening? That was Shirley. Calling to tell me she and Lucinda contacted everyone in the club to make sure they'll be at Wednesday's meeting."

"And?"

"They're all coming."

"That's great. I'll either have everything figured out by then, or I'll make such a fool out of myself you'll have to move to another retirement community. And if any of this is going to work, I really need Josie Nolan and her sunbathing entourage to attend. Plus Jeanette's pal, Leslie. Oh, and Jerry White. He needs to be there as well. So how do I manage that?"

"I'm sure you'll think of something."

"At least I'm pretty certain of one thing. There was no curse. Just a nifty little diabolical plan to turn an unknown book into a best-seller overnight. But I still need proof. Proof it was all about the money. The money . . . Oh, good Lord—the money! That's it! I've got to make a call."

Before my mother could say a word, I jumped up and reached for the cell phone in my bag. Then I scrambled for my contacts list and dialed Nate.

"Nate! Oh, I'm glad I didn't have to leave a voicemail."

"Why? What happened?" he said.

"My brain finally kicked into gear, that's what, and something dawned on me. Something we should have looked into days ago."

"Okay. Tell me."

"*The Twelfth Arrondissement* was self-published, right? By a Lily Margot Gerald, right?"

I wasn't giving Nate any time to answer as my mind raced ahead.

"Well, if you're self-published, the royalty payments have to go into your bank account, or an account you set up. Not to a publisher. Traditional publishers give you advances or quarterly payments. If you can find out where the money is going for every copy of that book, then we'll know who the real author is. And I, for one, am putting my money, so to speak, on Gretchen Morin. So can you do it, Nate? Can you find out before Wednesday?"

"Whoa, slow down, Phee. Take a breath. Without any prompting on my part, Rolo had already looked into Gretchen's bank accounts. There are no deposits from any book companies. The only income she receives, via direct deposit, is from her paycheck."

"Oh." I felt as if someone had just let the air out of all my tires. "I still think it's her."

"Then you'll have to shake the tree a bit more."

"Shake the tree? Where'd that line come from?"

"You've never heard that expression? Means you need to find more evidence."

"Phooey. You sound just like my mother. Look, what if some of these deaths are totally unrelated, yet somehow are connected? You know, like that old Hitchcock movie, *Strangers on a Train*. You should be familiar with that one."

Nate chuckled. "Yeah, it's a basic course requirement for criminology."

"Seriously? Hitchcock?"

"I'm just teasing. Sorry. But yeah, I've seen that movie and what you're saying makes perfect sense. Sometimes we find isolated events that don't seem to have any relationship with anything else, only to learn later on that they were connected after all."

"Nate, I need to find out where that money is being deposited. Who's pocketing it from every sale of that lousy book? I know this goes beyond cyphers and codes, and I don't want you to get in trouble, but you said Rolo had already looked at Gretchen's deposits. Does that mean he's looking elsewhere?"

"I'm sure of it. I can picture him now, slugging down some awful sludge from his new juicing diet and hacking into banking numbers, routing numbers, and God knows what else. If there's something out there, Rolo Barnes will find it. Heck, he'll probably unearth the latest book distribution numbers from Amazon and Barnes & Noble before their CEOs ever see a report."

"I'm at my wit's end, Nate. I need the info, but I don't want you or Rolo to be in any jeopardy."

"Calm down, kiddo. I won't, and Rolo's so far

ahead in this game no one's going to catch up to him. You still have forty-eight hours. Which brings me to my next question. What are you going to do on Wednesday?"

"A grand finale like Miss Marple or Columbo, but without the finesse or the bumbling."

"Ah, pick one and go for it."

I thanked him profusely, pushed the End button, and looked at the expression on my mother's face. I couldn't tell if she was awestruck or horrified.

"Whatever you do, Phee, do not embarrass me."

"Embarrass you? That's the least of my worries. What I need to do now is get a copy of Edna Mae Langford's death certificate. It won't be easy. Arizona is a closed record state."

"What does that mean? That it'll cost me an arm and a leg if we need legal records?"

"No, well, maybe, but that's not the point. Only family, lawyers, or private investigators can get a copy of the death certificate. I think it's going to show a connection between Jeanette Tomilson and Edna Mae. But I'll never be able to prove it without that death certificate. I'm sunk."

"Not necessarily. I have connections, too, you know. Bernie Alan from the SunGlow Mortuary. That's where they kept poor Edna Mae's body until they shipped it to Wisconsin. And, for your information, Bernie happens to like me."

"And you think because he likes you, he's going to give you a copy of the death certificate? He'll lose his job."

"I don't need a copy. I just need to see what's on it. Tell me what you're looking for, and I'll give Bernie a call."

"How can you be sure he'll do this?"

"That man has been asking me out for over a year. I'll just make it a prerequisite for a dinner date."

"Mother, you're horrible. I can't believe you'd do something like that."

"It's better than rooting through garbage. And besides, I haven't had a decent steak in months."

I couldn't believe my mother. Then again, I couldn't believe all the kooky things I'd done in the past week either.

Chapter 22

If I was going to pull off my grand Agatha Christie–style finale at Wednesday's book club meeting, I desperately needed Josie Nolan to be in attendance, along with Jerry White and Leslie Sackler. Somehow I'd need to convince all of them to attend, and I had less than forty-eight hours to accomplish that miracle. I was all but chewing my nails over this while my mother fixated on the television lineup.

"So, what do you want to watch on TV tonight? *Family Feud* comes on at seven. It's got to be about that time now since the Shih Tzu from down the street just went by with his owner. Every night like clockwork—pees on the mailboxes. I'd never allow Streetman to do that. Good thing for me is that by the time the Shih Tzu gets here, he's just lifting his leg to let out some air. So, what do you think?"

"About what? The Shih Tzu? The mailbox? The clockwork? Wait! The clockwork! That's it! The dog pees like clockwork. I could kiss you, Mom. Got to get over to the dog park right now. You just reminded

me of something. Jerry White is going to be there
with Izzy, and it's the one chance I've got to convince
him to be at that book club meeting on Wednesday."

"That's the man from the Italian restaurant,
right?"

"Right. Got to go. I'll be back in less than an hour.
Give my regards to Steve Harvey."

I reached for my bag and headed out the door.
Once again, no time to even run a comb through my
hair. Oh well. I doubted very seriously that anyone
got dressed up for the dog park. Especially at night.

If the number of cars was any indication of what to
expect in the dog park, I was in trouble. I was wearing decent sandals and really didn't want to step in
anything disgusting. The park was standing room
only, with at least fifteen people milling around a cav-
alcade of dogs, with another twenty or so wedged
next to one another on benches. I took my time eyeballing each and every one of them, hoping to find
Jerry White.

With all the movement from the dogs and their
owners, it was impossible to get a good look. I had no
choice but to walk in and try to be inconspicuous. So
much for that.

"Hey, lady! Did you forget your dog in the car?" It
was a man's voice, aimed directly at me. A tall guy,
standing near the entrance.

"What? No."

"Only checking, lady," he said. "It happens sometimes. Had a woman in here last week who spent a
full forty minutes on the bench before she realized
she left her dog in the back seat of the car. Good
thing it was at night and not in the heat of the day."

I nodded and mumbled something as I continued to look for Jerry.

Suddenly someone started yelling, and I turned around to see what the commotion was all about. A petite sandy-haired lady was shouting "Howard Elizabeth" as if it were one word. I figured she was looking for friends of hers in the dog park.

"Howard Elizabeth! Howard Elizabeth!" No one responded. The woman stomped over to a black and white mixed-breed toy that appeared to be eating dirt. She bent down and shouted, "Howard Elizabeth, what are you doing?" as if the dog were about to tell her. She shouted again. The dog looked up from the ground, dirt all over its face, and promptly ran in the opposite direction. The woman must have noticed me gawking because she quickly walked toward me and explained. "Howard Elizabeth, that's his name, likes to eat dirt. Very dangerous. Valley fever and all." I started to respond when I heard someone else shouting. This time it was a man with a comb-over that made Donald Trump look like Don Johnson.

"Who owns that curly black dog? He won't leave the other dogs alone. Just look at him, jumping all over everything."

"He's just a puppy," someone else shouted.

"Puppy or not, he's a nuisance. HOLY COW! Take a look at what he just did now! He stuck his paws in the water bowl and dumped it all over. Whose dog is he?"

I didn't want to find myself in the middle of a melee, so I took a few steps back, giving me a better view of the benches. Sure enough, there was Izzy.

Seated on Jerry White's lap and adoring every minute.

"Hey, Izzy boy!" I petted him. "Good, good boy."

Then I looked directly at Jerry. "Have you seen Cindy Dolton? I was hoping she'd be here."

"Cindy?" he asked. "No, she wouldn't be here at night. Says that there are too many dogs and it makes Bundles nervous. Claims the stress gives him diarrhea."

"Well, I wouldn't really know about those things." *Thank God.* "Oh well. Figured she'd be here. I wanted to let her know about the book club meeting on Wednesday. For some reason, in the back of my mind, I thought she wanted to attend the next meeting. She seemed interested in that whole cursed book deal. Say, that's a meeting *you* should attend. The last time we spoke, before I ran into you at the Bingo game, you had some pretty strong feelings about that book."

"I did," Jerry replied. "I mean, I do. I didn't want unnecessary harm to come to people, but I suppose it's too late. The media's made a mockery of this thing. No need for me to be there."

"Oh, I disagree. You really should attend. Who knows what's going to happen with the press there. I'm sure you wouldn't want to find out second- or third-hand."

"You've got a point. I suppose I could stop by."

"By the way, how did you like Gretchen Morin, the librarian? Interesting woman, huh? Glad I could introduce you at Bingo."

I tried offering up a smile, but just as I started to move my lips, Izzy jumped off Jerry's lap and raced to the fence, barking. I could swear the man looked relieved.

"It's nothing," he said. "Just a golf cart going by. Izzy goes berserk at golf carts."

"Maybe they're cursed, too." I tried not to laugh, but Jerry failed to see the humor.

"If that book didn't carry a curse, then it wouldn't have made the Associated Press."

"It made the papers because of its record sales in a matter of days."

"And that, my dear," he replied, "is because the book is cursed."

"All the more reason for you to be at the book club meeting. Think of it as your civic duty."

Suddenly a voice shot through the park like a bullet. "POOP ALERT! POOP ALERT! SOMEONE'S DOG IS POOPING!"

"Geez," Jerry groaned. "I wish they'd give that guy a tranquilizer. Every night it's the same thing. You'd swear the dogs were crapping explosives."

I was about to say something about land mines but didn't think Jerry was in the mood to appreciate it. Instead, I petted Izzy as the dog jumped back in his owner's lap.

"So, uh . . . have a good evening. See you Wednesday."

Two more dog owners were coming through the gate as I was leaving. One of them asked if I forgot my dog.

"No, I don't think so." I headed for my car before he could respond.

By the time I pulled into my mother's driveway, it was getting dark. I wasn't sure if I had gotten Jerry riled up enough to attend the book club meeting or if I had merely annoyed him. Maybe I'd have better luck getting the other culprits to be there.

"I'm home, Mom," I yelled as I came through the door.

"Don't you ever answer that cell phone of yours? I've been trying to reach you. Hurry up and sit down. It's on CNN. The commercial is almost over."

"What? What's on CNN?"

"*The Twelfth Arrondissement*, that's what. It's all over the news! Did you know there's a global e-book version? Well, there is, and people who read it in the UK and Germany are now dead."

"You have *got* to be kidding me."

"Shh, it's starting."

I watched, stunned, as CNN international anchor Erin McLaughlin covered the story in London. Apparently there were three deaths, and all three people had been reading or had read the book. In addition, there were four deaths in Germany.

"Is this hysteria, or is something else going on?" the reporter asked. Then, of all things, she mentioned the Booked 4 Murder book club and how the whole thing got started.

"Until they can unravel this phenomenon, which began in a small senior community in the United States, I'm afraid we're stuck with a greater mystery than the one that appears in this novel."

"Hmmph." That was all my mother said, but I knew what she was thinking.

"Mother, you know as well as I do that this is just a publicity stunt meant to increase sales. You started watching the news coverage before I did, so tell me, did they mention who the people were and the circumstances?"

"Car accident, stroke, and brain aneurysm in the UK."

"Coincidence. Coincidence. Coincidence. What about in Germany?"

"They didn't say."

"Well, I guarantee it's going to be very similar. Look, for whatever reason, people seem to be drawn to this kind of stuff—curses, magic, you name it. And it takes a shrewd marketer to create the snowball effect. When the truth comes out on Wednesday, that book will go back to obscurity."

"I wouldn't bet on it. So, did you figure out how to get those people to the book club meeting?"

"Not exactly. Unless I get the posse to drag them in. And one of them, Leslie Sackler, doesn't even live in Sun City West."

My mother gave me a quizzical look and smiled. "Leslie. The one we were talking about at lunch today? The beige SUV?"

"Yeah, her."

"Not a problem. Let me get Jeanette on the phone."

"You're going to come right out and ask Jeanette to bring her? She'll know we're up to something."

"Relax. I've got my ways."

I didn't doubt it for a minute, but I was still uneasy as my mother placed the call.

"Jeanette? Glad you're home. It's Harriet. Got a minute?" Pause. "You didn't happen to watch CNN just now, did you?" Pause. "Well, you're not going to believe it, but that book was on CNN. CNN! Unexplained deaths in Europe." Pause. "Uh-huh. Uh-huh. Well, anyway, that's not the reason I called. I met a woman today at the supermarket who lives across the street from Edna Mae Langford's house, and we got to talking. That checkout line was ridiculous. The store needs to hire more cashiers. Well, to get to the point, this lady told me she saw someone in Edna Mae's driveway acting suspicious. And that's not all. She saw the car. Said it was a tan wagon or SUV with writing on the back window, but she couldn't see that far."

Words spewed from my mother's mouth nonstop.

"Jeanette, are you still there? Uh-huh . . . No, she didn't call the posse. Why on earth would the posse come out just because someone was in someone else's driveway? The woman didn't realize what was going on and never expected Edna Mae to fall, much less break a hip. She blames it all on that book curse. Uh-huh . . ."

A quick breath and she kept on going. "So, I talked her into going to the book club meeting on Wednesday so she could tell everyone firsthand what happened."

Then, my mother paused. A pregnant pause.

"No, I don't think she got that close a look at the woman in the driveway. That's not the point. The point is, none of this would have happened if Edna Mae wasn't reading that book. Uh-huh . . . Yes, awful. Anyway, just thought you'd be interested. I'll see you Wednesday."

She lingered on the phone while Jeanette said a few more words. I was utterly speechless by the time my mother had finished.

"What? What's the matter, Phee? You think Helen Mirren is the only one my age who can act? And how did you like the way I wove everything back to the book curse? Pretty smooth for a woman my age, huh?"

"Yep, smooth. You can act and make up dialogue at the same time. So, do you think it worked? Do you think Jeanette will get Leslie to be there on Wednesday?"

"Yes, I do. Trust me. If Jeanette and her friend were responsible for Edna Mae's fall, then they're going to do everything possible to see to it the woman doesn't open her mouth at the meeting."

"You're not thinking Jeanette and Leslie would do anything to harm that woman? And by the way, her name is Bev. Bev Mortenson. And she isn't even going to be at the meeting. You made it all up."

"I know that and you know that, but they don't. Still, I think that Mortenson woman who lives across the street from Edna Mae will be fine. Those houses are so close together, it would be impossible to figure out which one is hers. Goodness. Elderly women probably live in all of those houses. Jeanette and Leslie would be hard-pressed to figure out which house belongs to the lady who spilled the beans."

"No one spilled the beans. You made it all up."

"Exactly."

My mother was pretty clever, but I'd never realized how conniving she could be. "Guess that leaves Josie Nolan and—Someone's pounding on the door, Mom!"

"Who on earth would be pounding on the door after dark? Unless it's Herb Garrett and something has happened on the street . . ."

"I'm up. I'll get it."

"Don't open the security door. Just the regular one," my mother yelled.

"I know. I know."

"And look down for snakes. They crawl around at night."

"I think you mean slither."

"Slither, crawl, whatever it is they do. Forget the snakes. Get the door."

Whoever was pounding also rang the doorbell and continued to ring it as I started to open the front door.

It was Shirley Johnson, and she was frantic. "Don Lemon! Don Lemon! At Bagels 'N More!"

Shirley looked as if she was gasping her last breath as my mother yelled for her to come inside. Streetman took off and hid under the couch as I opened the security door.

"Don Lemon! From CNN. He's here with photographers and who-knows-who. It's about the book curse. They're going to be at Wednesday's book club, and they're going to be interviewing people in Sun City West tomorrow. Lord Almighty! Don Lemon!"

"Slow down, Shirley, I'll get you something to drink. Iced tea okay?" my mother asked.

"Water will be fine. I stopped into the bagel place to get a dozen bagels and there he was, complete with his crew. People were swarming all over him."

"Here, take a sip of water," my mother said, handing Shirley a bottle of spring water from the fridge.

Shirley didn't merely sip the water. She guzzled it. I waited a second before asking her how she found out about Don Lemon's assignment here.

"Lord Almighty. In all my life, I never expected to walk into a bagel store and find Don Lemon there. I was standing right near the cashier when he told her about his assignment. Then it was total chaos. Here, look. I snapped a photo of him on my phone while I was waiting for my bagels. The minute he sat down, he was swarmed. Lordy, I got so nervous I almost left without my bagels."

Sure enough, there was Don Lemon, sitting at one of the tables surrounded by the twenty-something coffee drinkers and the late-night geriatric crowd.

"Which one is Don Lemon?" my mother asked.

"The cute one." Shirley and I both responded at once.

My mother didn't seem too phased. "Well, I'll get concerned when CNN sends Wolf Blitzer."

"I think they only send him out if it's a war or something." Shirley continued to talk about the book curse and how the whole thing was exploding all around us.

"I tried calling you, Harriet, but your line was busy, so I decided it would be easier to drive over. I've already called Lucinda and Cecilia. They were going to call people, too. Oh Lord! Do you realize what this means?"

It was impossible for my mother to utter a word. Shirley never let up. "It means they're going to film us at the book club meeting. I've got to get my hair appointment moved up to tomorrow. And my nails. I don't want my nails on national TV looking like chewed-up caramels."

"I really don't think anyone's going to be looking at your nails," I started to say, when my mother poked me and broke in.

"If word gets out, those salons are going to be packed."

"The phone's ringing again, Mom."

My mother darted for the kitchen as Shirley went

on about her hair and nails. All I could do until my
mother returned was to nod and mumble, "Uh-huh."

"That was Louise Munson, and she just found out
from her sister-in-law in Surprise that Fox News is
there, staying at the Hampton."

Shirley looked as if it was the next stock market
crash. "Good Lord! I have simply got to get a hair
appointment. I don't care if I have to drive all the
way to Phoenix. I'm not going to be on national,
no . . . make that *world* news looking like some retired backwoods schoolmarm. I'll call you tomorrow,
Harriet. I've got to run. And nice talking to you,
too, Phee."

Shirley was out the door before I knew it, but that
didn't mean the excitement was over for the night.
My mother's phone kept ringing, and each call was
more frantic than the last. CNN might have technology, but it was nothing compared to the rumor mill.
I leaned back on the couch and listened.

"No, I don't think you can lose ten pounds in
twenty-four hours."

"Why would they be sending the state police?"

"Tell your great aunt, Walter Cronkite has been
dead for years. Yes, I'm sure."

"I don't know if they will let you hold up a sign
promoting your pet sitting."

And on and on it went. Each call more bizarre
than the last. It was twenty after eleven when the
phone finally stopped ringing and my mother and I
could get to sleep.

"There's one good thing about this, Phee," she
said as we turned off the lights in the living room.

"What's that?"

"You won't have to worry about Josie Nolan and her crew showing up. They'll be there all right, front and center."

"How can you be so sure?"

"Because she's a realtor, and realtors will take advantage of any publicity. Why, I'll bet she's already put a large box of business cards in her car."

"What about the others?"

"Believe me, it'll be standing room only. That library will be filled to capacity as soon as the doors open."

"Mom, I don't know if I can go through with my, well, you know, my . . . conclusion. I thought I'd be in front of the book club and the suspects, not world-wide media."

"Ignore the camera. You'll be fine. Oh, and, Phee, whatever you do, don't wear anything too form-fitting. Martin Chomwitzer isn't the only one with a roving eye around here."

"Eeew."

Chapter 23

I must have been really exhausted because I slept until eight and never heard my mother's phone ring. She pointed to the coffeemaker as I staggered into the kitchen.

"Help yourself. Myrna Mittleson called about fifteen minutes ago. Frantic. Beside herself. It's her turn to conduct the monthly book club meeting, and she said she can't go through with it. Not in front of so many people and the press. Didn't want to make a fool of herself. I told her all she needs to do is follow the same dog-eared script we do each month, but she refused. Cecilia was next on the list, and she told Myrna that if she had to do it, she'd quit the club. So, that leaves me. My turn is third down the list."

"Mom, that's terrific. I hope you told her you'll do it."

"Like I have a choice. Shirley's turn comes after mine, and she's too petrified to even hold the book."

"Look, with you conducting the meeting, I'll be

able to step in and show them once and for all there's no curse. No murders either. What we have are opportunistic people taking advantage of a situation in order to cover up some deaths. Deaths they're responsible for."

"Wouldn't that be murder?"

"Not exactly. I still need time to flush out more information. The only problem is Nate. If he doesn't get back to me by the end of the day, I'll have nothing—just a big, fat, empty theory."

"From what you've told me, it sounds as if this detective is working overtime for you. So . . . any romantic interest?"

"With Nate? He's almost twenty years older than I am and no, there's no romantic interest. We've known each other for a long time, working for the Mankato Police Department."

My mother looked a trifle disappointed. "So what's left that you have to investigate?"

"A motive for Thelmalee's unfortunate encounter with the bees, the real author of *The Twelfth Arrondissement* (which is sitting on Nate's lap, so to speak), and the suspicious incident involving Jeanette's car left running in the garage the first night I got here. Oh, and not that it probably has any bearing on any of this, but the identity of the guy in the blue Mazda who I followed all the way into Surprise. The only surprise was he wasn't going home."

"Well, don't just sit there drinking coffee. Get showered. Get dressed. Get going. I mean, you do have some sort of plan to find those answers, right?"

"An actual plan, no, but I do have a good starting

place. Forget the shower. I'll take one at the pool. It should be open by the time I get there."

"What about breakfast?"

"I'll fend for myself and give you a call later, okay?"

My mother started to pour herself another cup of coffee when the phone rang again. As she took the call, I changed into a swimsuit.

"That was the library," she shouted. "They're calling everyone in the book club to let us know the meeting has been moved to the social hall in the recreation building. They anticipate a big crowd and there won't be enough room in the library."

"Ca-ching. Ca-ching," I said.

"What's that supposed to mean?"

"It means that with all the local TV stations and the national ones, that book is going to hit the bestseller list by the commercial break. Unbelievable. And I just thought of something else. Halloween's only a month away. Sales for that tome will skyrocket. I can just imagine the commercials now. *Want to send a Halloween curse? We've got yours all wrapped up in paperback or hardcover and e-book, too.*"

"All the more reason for you to expose those charlatans."

"And you know what the kicker is? That book was actually good. Really well-written and interesting."

"Yeah, yeah. You can tell it to the book club tomorrow. Meanwhile, you don't have much time left. And Shirley Johnson isn't going to be the only one with a new hairdo. I've got to call my beautician right away before I get caught up in something."

I rounded up a tote for swimwear along with my bag and keys before my mother had a chance to bring up the subject of my hair. Then I was off and my mind was racing. I could think of a million and one reasons why someone would want to knock off Thelmalee's family, but Thelmalee? Hard to say.

The trouble with not having a plan meant opening yourself up to anything and everything. That was exactly what happened when I got to the pool. It was packed. Packed with at least twenty-five to thirty women, all lined up in the shallow end. Someone yelled out to me, "Hurry up and rinse off, you don't want to be late."

I was about to say something when a voice came out of nowhere.

"Hi! I'm Bobbi Jean and this is the Wavy Wet Water Fitness Class. Make sure you're at least waist-deep in the water and arm's length from your neighbor. Slowly start jogging . . ."

The music picked up, and I looked around. It had to be a tape. And if I expected to get any information about Thelmalee, I would have to jump, kick, and jog my way around these ladies to do so.

I was, by far, the youngest member of the class, and the worst. I was out of breath somewhere in between "jump, kick, jump" and "twist, turn, twist." By the time the forty-minute tape was over, I was ready to collapse, and I hadn't even accomplished what I set out to do—chat with the pool monitors and sunbathers about Thelmalee. But, as luck would have it, everything changed in an instant. I caught part of a conversation and trudged my way over to two women who were still standing in the water. I wouldn't exactly call it eavesdropping, but it came close. I was glued to their every word.

"I know we shouldn't speak ill of the dead, but I have to tell you, it's been a lot more pleasant without Thelmalee here. I mean, you can actually use the space near the side without her claiming it was taken."

"I've never known a more territorial person."

"Thelmalee Kirkson?" I asked as they both turned around to face me.

"Oh, I hope we haven't offended you, if she was a friend of yours," one of them said.

I shook my head. "She wasn't a friend."

"That's a relief," the woman continued, "because, if the truth be known, she wasn't really well-liked around the pool."

Then the other woman added, "Well-liked? Try not liked at all."

It was time for me to step in, and I couldn't wait. "What do you mean?"

Both of them went on to explain how Thelmalee always got to the pool early so she could hog the entire space by the wall for her exercises. It was the only time she actually got in the water.

"And if that wasn't bad enough," the one woman continued, "I know firsthand she was downright miserable to the ladies who wanted to sunbathe in the afternoon."

I zeroed in like a vulture. "How do you know that?"

"Because I'm in a sewing club with one of those ladies. Thelmalee took up three lounge chairs and refused to give them to people. Used one for her towels, one for her lotions, and one to show off that body of hers."

My eyes all but bulged out of my face. "Couldn't the monitors do anything about that?"

"I don't think they wanted to get into a screaming match with her. And it wasn't as if there weren't other chairs. You know what was really strange, though?"

"No, what?" I was salivating at the thought I might actually be on to something.

"A few days before Thelmalee got stung, some of the afternoon sunbathers had had enough and went to the monitor to complain. And he told them that maybe they should figure out a way to scare her out of that place. Imagine that. Of course, they never had to, because the bees got to her first."

There it was. Right in front of me. The motive! Those ladies wanted equal billing when it came to poolside seating and literally took the monitor's advice.

"Do you know which monitor it was? I'm just curious. I mean, it was a clever response, huh?"

"David Blomgarten. He's the monitor on duty right now. The bald guy with the reddish beard. He usually has the morning shift Monday through Thursday."

"Interesting. Well, I'd better shower and get moving. It was nice exercising with you."

"Come back anytime. Bobbi Jean's always here at nine a.m. sharp on weekdays."

I headed for the locker room, showered as fast as I could, changed my clothing, and headed over to the monitor's spot by the entrance. David Blomgarten was busying himself with a Sudoku puzzle when I approached.

"Sorry to interrupt, but I'm curious. Especially when it comes to divine intervention."

He looked up.

"Huh?"

"Were you absolutely flabbergasted when those bees attacked Thelmalee Kirkson after you mentioned the only way to remove her was to scare her out of here?"

I swore the color drained from his face.

"I don't know what you mean, lady. I wasn't here at the time. That happened in the afternoon."

"Yeah, I know. But you did say that, didn't you? About giving her a run for her money, so to speak. I was talking with some friends, and they overheard you telling Josie Nolan and her crew the only way to remove Thelmalee was by scaring her out of there. Personally, I would have hired a bulldozer."

"Oh, that." The man suddenly seemed more relaxed. Was this how the police did it? Got the perpetrator to think they were on his or her side?

I paused for a moment to see what he would say.

"That Thelmalee woman was making everyone at the pool miserable. I made that remark jokingly. I mean, what were those ladies going to do? Put on masks and say, 'Boo'? Guess the only ones who took me seriously were the bees."

"Yeah, well, anyway, it worked. She was scared off for good. Tell me, was there any other way to remove her from the pool?"

"Sure. By formal complaint. Your friends would have to fill out a detailed complaint form and file it at the recreation center office. Of course, they'd have to wait for months until someone acted on it, unless, of course, the form got lost and then they'd have to start all over again. I got the feeling they wanted a quick and easy solution. As it turned out, they didn't have to wait very long."

"What do you mean?" I asked.

"The bee attack came a day or so later. I can't remember exactly. It was around the time everyone came in talking about that book curse. Anyway, maintenance has been here to spray the area."

"I see. Well, thanks for your time and good luck with your puzzle."

The guy grumbled something and then looked at his numbers as I headed back to the car. Was the motive that simple? Then I remembered the Bingo game and how some of those players were beyond territorial. Maybe Josie and her crew had had enough. It still didn't explain the relationship among the Nolans, Gretchen Morin, and Jerry White, but I felt as if I was getting closer.

I think the temperature must have risen at least ten degrees between the time I parked the car and the time I returned to it. I removed the windshield screen and was about to turn on the engine when my phone went off. It was my mother.

"I got what you wanted, Phee."

"What do you mean?"

"The name. The name on Edna Mae's death certificate. Bernie Alan just called me back. We're going to have dinner next week at the Arrowhead Grill in Peoria. Wonderful steaks. Fancy place. Anyway, I've got the name for you."

"It's Tomilson, isn't it? I was right, wasn't I?"

"No."

"That can't be."

"Do you want me to tell you the name or not?"

"What is it?"

She read the two-syllable name out loud and like a freight train jamming its brakes, the connection hit me in an instant.

"Thanks, Mom. You're an angel. Talk to you later."

The puzzle was starting to solve itself and I was along for the ride.

Chapter 24

After all that exercise, mental and otherwise, I was starving. What I really wanted was an honest-to-goodness breakfast, not a quick cup of coffee. I headed for the nearest little hole-in-the-wall restaurant that promised to deliver all of the above. Fortunately, I didn't have to drive far; there was a small diner just a block or so away. I had remembered spotting it in the same complex where my mother went food shopping. The turquoise and white sign in front of the place—PUTTERS PARADISE—looked bigger than the restaurant.

I made myself comfortable in the faded blue booth by the front window and glanced at the menu. Across from me were a few couples and in the middle of the room was a table for six, filled with men who apparently had just gotten off of the golf course.

In the corner on the right was a younger guy working frantically on a laptop. I glanced around and, sure enough, the sign above the cash register said, WE HAVE WI-FI. I took out my iPhone and scanned for messages. The waitress had already placed my order, and I figured I wouldn't have long to wait.

The conversation around the middle table never strayed from golf. Not that I was trying to listen. I wasn't. But it was impossible to ignore them. I glanced over at the guy in the corner, who was still working on his computer. Did it take that long for his food to arrive? I hoped not, since I was famished. Then he turned his head for an instant and I froze. Speechless. Dazed. It was the man from the blue Mazda. Not a single doubt in my mind.

It was difficult to guess his age the last time I saw him, in front of the blond woman's house on some cul-de-sac in Surprise. But I knew it was him—fabulous build, light blond hair, and the same tan khaki pants as before. I quickly spun my head around and scanned the parking lot. Sure enough, there was a blue Mazda a few rows from my car. I guess I hadn't noticed it earlier because all I could think about was eating.

Showtime. I'd better get off my butt and make my move. How many chances like this are going to fall into my lap?

The man's appearance took me completely off guard, and I was at a loss as to how to approach him. I figured I might as well be direct, even though flirting might have furthered my cause.

"Excuse me. I hate to interrupt your meal. That is . . . er . . . um, when it gets here, but I saw you in front of my neighbor Jeanette's house the other day, and I was wondering . . ."

"I'm sorry." He looked at me. No need to guess his age. He couldn't have been any older than thirty.

Is Jeanette really such a cougar? Is that what he thinks I am? I'll only know when he opens his mouth.

"My schedule is absolutely packed and I can't fit

you in for at least two weeks. Can it wait that long, or do you need someone right away?"

Oh my God! Is this guy a high-priced gigolo? Can what wait? Can what wait? Think fast.

"Um, uh—" Just then the waitress appeared and refilled his cup of coffee.

"So, how's it going, Josh? Think you can get the speed up on this thing? My boss is pitching a fit and doesn't want to buy a new computer."

"Yeah, I'm working on it. Did he know there was a virus? He's got to install a software program to prevent that."

"I'll let him know when he gets in later," the waitress said. "Oh, what the heck. Just install it. I'll tell him I authorized it."

"Sure he's going to be okay with that?"

"He'd better be if he knows what's good for his business."

"All right, then."

The waitress left and Josh turned back to me. "Sorry about that. So, as I was saying, my schedule is really booked up. Here's my card. Leave me a voicemail with all your details and I'll get you on my calendar. If it's really an emergency, I do work late at night and on weekends. Be sure to leave me a message. I won't remember anything if you tell me now. At least I can replay voicemail."

I was so relieved that I hardly knew what to say. This guy wasn't some escort, and he wasn't Jeanette's boyfriend. He was her computer guy. Her computer guy! So much for the jealous wife of the boyfriend theory. Great job, Mom, for having me chase all over the place. I took the card and put it in my bag.

/ "Thank you so much. I really appreciate it. Enjoy your coffee."

My meal was already on my table by the time I walked back to my booth—Applewood smoked bacon, scrambled eggs, and sourdough toast. At least it hadn't gotten too cold, but that didn't matter. I was too overjoyed to think I had literally stumbled upon one of the neighborhood mysteries and solved it without any effort on my part. I figured that by the time the book club meeting got underway tomorrow, I'd be able to put this whole fiasco to rest.

Unfortunately, the proverbial bubble burst the minute I walked into my mother's house. She was just getting off the phone and motioned for me to walk over. "You're not going to believe this, Phee. Not in a million years."

"What? Did someone confess?"

"No, no, but with all the attention this book curse is getting, one of the networks is sending Vivian Knowlton to the book club meeting tomorrow."

I shrugged. "Who's Vivian Knowlton?"

My mother looked at me as if I'd asked who George Washington was. "Don't you watch TV? Vivian Knowlton is the *Psychic Diva*. Her reality show is right up there with *Sister Wives* and that Honey Boo Boo."

"Sorry, Mom, but I guess I don't watch that stuff."

"Well, that's too bad, because once Vivian Knowlton gets here tomorrow, she's going to take over that meeting."

"WHAT?" I could literally feel my blood pressure rising.

"Oh, yes. It's been arranged with the library. Gretchen Morin invited Vivian to discuss *The Twelfth*

Arrondissement and any paranormal connections it may have regarding the cursing of people who read it."

"Oh, for heaven's sake. That meeting is going to turn into one big sideshow. I don't know how I'll manage to convince everyone it was a ruse. In case you haven't noticed, I've never been great at public speaking."

"Neither was that British king, what was his name? The one with the speech impediment? Colin Firth played him and was positively eloquent."

"I think that was King George the Sixth, but stuttering isn't my problem. It's going to be impossible if that psychic lady gets the crowd all riled up. I really thought I'd be able to pull all the evidence together like Miss Marple until the perpetrators finally break down. Look, I need to get ahold of Nate and try to piece things together."

"You know what would be good?" My mother continued on as if she hadn't asked a question. "A whiteboard and dry-erase markers. I'm going to give the library a call and make sure they bring a large whiteboard and markers to the social hall tomorrow. You'll need them in order to present your findings. Unless, of course, you planned on doing something fancy with the computer."

I was stunned and it took me a few seconds to respond. "You mean a PowerPoint presentation? I'm not giving a lecture on water rates or gardening in the desert. I want to present the facts as we know them and let people see for themselves who was orchestrating this entire charade and why."

"So, the whiteboard, then? Much more dramatic, I think. Draw big letters and be sure to underline when you emphasize something. And articulate when you speak. Articulate."

Honestly, she was beginning to sound like my tenth-grade English teacher. I looked her straight in the eye and enunciated every word. "I need to call Nate. Now. I'll talk to you in a few minutes."

"See, you've got the knack of it."

Groaning, I walked into the guest bedroom before my mother could say anything else. It was bad enough this meeting was going to be televised on major networks, but now this? It was as if that outrageous book had a life of its own and was manipulating everyone. And why should Gretchen Morin invite a psychic when she told Nina Alvarez there was no such thing as a book curse? Was she trying to exonerate herself at the book club or what? I grabbed my phone and dialed quickly.

Voicemail. Maybe Nate was still in the office. I dialed the switchboard for the Mankato Police Department and asked to be connected to Detective Williams. More voicemail. My lucky day. Meanwhile, my mother's phone rang. Mayberry couldn't hold a candle to this place.

"That was Herb," my mother shouted. "Look out the window. There's a news crew interviewing Jeanette about the attempted murder. They must have arrived right after you came in. They had the wrong address and went to his house first."

"This is worse than I thought. Those news crews aren't going to let up until they milk this thing dry. There'll be more spin-off stories than you can imagine. 'Who styled Thelmalee's hair?' 'What was Minnie Bendelson's last meal?' 'What kind of golf cart did Marilyn Scutt drive?' Right down to calling in some expert to discuss 'the pollination habits of the local bees in Sun City West.'"

"Hold on. That's the phone again."

I stared out the window as my mother took the call. A van from a local TV station was parked across the street. Jeanette was going to make the early evening news. I'd catch the segment later that night.

"That was Cecilia," my mother yelled. "She's at the library. They've got a news crew there interviewing people about their reading preferences. Said if I hurry, I can be on the news."

"You're not seriously thinking of going over there, are you?"

"Of course not. The only place I'm going is to the beauty parlor. I have an appointment in less than an hour, and I need to get a move on. You don't think I'd risk being on national television tomorrow looking like this, do you?"

"I . . . uh . . ."

"Say no more. I'm having my roots touched up and then getting a quick trim. Did you ever consider adding some blond highlights to your hair?"

"I have natural highlights."

"This is television, Phee. No one is supposed to look natural on television. Besides, your hair could use a boost."

I knew it. Harriet Plunkett couldn't keep her mouth shut when it came to my hair. If it was short, it should be long. If it was long, it should be curly. I learned to ignore the suggestions. "It'll be fine. I've got some more digging to do on the computer. If I decide to go out, I'll leave a note."

My mother grumbled and then proceeded to shuffle around until it was time for her to leave to go to her appointment. The TV van across the street was gone as my mother drove down the block. I was about to turn away from the window when I noticed Jeanette's garage door opening and her car pulling out. I was all but blinded by the shine on that KIA Sportage. *Well, I could have had one, too, if I was willing to trade mine in. Stop being so jealous.*

It did handle beautifully during my test drive. And those sleek lines looked nothing like the older models. Well, maybe something to consider when I get back to Minnesota . . . Oh, who was I kidding . . . ? Then, it was as if someone had lit a firecracker in front of me. Holy cow! Holy, holy cow! No one tried to murder Jeanette. No one! I should have realized this before. Vivian Knowlton or not, I was going to have my say tomorrow at the book club.

Chapter 25

With my mother safely out of the way at the beauty parlor and Streetman snoring on the couch, I pulled out my stack of notes and the charts I'd made, spreading them all over the kitchen table. The names of the victims reminded me of that old silly game we played as kids by pulling off the petals from daisies and saying, "He loves me, he loves me not," only this time I was muttering, "Dead, no foul play. Dead, with foul play." I still had the same results as before—foul play for Edna Mae and Thelmalee, natural circumstances for Marilyn and Minnie, and downright lying as far as Jeanette was concerned.

The only thing I was missing was the financial end, and that was paramount if anyone was going to believe me tomorrow. I stared at the kitchen clock, knowing it wasn't going to make Nate call any sooner. I'd asked him earlier to find out if Rolo checked the accounts for the Nolans since they all seemed to be connected. That had, apparently, pulled up a dead end as well.

"This is so damn frustrating!" I yelled out loud.

I was certain Lily Margot Gerald was really Gretchen, but if that was true, then the money trail would be leading to her and it wasn't. Nate had told me that Rolo scrutinized every conceivable derivation including Lillian, Margaux, and Gerauld. Not to mention all sorts of combinations for the initials LMG. Again, nothing. *Lily Margot Gerald.* I Googled her name to see what I could turn up, but all I found were a few Lily Margots, and they seemed to be in their twenties and living in France. Well, good for them. And no, I didn't want to connect on LinkedIn.

What a waste of an afternoon. The only thing I accomplished was to produce a neater set of notes for tomorrow's meeting, provided Vivian Knowlton didn't upstage me completely. I was staring at Lily's name, hoping a trance would come over me and give me the answer I needed when I emerged. That didn't happen either. Streetman must have heard my mother's key in the lock, because he jumped from the couch and stared at the foyer just as she came through the door.

"I'm back! Oh, there's my little man. Were you Momma's good little boy?"

The dog was jumping up and down, pawing at her legs.

"Isn't that cute? He should have a treat. So, what do think of my hair, Phee? I decided having her touch up the roots wasn't enough, so I had her add a few ribbons of creamy caramel to set it apart."

Creamy caramel? It sounded like a Halloween candy.

"It looks nice." *In an off-beat sort of way.*

"I thought so, too. I wanted something that would stand out. Everyone's going to be vying for attention. It was a circus at the salon. A circus. Do you know

that they put a sign out front that said, CAMERA-READY
LOOKS IN AN HOUR? The place was mobbed. Good
thing I made my appointment when I did. The only
saving grace was the fact the supermarket wasn't too
crowded. I ran into Herb Garrett, and he told me
he's decided to attend tomorrow's book club meeting. Can you imagine? Herb. I don't think he's
picked up a book in thirty years! Oh no! Would you
look at the time? It's close to dinner. I got us some
stuffed cabbage from the deli. It was on special."

The fifteen or twenty minutes we ate dinner was
the only break we had from a relentless string of
phone calls that began at five-thirty and didn't end
until well past ten, when my mother swore she was
going to unplug the landline. It was worse than the
day before. Again, I listened as my mother responded
to each caller.

"What? Your church choir decided to come? All of
them? And they want to sing?"

"No, I have no idea if Anderson Cooper will be
there."

"Movie rights? Movie rights to what? That book or
Sun City West? You're not making any sense, Shirley.
Where did you hear that? . . . Uh-huh. No wonder."

"Refreshments? No, I don't think we'd better
bring refreshments this time. It would be like feed-
ing a stadium."

"Tell her that dogs are NOT allowed in the social
hall. Even if they are small. And besides, a twenty-
five-pound beagle isn't my definition of small."

Unfortunately, none of those calls was Nate, and
by eleven I was more than a little twitchy.

"This is a nightmare, Mom. A veritable nightmare.
Nate hasn't called and that's because Rolo Barnes

wasn't able to track down the money. I can't pin this on Gretchen or anyone else, for that matter, if I don't know whose account is receiving the money from online sales. The only thing I'm fairly certain of is there is NO Lily Margot Gerald."

My mother let out a sigh and muttered, "I know," before turning up the volume to the TV. "Can you believe this? They're showing the original Disney *Snow White and the Seven Dwarfs* at midnight. I haven't seen that since you were a little girl."

"There's a reason for that. And don't tell me you're going to stay up and watch it now."

"No, I'm too exhausted. Besides, we've both out-grown that tired theme of the lily-white princess who has to be rescued by the handsome prince. Even though I wouldn't mind hearing a rousing chorus of 'Heigh-ho, heigh-ho.'"

"What did you just say?"

"I said I wouldn't mind hearing a rousing chorus of—"

"No, no, before that. Something about the princess."

"I said the theme of the handsome prince having to rescue the lily-white princess is getting pretty old."

"That's it! That's it! And it was right in front of our eyes. How could I be so dense? I don't care if it is midnight in Mankato, I've got to get ahold of Nate!"

"What? What was in front of our eyes?"

"Not what. Who."

"Jerry White, that's who. Look at the name—Lily Gerald. Gerald is formal French for Jerry. And Lily. What's the first thing that comes to mind when you think of that name? White. Lily White!"

"But isn't that author's name *Lily Margot Gerald*?"

"Yes, it is. And I'll bet dollars to donuts that

somehow *Margot* translates to *Gretchen*. Turn on your computer, Mom, and go to Google translate. Try French and German while I call Nate."

My mother lasted about twenty minutes on Google Translate before declaring she was too tired to think in English, let alone another language. Meanwhile, I managed to wake up Nate, and in his stupor he agreed to place a call to Rolo.

"Do it now, Nate," I said, "Don't go back to sleep."

A garble of incoherent words followed and, just like that, the conversation was over. The rest of the night I wondered if he placed the call. The next morning, I got my answer.

Chapter 26

It was six a.m. Arizona time, and I was the one who was groggy when my phone rang. Sure enough, Rolo had been up all night working on this. Unfortunately, the results turned out to be a big fat zero.

I was all but whining. "Are you absolutely sure there are no accounts linked to Jerry White?"

"I'm sorry to disappoint you, but no monies are being cyphered into Jerry White's account from any book sales."

"And I was so certain it was him. I would have bet my life on it."

"Hey, it was a good lead. Heck, more than a good lead. It just didn't pan out. Things like that happen all the time."

"My God, Nate. That must be so frustrating. And I'm so sorry that Rolo lost a night's sleep."

"Don't worry about it, kiddo. I don't think that guy sleeps anyway. Look, given the info you have, you can still shoot down that book curse. Plus, you have the evidence to incriminate Josie Nolan for Thelmalee's death, plus some decent circumstantial evidence to point a finger at the people responsible for Edna Mae Langford's death. I'd say that was pretty darn good for a week's work."

"I suppose. Anyway, I can't wait to get back to Minnesota tomorrow night. I'll give you a call after this book club fiasco is over."

"Don't forget to smile at the camera. I'll be tuning in to CNN and Fox this afternoon. Should be a doozy."

"That's one word for it. Which reminds me, ever hear of a Vivian Knowlton from *Psychic Divas*?"

"Not a show I watch. I think that's all a bunch of crap. But hey, showmanship is everything, so I hear."

"Thanks, Nate. And thanks for not being too mad at me for waking you up. And thank Rolo, too."

"No problem. When this is over, you can buy Rolo a Cuisinart or whatever the latest juicing machine happens to be. Catch you later."

I jumped into the shower and rehearsed what I would say when the meeting started. I knew Gretchen would introduce Vivian first. I just never expected what would come next.

My first clue we were in for trouble should have been the traffic as we headed to the social hall. My second came later.

"Can you believe this?" my mother said as I pulled into the parking lot. "Our book club meeting doesn't start for another hour and a half, and it's already impossible to find a spot. This place is packed tighter than a can of sardines."

It was more than packed. It was crammed. Cars, minivans, golf carts, emergency response vehicles, and a full fleet from the sheriff's department. Worse yet, television crew vans from at least four stations were front and center.

"I don't have a good feeling about this. Like things might get out of control or something."

"Don't be ridiculous. It's not like senior day at the supermarket. They're not giving away anything. And look, there are a few sheriff cars parked here, too. Everything will be under control. Just take out your notes and articulate. Remember, underline the important stuff on the whiteboard."

I sighed and pulled up to the front of the social hall. "I'm going to let you out so you won't have too far to walk. Then I'll park the car and meet you inside. At least we don't have to worry about getting a seat. Our table should be in the middle, right?"

"Yes, it's all set. I made those arrangements for the meeting days ago."

"Good. Then I'll see you inside."

"Oh, look, Phee! At the bus. It's the *Psychic Divas* bus and it's huge."

Sure enough, a bus the size of a large Greyhound was off to the side of the main entrance. Its façade was painted pink and lavender with cutesy curls and flowers that formed the words *Psychic Divas*. I wanted to throw up. That was before I caught sight of the other vehicles—shuttle buses and limos from every resort and retirement hotel in the area. I could see The Golden Heritage, The Royal Lifestyle, The Monte Carlo, and of course, The Lillian. And those were only the ones parked on that side of the building. In addition to its shuttle, The Lillian had four or five white stretch limousines, the largest one with ornate signage that read, GRACEFUL LIVING FOR DISCERNING

RETIREES. At that point, I wanted to throw myself under its tires.

"The entire state of Arizona is here! This is horrendous."

"Horrendous? It's a wonderful turn-out. Maybe more people will enroll in the book club."

Or turn on us like those peasants from the horror movies.

At least a dozen people were making their way to the entrance and my mother was about to join them when she noticed something. Actually, someone.

"Look to your right, Phee. Look to your right. It's that wretched Miranda Lee from Bingo along with Paula Darren. Those two are joined to the hip like nobody's business. What are they carrying?"

"Looks like bottled water to me. Those huge containers."

"I'll bet it's that ridiculous Fiji water they bring to the Bingo games for good luck. I hope they don't plan on sprinkling it around at our meeting. Cleansing properties or not, none of us want to be doused with water."

"I doubt that's what she has in mind. And I don't think it has more cleansing properties than tap water."

"Quick. Unlock the passenger door. I'm getting out. I'll walk behind them and see if I can hear what they're up to."

"Let it go, Mom. They probably brought water in case they get thirsty."

"Oh, I suppose you're right. See you inside."

I pulled away from the curb and scanned the lot for a parking space. Who was I kidding? I'd have to walk from hell's creation and back the way this place was filling up. Suddenly, I remembered something.

I could park on the other side of the building near the dog park and walk around. It would be much shorter and not as packed.

As I rounded the corner of the complex, I saw a few people with their dogs, and the parking lot wasn't as crowded. I grabbed a spot next to a minivan and started to walk toward the social hall when something caught my eye. It was a license plate that read, MISSYGRL, and I knew, in that split second, exactly where the money was being funneled. Jerry White had another name for this bank account, and I wagered he had a fake social security number to go along with it. I reached for my cell phone and took a deep breath. Voicemail. My second clue that this wasn't going to go well.

"Don't shoot me, Nate, but this time I think I've got it. Find Rolo. Tell him to look up anything under Izzy, Izzy Boy, Izzy Baby Boy, Izzy Dog, Izzy White, or any combination of Izzy and dog that you can think of. Promise him a juicing Ninja if you have to, but get him to check it out. And call me as soon as you hear this voicemail."

I knew the process would be expedited if I had a social security number or a bank routing number, but at least with a name, Rolo might be able to track down the money. From what Nate told me, Rolo was like a shark. Once he bit into something, he wasn't going to release his jaw anytime soon.

By the time I walked to the front door of the social hall, the crowd had swelled. It took me fifteen minutes to get inside. Thirteen of them were spent in a conversation with Trudy and Gertie from the plane. They had arrived along with twenty or so others from The Lillian and were dressed as if it was a cocktail party—silky white dresses and sage green hats with taffeta bows. Gertie grabbed my wrist as I tried to get to the front table.

"Remember us? From the airplane? We thought we recognized you. Phee, right?"

"Um, sure. Of course. Gertie and Trudy. Uh, how've you been?"

"We were fine until this book curse found its way to our community. I must tell you everyone at The Lillian is on edge. Last thing we need is to bring something like that into our home. Isn't that right, Trudy?"

Trudy locked her hand around my other wrist and I was stuck. She gave her sister a nod of approval as people elbowed their way around us. Then she spoke directly to her sister as if I wasn't there.

"It's Aunt Hortensia's cursed wedding ring all over again."

"What are you talking about? The ring wasn't cursed. The marriage was."

"Listen to me, Gertie, the marriage wouldn't have been cursed if it wasn't for the ring."

"The marriage was cursed because Uncle Ambroise dallied around with other women."

"He wouldn't have done that if it wasn't for the ring. Who buys a wedding ring that has pearls in it? Pearls bring bad luck."

"Says who?"

"Says everyone."

I tried to shake their hands from my wrists, but all I succeeded in doing was flapping my arms about like a cartoon chicken. It didn't help matters any that my shoulder bag was flinging itself all over the place. Finally I raised my voice. "Stop it, please. Both of you.

There is no curse. You'll see. Take a seat and relax, okay?"

I heard two audible sighs and felt badly for my outburst. "I'm sorry, ladies, but this curse thing has gotten out of hand. You have nothing to worry about. Maybe we can chat later."

My words seemed to appease them. Luckily Gertie spotted two empty seats and hustled her sister over there. I'd never seen such chaos in all my life. People were pushing and shoving from all directions. Compared to this scenario, Bingo night was small potatoes. Off to the right was a giant table with a banner over it. It said, SIGNED COPIES OF *THE TWELFTH ARRONDISSEMENT*. The line in front of that table wound down the corridor toward the restrooms.

My mother was already in the front of the room by the table that had been prepared for the book club. Even though the membership had dwindled, they had placed at least fifteen chairs around it. And sure enough, the whiteboard was off to the side, a few feet from the head of the table. Most noticeable were the microphones that seemed to be everywhere. Behind me, seats were filling fast. This was going to be SRO in a matter of minutes.

The chairs for the audience were arranged as if they were going to be watching a major theatrical production. I doubted opening night for an Oscar Hammerstein musical held as many people. That wasn't the worst of it. As I made my way toward my mother, I witnessed what best could be described as "a field day" for every realtor and funeral parlor business in the area. Business cards were being handed out, along with pens and assorted novelties. A carnival barker would've been right at home here.

Unfortunately, I wasn't. My mouth was dry and I had used up the last of my mints a few days ago.

I wormed my way over to the table and gave a wave to the book club ladies who were already seated—Cecilia, Shirley, Lucinda, Jeanette, Louise, and Myrna. Jeanette kept looking over her shoulder, and I realized why. Apparently Leslie Sackler had taken a seat in the audience a few rows back.

And I was worried she wouldn't show up. I casually turned around and scanned the place, trying to not look too obvious when I found myself eye-to-eye with Josie Nolan. She nodded as if to acknowledge me and then turned her attention to the people sitting near her. Next to her was an empty seat I presumed was for her husband, who was probably handing out business cards. A few rows away from them were Gertie and Trudy. I wondered if they were still arguing over the cursed wedding ring. As I took in the entire room, I was beginning to feel nauseated.

No sign of Jerry White, but it was, after all, a huge social hall, and he could be anywhere. My mother's voice reached me and I turned around.

She was busy yacking with Herb Garrett. "Why are you standing like that? It looks like you can't breathe, Herb."

"I'm sucking in my gut, Harriet. There are TV crews everywhere. Those cameras add at least ten pounds, you know."

"Hey, Herb!" someone yelled. "I saved you a seat. Hurry up!"

"See you later, Harriet. That's Eddie from pinochle."

I couldn't catch the rest of the conversation since the noise level was getting worse by the minute. Those microphones were a good idea after all. I

started to take a seat next to the head of the table
where my mother would be conducting the meeting.
My rear end hadn't even made contact with the chair
when I heard the unmistakable voices of Thelmalee's
family. They were making their way to the front of
the room and, in that second, I knew we were in for
a disaster.

"Are you ready for this?" my mother whispered as
she leaned toward me.

"I, um, er . . ." I muttered, but before I could say
anything, Gretchen Morin stood over us like a sen-
tinel. I didn't even see her approach.

"I'm going to get the meeting started, Mrs. Plunkett, and I'll be introducing Vivian Knowlton. Once
she says a few words, you can go ahead and run the
book club, same as always."

I glanced up, but my eyes moved right past
Gretchen to Vivian Knowlton. She looked the same
as the artistic rendering on the side of the bus—
flaming red and pink hair with some sort of a tiara
and a dress that probably traveled with the Grateful
Dead's entourage in the sixties. I didn't realize it, but
my jaw had opened to the point where it was obvious.
My mother gave me a nudge with her foot, and I
immediately turned away from Vivian.

"You don't want the cameras to catch that, Phee."
My mother's voice was barely audible, but because
we were sitting right next to each other, I heard every
word.

Without wasting another second, Gretchen walked
over to the tallest microphone. "May I have your attention please? Your attention please!"

With the exception of Thelmalee's relatives, who

were still elbowing their way to the front of the room,
literally everyone seemed to quiet down.

"Welcome, everyone, to the Sun City West's
Booked 4 Murder book club. I'm Gretchen Morin,
director of our library. Normally, this would be a
small meeting of the club and it would run itself. All
I do is reserve the library space."

I started to roll my eyes but thought better of it.

"However, given the magnitude of events that have
transpired, I felt I should provide some background
and introductions. You see, the book the club selected this past month has met with . . . shall we say,
some inexplicable circumstances."

"IT DAMN WELL KILLED MY GRANDMOTHER,"
someone yelled, and I knew that Thelmalee's family
had finally made it to the front of the room.

Gretchen stood steadfast. The fact one of the sheriff's deputies was moving toward the guy must have
added to her already inflated sense of bravado. Too
bad she didn't realize the Kirksons outnumbered the
deputies.

"WHEN WE GET DONE SUING YOUR ASS, THERE
WON'T BE A BOOK LEFT IN YOUR LIBRARY!"

I turned my head to see a scraggly looking kid
about sixteen or seventeen.

"SHUT THE HELL UP, FRANKIE. I WANNA
HEAR WHAT SHE HAS TO SAY. THEN WE'LL SUE
THE CRAP OUT OF HER."

Frankie. That must have been the brother who
was "on the pot" the day I stopped by Thelmalee's
house. And the man who was yelling at him had to
be the father. If anyone was trying to have a private
conversation during Gretchen's "introduction," it
would have been impossible.

Without blinking so much as a single eyelash, she cleared her throat. "As I was saying, the book club selected a gothic romance-mystery by a new author and unfortunately, a number of its readers met with their demise shortly after, or even while they were reading the novel."

She went on to provide details and facts leading up to the book's reputation of being cursed. That's when she introduced Vivian Knowlton from the reality show *Psychic Divas*. At least that shut Frankie up for a few minutes. *That*, or maybe the fact his father was only one fist away from the kid's mouth.

"And so, it gives me great pleasure to introduce a lady who really needs no introduction for those of you who watch her top-rated TV reality show. Please welcome Vivian Knowlton from *Psychic Divas*."

The applause was thunderous as Vivian took the microphone. She held a copy of *The Twelfth Arrondissement*. For a woman who was a psychic, she seemed to have no clue what was about to happen. No sooner did she utter the words, "Thank you, Gretchen, it's my pleasure to be here today," when all of a sudden a heavyset woman with short, curly brown hair and a floral duster ran to the front of the room and yelled, "Vivian, Vivian, can you please channel my late husband, Morty?"

If that wasn't enough, another woman stood and screamed, "My grandmother Eunice. Eunice Baker. Please contact her from beyond. Eunice! It's Eunice Baker. From Pocatello, Idaho."

Just then, a balding man wearing a Hawaiian shirt waved his hands in the air as he pushed his way to the front table. "We need to find out where my crazy old uncle Harry hid the money! Harry Petrillo. From

New Jersey. He mentioned money in the will, but the old codger never told us where it was. Can you find out?"

It was like watching a dam break. More people. More shouting. More demands for Vivian to speak with the dead. But the worst was when Miranda Lee stood up, unscrewed the top of her water bottle, and began to slush it around, resulting in a near riot.

"If you're conjuring up the dead, you'll need Fiji water for purification," she yelled.

I looked at the stricken expression on my mother's face.

"Now will you believe me?" I said. "It's totally out of control."

I closed my eyes and moved my head from side to side. My mother gave me a nudge.

"Let the Psychic Diva deal with it."

Before Vivian could say a word, the Kirksons were back in the game.

"CONJURE UP GRANDMA NOW!" Maisy-Jayne screamed. "I WANT TO GET OUT OF THIS STINKIN' PLACE!"

"You know what, Mom?" I whispered. "I think I do, too."

Chapter 27

It took five deputies and more than a half dozen firefighters to get the room to settle down before Vivian Knowlton could continue to speak. When she did, I wasn't so sure it was to address the matter of the book in question, or to promote her TV show.

"Thank you. Thank you for your trust in my psychic abilities. Unfortunately, we don't have the time in this venue to address all of your needs, but I urge you to continue watching my show and sending your requests to my producer. Visit the Web site at PsychicDivasTelevision.com and be sure to mention Sun City West."

"When is she going to get on with this?" Lucinda leaned across the table. "I thought we were here to discuss the book and listen to whatever stuff Harriet and her daughter uncovered."

"I don't think she'll be too long," Myrna replied. "She already got her photo op."

Some brief static from the microphone jolted us for a second. Vivian held the book high in the air and leaned her head back as if the book were about to jump at her. "Aside from the plot of this intriguing novel, I sense there is a great deal more to the book itself. Something ephemeral. An enigma, if you will. I doubt the author set out to cast a curse on her readers, but the book, it seems, has taken on a spirit of its own."

"Oh, brother," I said. This time my mother didn't nudge me or give me a kick under the table.

Gretchen moved closer to Vivian and took the microphone.

"Are you saying the book is indeed cursed?"

"I'm saying the book is more than words and paper. More than the plot and characters. Somehow, a fusion of elements has resulted in a dynamic that no one could have predicted. Not even the author."

"Good Lord. What the heck is she saying?" Shirley whispered.

My mother and I shrugged at the same time.

Meanwhile, Vivian gushed on with her commentary. "So you see, what we have here is a tome that holds a power of its own. Something sinister, I fear. Something that demands our respect and our caution. Whoever Lily Margot Gerald is, she has unleashed a true gothic horror upon all of us."

"I can't take it anymore. I'm stepping in." I stood. With or without the true identity of the author, I still had enough evidence to put a stop to this charade. Nevertheless, I made sure to put my cell phone in my pocket in case Nate called. I desperately wanted my hunch about Izzy dog to pan out. Then I walked over to one of the microphones that had been set up behind our table and took it, hoping no one would see my hands were shaking.

"I am so sorry to interrupt you, Miss Knowlton, but I can't let this go on anymore," I said.

The collective gasps coming from the audience set me on edge. I had to speak eloquently, clearly, and directly. And I had to speak fast before they yanked the microphone away. As if on cue, my mother slipped out of her seat and moved the whiteboard closer to the table. I swallowed once and began what Miss Marple would have called the "Big Reveal." For me, it was "hurry up and get it over with before they all turn on you like a pack of rats."

"My name is Sophie Kimball. I'm Harriet Plunkett's daughter. I also work for the police department in Mankato, Minnesota, and I came here at my mother's request to investigate the series of unexplained deaths and near encounters with death." I made sure to look directly at Jeanette. *So far, so good. No one knows I'm in accounts receivable.* "Like many of you, my mother was convinced this novel, *The Twelfth Arrondissement,* was cursed. But that book is no more cursed than this table, these chairs, and the very microphone I'm speaking from."

"THAT'S BULLSHIT, LADY, OR MY GRAND-MOTHER WOULD STILL BE HERE!"

I didn't have to pan the room to figure out Frankie was back at it. I wasted no time getting to the point. "Your grandmother wasn't killed by this book. She died as a result of uncontrolled greed and a series of opportunistic actions taken by more than one person in this community."

"SPEAK ENGLISH, LADY!"

My face turned beet red, and all I could do was scream out, "It was a setup! Is that good enough English for you?"

"YEAH, I'M LISTENING."

Then, without warning, Gretchen Morin took the mic from Vivian. "We cannot have people popping up out of nowhere and spouting off anything and everything that comes into their mind. Now, Miss Knowlton was kind enough to travel all the way here from Los Angeles in order to shed some light on the book, and I feel we need to give her a chance."

"I WANT TO HEAR FROM THE OTHER LADY. THE POLICEWOMAN WITH THE UGLY CLOTHES."

Under ordinary circumstances, I would have been insulted since I was wearing something I deemed highly fashionable. But, given the fact that it was Maisy-Jayne speaking, I let it go. I also didn't bother to clarify that I wasn't a policewoman.

"Thank you. I'll try to be brief."

Gretchen started to say something, but Shirley Johnson grabbed the microphone away from her, and for a minute, I thought they were actually going to get physical. Instead, Gretchen motioned for someone to get over to the table, but I couldn't see who. At the same time, my mother shoved a dry-erase marker into my hand and turned her head to the whiteboard. It was "showtime."

Small beads of sweat formed on my forehead and I brushed them off with the back of my hand. "Please listen carefully, everyone, and I'll try to explain why there is NO book curse."

The audience got quiet for a second, and I went full speed ahead, hoping to avoid any more interruptions.

"As many of you may know, it's very difficult to have a book published these days. The competition is fierce, from what I understand, and the likelihood of finding a literary agent is next to impossible. So, burgeoning authors sometimes self-publish, the way Lily Margot Gerald did when she wrote *The Twelfth Arrondissement*. The trouble is, no one knew who she was, and that made it less likely anyone would read her book."

I was on borrowed time with my explanation and sure enough, Frankie broke in.

"WELL, GRANDMA MANAGED TO READ THAT THING AND NOW SHE'S PUSHING UP DAISIES!"

His father squelched his attempts. "SHUT YOUR TRAP, FRANKIE, AND LET THE WOMAN SPEAK!"

"Um, er, as I was saying, it was very unlikely anyone would read the novel. There was no publicity, no advertising. Nothing. Then it suddenly appeared on the Booked 4 Murder reading list. And that meant at least fifteen people would get their hands on it. Word spreads quickly in small communities, so if the book was any good, it would have a start. But here's the interesting tidbit—no one in the book club recommended that book. So how did it get on the reading list? My guess, and it is simply a guess, is that someone from the library put it there."

I didn't exactly point fingers. I was waiting for a more opportune time.

"Then a series of unfortunate events happened. Well, deaths, actually, for a few members of the book club. Members who were reading the book. First, Marilyn Scutt had that awful golf cart accident and died. The only item that was found intact on the street was her copy of *The Twelfth Arrondissement*. Shortly afterward, Minnie Bendelson passed away at the hospital, while reading the same book. And that's when someone came up with a brilliant idea to sell that book. Not only sell it, but catapult it to the *New York Times* best-seller list. And what could be more throat grabbing than the thought the book was cursed!"

I took a deep breath. I had the full attention of the audience. Not only that, but I finally located Jerry White sitting off to the side, near the exit. I wasn't about to lose my momentum.

"Here's where it gets tricky. While the author of the book, whoever that may really be, since no one can seem to find a Lily Margot Gerald, was just out to make her novel famous, other members of the community used that premise of a cursed book to take care of their own agendas."

"WHAT ARE YOU SAYING, LADY?" Maisy-Jayne shouted. "THAT MY GRANDMOTHER WAS MURDERED?"

"Whoa. Hold on. I'll try to get to everything."

Just then, Gretchen pushed her way toward me and grabbed the microphone out of my hand. "This is absolutely ridiculous. Pure speculation. I insist we go back to our regular program agenda."

"The hell with your agenda," someone shouted. And it wasn't a Kirkson. "We want to hear what that police lady has to say."

"Yes, give her a chance," came another voice.

And suddenly, the entire audience was up in arms, shouting for me to continue. Gretchen had no choice but to relinquish the mic and let me speak.

"Edna Mae Langford was the next member of the club to die. She was elderly, hard of hearing, legally blind, and more than just a little forgetful. Her family had been trying for years to get her into assisted living, but she would have no part of it. Her house was a veritable deathtrap, yet somehow she managed to live day by day. Her family was scared to pieces she would fall in the shower or, worse yet, turn on the stove, forgetting that she put the mail on top of one of the burners. Edna Mae refused to get one of those medical alert buttons and wouldn't hear of letting anyone into her house to help her with her daily chores. And that's when her daughter and a close friend hatched a plan to force Edna Mae out of the house. They would use the idea of a book curse to cover up what really happened."

"She's good," Vivian Knowlton whispered to Gretchen. "I should get her on *Psychic Divas.*"

"Try to get her away from the microphone," Gretchen hissed back.

"By tossing gravel near Edna Mae's mailbox, Edna would certainly trip and fall on the pieces of rock. She was too blind to see them. Her daughter hoped it would be a "wake-up call" when Edna Mae found herself lying in the driveway. The daughter never expected Edna Mae to break a hip, much less wind up in the hospital and die of pneumonia. In fact, according to an eye witness, Edna's fall was timed so that the UPS driver would be coming down the block shortly after the mail truck. Edna Mae would be seen and helped right away." I looked directly at Jeanette and then moved my gaze to the audience, where Leslie Sackler was seated. Both of them were poker-faced, but I could tell by looking at Jeanette's hands that she was shaking.

"Now there were three deaths. And all three of the women were reading that novel. The idea of a book curse was firmly hatched. As the rumor started to spread, some people in the community went out of their way to tell anyone and everyone they should stay away from that book." I stared directly at Jerry.

"In fact, one such vigilant man got escorted out of the swimming pool for harassing people reading the book. Let's face it, we're all like kids and if we're told not to do something, we immediately want to go ahead and do it. Reverse psychology was working well for this book marketing campaign."

"WHAT ABOUT MY GRANDMA? YOU HAVEN'T SAID ANYTHING YET ABOUT HER!" Maisy-Jayne wasn't giving up and neither was I.

I cleared my throat and, at that moment, my mother stood and gave me a poke in the arm.

"Use the whiteboard. Start writing names and information."

"I think a timeline would really help, so give me a second," I said to the audience as I began to write. I made sure each name was printed clearly and large enough to be seen on TV. The camera crews were all over the place. By now, my heart was palpitating, and I prayed I could get through this without falling apart.

Suddenly, Lucinda Espinoza started sobbing at the table. "It's all my fault. It's all my fault."

"What is?" Shirley asked.

"It's my fault Edna Mae is dead."

Chapter 28

Lucinda's confession came out of nowhere and, for a second, I was stunned. Before I could form words, Shirley pressed Lucinda for the sordid details.

"Tell me, Lucinda. What did you do? Were you working in cahoots with the daughter?"

"What are you talking about? No, nothing like that. I didn't even know she had a daughter."

"Good Lord, why did you say Edna Mae's death was your fault?"

At this point, someone moved two microphones closer to the table.

Lucinda blew into a tissue and the noise reverberated off the walls. Amid her sobbing, she was able to sputter out a few words. "I was supposed to take Edna Mae to Costco's that day. I was going to pick her up at ten but decided instead to go to the Casino in the Pines. My neighbor, Doris, called and there was an extra seat on her church bus. I figured I could take Edna Mae to Costco's anytime. Oh, I feel so awful. So absolutely awful. It really was my fault."

My voice was getting stronger as I leaned into the

mic. "No, it wasn't your fault, Lucinda. If Edna Mae hadn't fallen on that day, it would have happened the next. Or the day after that. The point is, it was going to happen because her family had reached their breaking point and were desperate to move Edna Mae out of her house."

"ENOUGH WITH EDNA MAE. I WANT TO KNOW WHAT HAPPENED TO THELMALEE KIRKSON!"

This time it was a different voice. A woman's. Carleen or Almalynn? It didn't matter. It was all coming from the same tribe.

"Fine. I might as well get to that," I said.

The relief on Jeanette's face was obvious. She was off the proverbial hook, for at least a few minutes, as the Kirkson clan began to circle around the table as if we were a wagon train and this was the Wild West.

"Everyone will need to step back," my mother said. "The audience needs to hear and see what's going on, and the media is trying to film it."

The Kirksons fanned out a bit, but I was certain their breath could be felt on the necks of the ladies sitting at the table. I immediately underlined Thelmalee's name and started talking before Gretchen decided to make a move.

"Thelmalee Kirkson, as we have been informed, died of an allergic reaction to a bee sting while she was sunbathing at the recreation center swimming pool. At least that's what the official report says. However, it took more than one bee to sting Thelmalee, and it was no accident."

"I TOLD YOU SOMEONE OFFED THE OLD COOT!"

This time it was one of the sons-in-law, but I couldn't tell which one. "No one meant for Thelmalee to die.

No one expected her to die. Those responsible for her demise just expected her to . . . well, not hog an entire section of the sunbathing area. You see, I'm sure Thelmalee was a lovely and delightful person, but when it came to sunbathing, she was quite territorial."

"Damn straight she was. Not to speak ill of the dead, but, my God, that woman hogged the best spot in the pool for years and wouldn't let anyone take it!"

I looked out in the audience to see who said that, but it was impossible to tell. I only knew it was a woman's voice.

Before I could say another word, someone else blurted out, "You can say that again! She once threw ice water at me when I tried to move my lounge chair near her spot."

Cecilia leaned her head into the center of the table and whispered, "Sounds like Thelmalee, all right."

I didn't want to lose control of the situation, and I was afraid that was the direction in which we were going. I raised the pitch of my voice. "Thelmalee apparently made life unbearable for the other sunbathers at the pool, especially a group of women who frequented that spot every afternoon. So, when they found out Thelmalee was reading *The Twelfth Arrondissement*, and that three other book club members had died while reading the same novel, they saw an opportunity and took it. They wanted everyone to think she got stung by bees as a result of the book curse. They had no thought that she would die. However, those bees didn't attack Thelmalee at random.

Someone went to a lot of trouble to make sure the bees would swarm her."

One of the sheriff's deputies standing in the back started to make his way to the front of the room. Then he looked right at me. "Are you accusing someone in this community of murder, because if you are, you'd better have some evidence."

"Not murder. Like Edna Mae, no one planned to murder Thelmalee. All they wanted to do was give her a good scare so she'd stop hogging the coveted chaise lounge site. And how they went about it was quite clever. You see, there are bushes behind the pool and lots of them. Honeysuckle. Boxwood Beauties. Lantana. Bougainvillea. Bees normally mill around the bushes. So how could someone ensure they'd be right by the very bush where Thelmalee's chair was? Simple. Dig a small hole and fill it with sugar. And that's exactly what they did."

The deputy sheriff had moved a few feet closer. His voice was loud enough so that he had no need for a microphone. "Can you prove that?"

"Yes. Yes, I can." I opened my mother's big Vera Bradley bag and took out the small piece of cardboard. Then I held it up in the air. "You see this piece of cardboard? It's from a cane sugar box. Common brand. Found in every grocery store. This particular piece was found under the bush when I went to investigate. There was a small hole where sugar had been poured. Someone forgot to remove the evidence."

For the first time, the audience was speechless. Even the Kirksons.

The deputy sheriff, however, had a few words to

say. "It may be evidence, but it's not going to be admissible in court and it doesn't lead us to the perpetrators."

"No, not by itself. However, it does match exactly to the box from which it was taken."

At that moment, I pulled out the entire box I'd found while sifting through the garbage behind Nolan and Nolan Realty that night.

"This is the box where it came from, and I found it in the garbage Dumpster behind Nolan and Nolan Realty, along with a number of other items and correspondence from their office."

Josie Nolan shot out of her seat like a missile. "That doesn't prove anything!"

"It proves the box came from your company. And that's not all I found in that Dumpster. Let's see, where did I put that note . . . ?" I thumbed through the Vera Bradley.

By now, Josie Nolan was getting frantic. "I don't care what you found. Nolan and Nolan Realty did not murder Thelmalee. I certainly didn't plant that sugar behind the bush. I mean, all of us sunbathers talked about it, but we didn't do it."

Then the deputy sheriff stepped in. "I'm afraid, Mrs. Nolan, you'll have to come with me. Admissible or inadmissible evidence, you've got some questions to answer."

"But, but . . ."

As the deputy started to escort Josie to the exit, another lady stood. It was Joanne. I recognized her as the woman with Peg at the pool. She grabbed Josie by the elbow and looked directly at the deputy. "Josie is telling the truth. She didn't have anything to do with planting the sugar. It was me. I did it."

Like the flick of a switch, the noise in the room dropped.

Hallelujah. A confession. I did it. Even with inadmissible evidence.

Joanne took a deep breath and then rambled on a confession I swear was longer than the Declaration of Independence. "None of us meant for Thelmalee to die. Especially me. I'm not a killer. I just wanted to enjoy the sunshine, like everyone else around here, and Thelmalee was making that impossible. She was particularly obnoxious the week before her bee sting. So when Peg and I stopped in at Nolan and Nolan for a cup of coffee, which we do from time to time since Peg is Tom Nolan's sister and likes to visit, I saw the sugar cane box on the counter and decided to do something that day. The box was only half full and there was enough sugar in the bowl, so no one would notice if it went missing. I shoved it in my tote bag and 'borrowed' it. I brought it back the next day after I had poured some of the sugar under the bush. It wasn't pouring out fast enough, so I ripped the tab from the other side. It must have fallen off."

Then one of the other sunbathers spoke up. "Joanne didn't act alone. We're all responsible. You can arrest all of us. We all came up with that plan."

One by one, they started to stand. That was when Peg held her arms straight out in front as if she were directing traffic. "Arrest all of them. I didn't have a part in any of this. And for heaven's sake, Joanne, why couldn't you have used your own sugar? It's not that expensive."

"I'm sorry, Peg. I don't have sugar at home, just Splenda."

Peg shook her head, straightened her hair, and

stared into the nearest TV camera. "I knew this was going to get out of hand. I told my sister-in-law I thought it was a stupid idea and that we should just follow the rules and file a complaint at the rec center. Didn't I, Josie?"

Josie didn't say a word.

"Well, didn't I? Didn't I?"

By now, Peg was getting really adamant.

But instead of answering her sister-in-law's question, Josie made her own announcement. "THOMAS NOLAN, IF YOU'RE STILL IN THIS AUDIENCE, QUIT HANDING OUT BUSINESS CARDS AND CALL OUR LAWYER! JOANNE NEEDS A GOOD DEFENSE."

One of the sunbathing ladies put her arm around Joanne. "It was a stupid thing to do, a prank. Each one of us thought someone in our group did it, but no one wanted to ask who. In a way, we're all responsible for what happened to Thelmalee. So, when we found out about the book curse, it was serendipitous. It would take any suspicions away from us. We all agreed to keep that rumor going."

Another deputy walked over to the deputy, and they spoke quietly before escorting the ladies to the exit doors. As they walked out of the social hall, Maisy-Jayne let out a clarion cry that could be heard for miles. "THERE'S GONNA BE A LAWSUIT!"

In less than thirty seconds, the entire room erupted into bedlam. Complete and total chaos. The Kirksons were shoving chairs and people out of their way in order to get to the doors. Members of the frantic audience tried to get away.

At one point, an elderly woman fainted and someone yelled, "Can we get some assistance?"

Unfortunately, her words were drowned out by the Kirksons, who had a few choice words as they stormed to the exit.

"LAWSUIT, HELL. I WANT TO WRING THAT SKINNY WOMAN'S NECK!"

"TAR AND FEATHER HER!"

"SHUT UP, FRANKIE. THAT'S AGAINST THE LAW IN ARIZONA!"

"SAYS WHO?"

"GET HER! SHE'LL PAY FOR THIS!"

A few posse members from the sheriff's department tried to run after them, but they were no match. The firefighters took off as if they were about to battle a three-alarm fire. Meanwhile, the audience was in turmoil.

"It *is* that book, you know," Vivian Knowlton said as I stared straight ahead. "Only a powerful curse could do something like that."

"Not a curse. Bad upbringing."

I had no idea how I was ever going to continue, because the Kirksons lit a spark that ignited the entire room. People were yelling at one another, pushing, shoving, and swearing. It was Sodom and Gomorrah. Unfortunately, it was being televised.

The camera crews moved in like they were covering a war zone. And suddenly, all of the ladies sitting quietly at the table began to stand and head toward the nearest reporter.

"Pardon me, Phee." Lucinda edged behind me. "I didn't get my hair done for nothing."

Then Myrna Mittleson elbowed Lucinda. "Forget your hair. I spent half my social security check on this dress. Out of my way, Lucinda!"

"PHEE!" My mother yelled. "PHEE! Your phone's ringing. I can hear it from here. Answer it."

It was as if my mind was working on a ten-second delay. I was so intent on processing the chaos that had erupted around me that my hand couldn't seem to reach into my pocket fast enough to get the phone. It was too late. I had lost the call. Frantic, I tried dialing Nate's cell number, but all I got was voicemail. I left a brief message, knowing he'd hear the panic in my voice. "No time to explain. TEXT ME with any info."

My mother gave me a funny look and shook her head. "I thought you don't like to get text messages."

"I don't. And I don't like to send them, but I'll never hear Nate with this calamity going on."

I couldn't tell which part of the three-ring circus was worse—Vivian off to the side interviewing with a reporter from Fox, the three local channels weaving in and out of the confusion as they tried to get comments from the public, or Gretchen Morin making her way to the cameraman from CNN.

"I've got to do something, Mom. I can't let this go on. I've got to finish what I started."

Then it dawned on me. I was the one who started this. It happened the minute I revealed who was responsible for Thelmalee's death. I should have gone to the sheriff's department the second I uncovered the matching cardboard piece from the cane sugar box. But nooooo . . . I had to have the spotlight, like all those famous detectives. And where did that get me? Standing in front of a disaster zone, not knowing what to do next.

"It's not too late." My mother pointed to the doors.

"Look. See for yourself. The deputies have removed the Kirksons, and the firefighters are coming back into the room."

"You really think I can pull this off?"

"I don't think you have a choice."

Chapter 29

The social hall looked more like a junior high school dance gone awry, but at least the Kirksons were out of the way and the screaming had stopped. I tapped on the microphone to try to get everyone's attention, but it wasn't working. My mother looked as frustrated as I felt.

"Remind me, Mom, to never, ever, under any circumstances become a school principal, because the last thing I want to do is to try this in front of an auditorium filled with kids."

"Quit tapping on the mic and tell everyone to take a seat. Speak like you mean business, Phee."

I held the mic at my chin and articulated each word. "I need everyone's attention and I need it NOW. Please return to your seats."

In the meantime, my mother had scooted off to where Herb Garrett was standing and, the next thing I knew, he was directing people to sit down. Between the two of them, they were able to restore some semblance of order so I could continue to explain why there was no book curse. As I reached for the microphone, Jeanette grabbed me by the wrist.

"You're not going to mention Edna Mae Langford anymore, are you? I mean, that ship has sailed, hasn't it?"

"Sorry, Jeanette, but that ship is about to crash on the rocks."

Before she could utter another word, I was back on the mic. "This won't take long, but I will be able to clarify a few things regarding those deaths. As I mentioned earlier, the book curse was the perfect ruse to disguise the fact that a number of people were responsible for what happened to Thelmalee and Edna Mae. Listen carefully."

"Edna Mae Langford was born Edna Mae Tiltonbury. She was married twice and outlived both of her husbands, Fredrick Langford and Jackson Sackler. She kept Langford as her last name but Sackler was the name on the death certificate. I found out from snooping around with her neighbors that she didn't want to deal with the paperwork associated with another name change. It must not have mattered to her second husband. She had one daughter from her most recent marriage, Leslie Sackler, and a number of nieces and nephews."

"Lord Almighty, what does any of this have to do with her death?" Shirley said, loud enough for her voice to carry into the mic.

"I'm getting to that," I said. "Excuse me. Um, uh, as I was saying, Edna Mae's relatives were more than just a little concerned about her. Especially her daughter. Fortunately, well, I'm not so sure fortunately is the word, but anyway, her daughter had a close friend and ally who helped her with a scheme that was supposed to make Edna Mae realize it was time to give up the house and move to assisted living."

Someone at the table gasped, but I kept talking. "Leslie's girlfriend, and former college buddy from Lawrence University, class of nineteen eighty-two, thought all they had to do was put rocks in front of the mailbox, and Edna Mae would tumble into her new life in a safe environment. Isn't that right, Jeanette?"

Jeanette Tomilson looked as if she'd been caught red-handed breaking into a bank vault. At first she didn't say a word. Then, the drama act began. "That's ridiculous. Utterly ridiculous. I, myself, was a victim of that book curse. You know that. You know someone got into my garage, took my car keys, and left my car running so my house would fill up with carbon monoxide. You were there that night! Along with the entire street!"

"That's true. Very true. Except for one small detail. It took me a while to figure it out, but I eventually did. You created the fake attempt on your life to throw off any suspicions about your involvement in Edna Mae's death. No one would connect you. After all, why would anyone care that a beige SUV with advertising for West Valley Home Mortgage Solutions was at your house so often? That company belongs to your old college friend, Leslie Sackler, Edna Mae's daughter."

"You still can't prove anything," Jeanette said as she glanced toward Leslie.

"That's where you're wrong. You told a deputy sheriff, on the night of the incident, that your car key was on the same keychain as your house key and that in order to let yourself into the house, you had to turn off the car. You insisted that someone got into your garage from the side door and somehow snuck into the laundry room to retrieve the car keys, turn on the car, and leave out the same side door."

"Don't say anything, Jeanette," came a voice from across the room. It was Leslie Sackler. She stood and started heading toward the table.

I had one more final "punch," and I was going to use it. "Here's the interesting part—your car doesn't use a key. It has a keyless remote. It's a brand-new KIA Sportage SX and, not only that, but no keys are required to open the doors. It's all remote. I should know. I test-drove one a few weeks ago, thinking I might be ready for a new car. I just wasn't ready for a new car loan. If someone did break into your garage, like you said, they wouldn't be able to start your car. It has voice recognition and a number of other neat things I can't afford right now."

Leslie Sackler had pulled an empty chair over to Jeanette and put her arm around her friend, who had now started crying. I felt awful. Did Miss Marple ever feel bad when she revealed who the responsible parties were? I doubted it.

"You have no idea how tormented we are over what happened. We wanted to help my mother, not watch her die." Leslie's voice was beginning to crack.

"So you used this book curse thing to cover up what really happened."

"Excuse me, Phee," Cecilia said. "I don't think any of the deputies are left in the room. They all went with the Kirksons."

"We're not killers," Leslie said. "And we'll make our own way to the sheriff's office."

Gretchen Morin seized that minute to return to the microphone. "Well, under the circumstances, I guess this about sums up our book club. No sense in keeping anyone any longer."

"But we haven't even discussed the book," someone said.

Suddenly, my phone began to vibrate, and this time I grabbed it immediately. I had received a text message.

I was staring at three words that could change everything, and my heart started to race.

"Don't leave yet, folks! The best part is coming!" I shouted.

Lucinda poked my mother in the elbow. "Is your daughter always this dynamic?"

"No, she's really kind of mousey when it comes to public speaking."

I ignored the conversation at the table and stood as tall as I could. "I am about to end that book curse right now, so LISTEN UP!"

In the background, my mother mumbled, "Remember to underline."

"The author of *The Twelfth Arrondissement* deserves far more credit as a marketer than a writer. Although, the book itself is really quite decent."

I tried to read the expression on Gretchen's face, but it was blank.

"Lily Margot Gerald is a pen name. No one by that name wrote the book. But, interestingly, the royalties from all book sales are being deposited to a bank account under the name of IZZY BAY BEBOI."

"Izzy Baby Boy? Izzy Baby Boy? Jerry White's dog? You're saying Jerry White's dog wrote that book?"

Cindy Dolton stood, hands on her hips, shaking her head and trying to keep herself from laughing.

"Not the dog, but the owner," I said. "And he wasn't working alone."

I turned to the whiteboard and wrote *Lily Margot Gerald* in big letters. Then, underneath, I wrote, *White Gretchen Jerry.*

"You see, Margot is French for Gretchen, and Gerald is, well . . . Jerry. And we all know Lily is synonymous with white. So, there you have it. The tag team of our own librarian and her companion worked together to launch their first novel."

"I ought to have you sued!" Jerry shouted. Although, compared to the Kirksons, it was more like a loud statement.

"For what? You're the ones who deceived the public and created the hype about a book curse. In fact, if it wasn't for you and Gretchen, Josie Nolan and her pals would never have gotten the idea to use the book curse as a cover to explain how Thelmalee got stung by those bees. She had no choice but to keep that book curse rumor going because, without it, her plot would have unraveled pretty quickly. Josie knew all the details, seeing that she and her husband were frequent dinner companions of yours."

Then Myrna Mittleson pointed a finger at Gretchen. "It was you! It was you all along who selected that book to read. Our club could have you arrested for fraud."

"Psst! Myrna! Psst!" It was Louise Munson. "I don't think that counts for fraud."

I was about to pat myself on the back for my keen investigative instincts, but I knew it didn't take a genius to tap into Ancestry.com, e-yearbook.com (at the $4.95 monthly subscription), and every other site I'd used to gather data. And, without Nate and Rolo's help, I wouldn't have been able to prove who really wrote that book. I was as much of an investigator as Izzy Bay Beboi was a writer. Still, I did manage to put an end to the book curse. Or so I thought. I was about to thank the audience and go back to my mother's house when, out of nowhere, Vivian Knowlton grabbed the mic.

"Please welcome our latest addition to *Psychic Divas*! The little sleuth from Minnesota is more psychic than sleuth and she belongs on our show!"

The social hall erupted in applause and I wanted the floor to open up and swallow me.

"Wait. No, I'm not a psychic, and if the truth be known, I'm not a policewoman either. I mean, I do work for the police department, but—"

"You stinkin' detectives are all the same. Once you pass that test, you forget where you came from."

It was a voice I thought I recognized, but I wasn't so sure. It was certainly loud as if the guy behind it was a linebacker.

Vivian and I were speechless.

"Well, I'll tell you something, my brother Milton's a police officer in Boston and proud of it."

Before I could even clarify, someone else stood and spoke. "That's right. My cousins, Mario and Nicholas, have been police officers in Trenton for over twenty years, and it's good enough for them."

"Yeah," someone shouted, "my father, rest his soul, was a beat cop in New York City, but I guess that's just how it is. You make the grade and the next thing you know, you're a detective or an investigator or whatever title they give you."

For a minute I wished I could bring back the Kirksons. All of them. Then, thankfully, Vivian grabbed the microphone again. "The spirit of *The Twelfth Arrondissement* is still in this room, and that's why no one can rest."

"Oh, brother," Shirley blurted.

Then Gretchen took over. "Ms. Kimball is right. There is no book curse. More importantly, Mr. White and I were never part of any conspiracies to cause harm to anyone. We only wanted to promote our book, which, by the way, is still on sale by the door."

Just then, Josie Nolan's husband, Tom, raced to the front of the room faster than the Kirksons on their way to a free meal. In a matter of seconds, he had grabbed Gretchen by the shoulders and began to shake her. "YOUR BOOK? YOUR BOOK? YOU UNSCRUPULOUS LYING LITTLE WITCH! YOU DIDN'T WRITE THAT BOOK! ALL YOU HAD TO DO WAS SNEAK IT ONTO THAT BOOK CLUB LIST. THAT WAS OUR AGREEMENT. IN RETURN FOR A PORTION OF THE ROYALTIES."

Then, like one of those scenes straight out of a horror movie where the madwoman runs tearing through the mansion, Peg from the sunbathing group stormed up to her brother and gave him a shove in the chest. "HOW DARE YOU GIVE HER A PORTION OF THE ROYALITES WITHOUT CON-SULTING ME FIRST! I'M THE ONE WHO CAME UP WITH THE IDEA FOR THE BOOK. PLOT. CHARACTERS. EVERYTHING!"

"YEAH, BUT IF IT WASN'T FOR JERRY AND ME, THAT'S ALL YOU WOULD HAVE HAD. SO, GIVE IT UP, MARGARET. WE AGREED IT WAS A THREE-WAY DEAL."

In that split second, I swore the room lost a fair amount of oxygen as everyone gasped.

"Looks like you got it wrong, Phee," my mother whispered as I tried to figure out what on earth was happening. "So much for Margot translating into Gretchen."

"At least I wasn't way off base like your lunatic theories about jealous wives," I told her.

I wanted to say more but couldn't get above Thomas Nolan's voice. It could drown out the United States Marine Band. He turned to Jerry White and, for a minute, I thought he was actually going to take a punch at him. "WHY DID YOU JUST SIT THERE AND LET THE LIBRARIAN TAKE THE CREDIT?"

"BECAUSE YOU DIDN'T WANT YOUR WIFE TO KNOW WE WERE WRITING THIS BOOK TOGETHER!"

"WHAT?" came a high-pitched voice from the rear of the social hall. It was Josie Nolan. She was back. Somehow she'd managed to elude the deputies. "I could hear your voice, Tom, all the way out in the parking lot. I nearly broke an ankle trying to run from one of the deputies and get back inside. *You* took Peg's idea and wrote that book? *You* were the one responsible? You and Jerry? You told me the two of you were working on investments. Investments, for crying out loud! I wondered why our finances weren't improving. You were working on that book instead of our wealth management. Why didn't you tell me?"

"Because you were too busy working on your tan. We were losing clients."

Jerry took a step toward Josie and cleared his throat. "He didn't want to tell you because he invested a lot of money into that book, what with formatting costs, special cover design . . ."

Then, as if on cue, Josie turned her anger away from her husband and she slapped Gretchen right in the face. "Don't plan on getting any royalties. It's bad enough we'll have to split them with his sister and Jerry."

My mother poked me in the arm and leaned toward me. "I never saw *that* coming, did you?"

"Apparently not," I replied.

"Now can we discuss the book?" Cecilia said. "I want to know why the mistress hid the fact she was the governess's sister."

I was about to say something when the CNN news crew headed straight toward Gretchen. Sure enough, it was Don Lemon. More adorable in person than on-screen.

"Oh my God!" Lucinda yelled. "It's the cute one from CNN!"

The noise level in the room increased dramatically as people stood to get a good look.

The TV anchor, apparently used to these situations, walked over to Josie and asked if they could interview her and her husband.

"Whoa! I'm right here!" Jerry White shouted as he made his way toward the camera crew. "Someone better interview me!"

"There would be no book without me," Peg yelled. "If anyone should be interviewed, it should be me!"

I turned off the mic and leaned over to the table. "I don't know how anyone else feels, but maybe the club should discuss the book at a different place and time."

"My daughter's right. It's way too chaotic in here.

Let's meet on Friday at Bagels 'N More. How about at ten?"

A consensus was reached in less than five seconds.

"So, that's it," my mother said. "Ten a.m. on Friday. And don't tell anyone. We don't need another side-show."

Next, my mother took the microphone and ended the program faster than the career of a politician who'd just been caught cheating on his or her spouse. "I'm afraid this concludes the monthly meet-ing of Booked 4 Murder. New members are always welcome. Please sign up at the library. There are at least four or five news crews in the social hall, not to mention the newspaper reporters, and I'm sure they'd love to hear from the public."

"Come on, Mom," I said. "Let's get out of here while we can."

There was a small exit door down the corridor to our left, and we moved quickly, followed by Myrna and Shirley. I didn't turn around to see who had decided to stay. I figured it would either be on the news that night or in the morning paper.

Chapter 30

"Oh my God, Mom. That was horrendous. I'm glad you offered to drive us home. Can you get us out of this parking lot any faster? My head is spinning. It was awful in there. I never expected it to be so . . . so . . ."

"Catastrophic?"

"Yeah, that's a good word."

"Look at the bright side. You were on the right track, Phee. Even though you did get it wrong in the end."

"I know. I know. So much for the 'Big Reveal.' And all this time I was certain Gretchen Morin was the brain trust behind the book. Huh. Turned out she was only a small part of the scheme. Imagine that. Thomas Nolan wrote the book with Jerry White. And they got the idea from Tom's sister, Peg. I should have realized Peg is a nickname for Margaret. And worse yet, I didn't even connect Izzy's dog hairs on Tom's trousers that day at Nolan and Nolan Realty. Jerry White must have lied to Tom as well about Izzy being a pure-bred Coton de Tulear. Those dogs don't shed. I told you I wasn't cut out for this sort of thing."

"Who says you're not cut out for investigating? You figured out how Jeanette and Edna Mae's daughter were responsible for Edna Mae's fall. Not to mention that ugly business with Thelmalee and the ladies from the pool."

"I didn't exactly get that right either. Josie Nolan wasn't the one who put the sugar under the bush. It was Joanne. And you know what else I didn't solve? That cryptic e-mail all of the members in your book club received. The one that said, 'Death lurks between the lines.'"

My mother's face began to flush. "Oh, that. I completely forgot. In all this turmoil, it absolutely slipped my mind. It wasn't a cryptic e-mail after all. It was an announcement for the Sun City West Theater's fall production of a new play, *Death Lurks Between the Lines.* Eunice Berlmosler, the publicity chair, called me a few days ago. They sent the e-mail but forgot to include the message. Can you believe it?"

"Yeah, at this point, I can believe anything. Listen, I don't think I'm going to be too welcome here in Sun City West this Christmas. Maybe you should visit me in Minnesota."

"Are you crazy? With all that snow? I don't do snow anymore, Phee. I only like to see it on The Weather Channel and holiday cards. Besides, I already bought tickets for the three of us to see *The Nutcracker Suite* ballet in Phoenix this December."

"Three of us?"

"You didn't think I wasn't going to invite my only granddaughter?"

"She'll love it. And the timing works great with her teaching schedule."

She beamed and it felt good.

"So, do you feel like getting a bite to eat, Phee? We don't have to drive right home."

"Sure. As long as it's out of 'the compound.'"

We were in luck and got a great corner table at Olive Garden, and I finally reached Nate on the phone. I think my mother was more anxious than I was to see what he'd found out. She kept moving closer and closer to me as I was fielding the call. When I thanked Nate and clicked the End button, my mother jumped in.

"So, what did he say? How they'd figure it out? Is the money in some bank account in the Caymans? You know, they always hide money in the Cayman Islands."

"No, Mother. According to Nate, it was a regular bank account with a national bank. The account holder was Izzy Bay Beboi, and it had a tax identification number, not a social security number. The three of them must have set up a fake company. That's why it was virtually impossible to find. And technically, no crimes were committed. Not by them, anyway. I tried not to picture Rolo getting arrested for computer hacking. So unless Jerry, Tom, and Peg don't pay taxes, they'll be off the hook. By the way, do you think Jeanette and Leslie are going to be in a lot of trouble? And Joanne? And what about the pool ladies?"

"Nah, they'll probably all get probation. That's all anyone gets these days. What time's your flight tomorrow?"

"Five-seventeen. Terminal Three. I need to be on

the road by two in order to return the rental and give myself enough time to get through security. By the way, I'm really glad you insisted on my visit. In spite of all the craziness, this was a heck of a lot of fun."

My mother smiled and helped herself to the salad. For the first time in a week, we had a leisurely afternoon and a nice, relaxing evening. I made sure of that by taking the phone off the hook when my mother wasn't looking.

Of course, the book club event was televised on all four local stations. I appeared for less than five seconds, compared to Vivian, who got lots of airtime.

"Don't worry about it, Phee. It's that way with celebrities."

"Believe me, the less publicity I get, the better."

I meant it, too. I wanted to return to my normal routine in accounts receivable. Yet, oddly enough, things don't always work out the way you have them planned. The next morning, when the paper arrived, there was a little feature notation on the top of the front page. It read:

BOOK CLUB CURSE CRUMBLES UNDER MN SLEUTH'S SCRUTINY

In the split second it took for me to read it, I knew my life would take a different turn. What I didn't know was how.

Chapter 31

Two months later
Mankato, Minnesota

I was sitting at my desk, back in accounts receivable, and sifting through some department receipts. I was so engrossed I didn't even hear Nate approach. It was good to get back to normal. Although, I had a nagging feeling something was missing. My work seemed dull in comparison to the exhilaration I felt when I was tracking down the book curse. I hated to admit it, but I missed the excitement.

My mother had told me Gretchen resigned from her position as librarian and was on a book tour with Jerry White, Thomas Nolan, and Peg Nolan, promoting their latest endeavor, a self-help book for self-published authors, entitled *Unconventional Marketing Strategies for Self-Publishing*. She neglected to tell me just how popular they were.

"Have you seen this, Phee?" Nate announced as he

slapped a copy of *USA Today* on my desk. "Thought you'd get a kick out of it."

I was startled for a second and then took a look at the paper. I was staring at the business section, where the lead article read, "Unconventional Marketing Strategy Pushes Novel to NY Times Best-Seller List." *The Twelfth Arrondissement* had reached number one.

"Guess whoever came up with that marketing strategy knew what they were doing," Nate said as I read the article for the second time.

"Yeah, it's just too bad two people died as a result of their ambitions."

"I don't know. I think the book curse idea was the cover up, but the actions would have happened anyway. Listen, I didn't stop by just to show you the article. There's something I wanted to talk to you about."

"Sounds serious."

"Serious. Not fatal. I wanted you to know I put in my retirement letter, effective January one. I'm starting my own business in private investigating. I even put down a deposit for office space."

"Wonderful, Nate! You'll be spectacular."

"That's not all. I want you to consider joining me."

"To do your accounting?"

"Uh-huh. I wouldn't trust anyone else. But here's the caveat—it's in Arizona!"

"What???"

"That office I'm renting is not too far from Sun City West."

As soon as he said those three words, my stomach began to churn. It would mean I would be living so close to my mother she'd think nothing of coming over to rearrange my kitchen cabinets or vacuum the rug.

I'm sure Nate could see the tension on my face. "Come on, kiddo. Give it a try. I always told myself when I retired I'd move to a place where I wouldn't have to put up with ice or snow. You could easily rent out your house to one of the officers in Mankato."

"I, uh, um . . ."

"Look, you don't have to commit right away. Think about it. You could take an unpaid leave of absence for a year and work for me. I'll match your salary and benefits. Oh, what the hell! I'll do better than match them. You see, I've been saving up for a long time and, thanks to a few very healthy investments, I'm able to pull it off. If you don't like it, you can always return to your present job. If you do like it, and I know you will, you can take early retirement from Mankato. You've got twenty years into this place. So, what do you say? Will you give it some thought?"

I was stunned. Flabbergasted. All I could do was stare at Nate with my mouth open.

He chuckled. "I'm just asking that you give it some real thought. Okay, kiddo? Besides, you don't want a repeat of the Super Target incident last winter when you fell facedown on the ice. There's no ice in Phoenix."

The Super Target incident. Why did I ever tell him about it in the first place?

I paused for a second and took a breath. "Just the accounting, right?"

"Right."

"I'm not an investigator."

"I know."

"I want my own office. Or at least my own cubby-hole."

"Done!"

"And call monitoring so I'll be warned if my mother's on the other end."

"Done!"

"And one more thing."

"What's that?"

"That you never accept a case from my mother."

"Done!"

As things turned out, two out of three wasn't bad.

If you enjoyed BOOKED 4 MURDER
by
J.C. Eaton
More Sophie Kimball Mysteries
are on their way!
Don't miss

DITCHED 4 MURDER

in December 2017!
Turn the page for a sneak peek!

Chapter 1

"Listen to your mother for once, Phee. Hold off on turning on that air conditioner. You should wait as long as you can so you don't pay a fortune to those utility companies."

"Maybe you can put it off, but you've been living out here for at least a decade. Your blood's probably as thin as water. Mine's not."

"Well, it won't thin out unless you put it to the test."

"I'm not going to sweat to death to prove a point," I said. "I've only been out here a few months and my blood's as thick as sludge. Heavy Minnesota sludge. Or have you forgotten what it's like back there?"

"Forgotten? I can't even look at a Norman Rockwell holiday card without shivering. Trust me, honey, you'll get used to the heat."

This, from the woman who installed a small portable air conditioner in her back bedroom for the dog.

It was a conversation I'd had a few days ago with

my mother, Harriet Plunkett, and it was a typical one
for us. Very little had changed since then. Until the
murders. But I'm getting ahead of myself. I stood at
the thermostat, debating whether or not to break
down and turn on the air-conditioning like I did
every summer back in Mankato, Minnesota. But
this wasn't summer. It was late April. April in Peoria,
Arizona, and approaching ninety-five degrees. The
ceiling fans in my small rental casita could only do
so much.

I made the move to Arizona so I could handle the
bookkeeping for a friend of mine, Nate Williams. He
was a retired police officer from Mankato who started
his own private investigation firm near Phoenix. Nate
convinced me to take a year's leave of absence from
my job in accounts receivable at the Mankato Police
Department and move to a place where I'd never be
bothered with snow or ice again. All he had to do was
remind me of the Super Target incident the winter
before and he knew I'd jump at the chance to move
to Arizona.

The humiliation of opening my car door, taking
a step, and falling face-first on the icy pavement still
appeared in my nightmares. The worst part was
being unable to stand and having the two twenty-
something guys from the car next to mine hoist me
up and plop me back into the driver's seat. Worse
yet, they kept calling me "ma'am."

Ma'am. When did I become a *ma'am*? I was only in
my forties. *And I can still pull off a two-piece at the beach.*
Maybe if it wasn't winter and I didn't have a bulky
coat and long scarf covering up my figure, they
wouldn't have used that awful word. And why did I

tell Nate about the stupid incident in the first place? It gave him leverage. Leverage he used to talk me into moving near my mother in Arizona. I still remembered every word he said.

"Come on, kiddo. You don't want another icy parking lot incident, do you? You've got nothing to lose. Your daughter's teaching in St. Cloud, your ex-husband has been off the grid for years, and nothing is holding you back. Besides, you'll love the area. And you've got the advantage. You're already familiar with it."

"I'm familiar with my mother's small retirement community. And it's a wacky one at that. Or have you forgotten?"

"How could I possibly have forgotten about Sun City West's book curse and all those unrelated deaths that scared everyone in a fifty-mile radius of the place? We can thank your mother's book club for that."

"So now, you want me to live there? Near all of my mother's friends? The same batty crew from Booked 4 Murder? That's the name of their club, you know. I think my mother thought it up. Anyway, those women had me chasing all over the place a year ago to find a nonexistent killer. That's where you want me to live?"

"Not there. Near there. You're much too young to think about retirement communities."

"If that's your way of buttering me up, you need to do better."

He did. Nate Williams upped my salary, helped rent out my house to a young police officer and his family, and paid for all of my moving expenses. He also helped me find a fabulous casita in Vistancia, a multigenerational community in Peoria, not too far from Sun City West.

Now I was standing in front of my thermostat wondering how I could have been bamboozled into relocating to an area where a hundred and three degrees was described as "warm." As my fingertip reached for the button on the thermostat, the phone began to ring. An omen. An omen telling me to wait another few days and save on my electric bill.

Unfortunately, it wasn't a sign from another realm; the caller ID made it clear it was my mother. I massaged my right temple and stared at the phone. My mother was calling to moan and groan about the latest disaster in her life—my aunt Ina's wedding. As if I didn't get an earful yesterday. At least it wasn't as bad as the day before, when my mother went on a tirade insisting Aunt Ina was trying to take over the book club. That was a one-sided conversation I could've done without.

"Your aunt Ina will drive us all to the brink with her endless lists, her obscure authors, and her constant need for attention. Be happy you're an only child."

An only child who gets 100% of Harriet Plunkett's complaints.

"We've told her time and time again we like to read cozy mysteries. Maybe a British whodunit once in a while, and what does she suggest? I'll tell you what she suggests—mysteries translated from godforsaken languages like Hungarian or Romanian. Romanian. That's a language, isn't it? Well, one thing's for sure, reading those things would be like

watching a Swedish movie with subtitles. We'd be
snoozing before they even found a body."

"Um, yeah, well . . ."

"And one more thing, she suggested having us
arrive in the attire of the day, according to the book."

"Huh? The what?"

"Oh, you heard me. She wants us to dress up like
the characters in the book according to when that
book was written. Honestly, the library committee
would have us locked up if we arrived to our meetings looking like we stepped out of another century.
Even Shirley thought it was extreme, and she goes
for all that new age stuff. Then Ina goes and says it's
no different than the Red Hat Society. No different?
We'd be known as the lunatic fringe ladies."

The phone was now on its fourth ring and I had
to make up my mind. In a moment of weakness I
picked it up. I should've pushed the thermostat
button instead.

"Phee! It's about time you got home. You never
worked so late when you were in accounts receivable.
This new accounting job is really eating up your
time. Anyway, I just wanted to give you the latest on
the wedding. Your aunt Ina decided to wear white.
White. I honestly don't know what's come over my
sister, but all of sudden she's acting like she's twenty
instead of seventy-four. And white! She's not supposed to wear white. This is her second marriage.
Before I forget, your cousin Kirk and his wife are
flying in from Boston. I wonder what he has to say
about this. . . ."

Finally, a pause. My mother actually paused, and I
could say something.

"I'm sure Kirk is thrilled for his mother. Look, Aunt Ina was always a bit eccentric. It was Uncle Harm who kept her in line all those years, and even he could only do so much. I say if she wants to wear white, let her wear white. It's not like there are any rules or anything. So, are all the other arrangements made? The invitation wasn't too specific."

"Not too specific" was an understatement, even for me. The invitation was a coiled message written on a small, round piece of parchment paper. It reminded me of an enchantment bowl I had seen once in the ancient cultures section of the Art Institute of Chicago. Unfortunately, we didn't have a docent on hand to explain my aunt's invitation. It read:

The fusion of our lives will meld in the
glorious sunrise at Petroglyph Plaza,
14th of Sivan, 5778,
nine days past the counting of the
Omer as Ina Stangler and Louis Melinsky become one.
Join us for this celebration of eternal bliss.

It took my mother a half hour to figure out the 14th of Sivan was a date on the Hebrew calendar that coincided with May 28. Then another half hour to complain.

"Who writes a date like that? At first I thought Sivan was Aztec or maybe Incan. Possibly Tibetan. Finally, I dredged up the Jewish calendar from the Sinai Mortuary and lo and behold—it was Hebrew."

I took a breath as my mother continued to vent about my aunt.

"The arrangements? You want to know if the arrangements were made? Oh no, that would make it too easy for the rest of us. And her husband-to-be seems just as fly-by-the-wind as she is. He's a musician, you know. Plays the saxophone. Worked for years in one band or another on cruise ships. Divorced three times. Three times!"

As much as I hated to admit it, my mother was right about my aunt Ina. Every family has one member who, shall we say, "dances to their own drum," but in Ina's case, she's been pounding on the entire percussion section ever since I've known her. My aunt Ina had never grown out of the "hippie phase," as my mother referred to it. From the gauzy white skirts she wore with peasant blouses and fetish necklaces, Aunt Ina had a style all her own. At seventy-four, she still braided her long gray hair and wrapped it on top of her head like the old German women did in the eighteenth-century paintings. Only they didn't put flowers, ribbons, or bits of tinsel in their braids.

I was picturing Aunt Ina with a floor-length gown and white tinsel in her hair when my mother continued to complain.

"And when does she pick to get married? When? One of the hottest weekends in the valley—Memorial Day! She picks Memorial Day. That'll cost your cousin Kirk a fortune on airline tickets. And that's not the worst of it, Phee. Not by a long shot."

"Why? What do you mean?"

"You said the invitation wasn't specific. Well, here's specific for you—They're getting married at dawn in the Petroglyph Plaza in the White Tank Mountains."

"The Petroglyph Plaza? You mean the old Indian ruins in the state park?"

Even I was getting concerned. This was extreme, even for Aunt Ina.

"Oh yes. We can all sweat to death as we schlep up the mountain. And I emphasize 'death.' Who's going to come?"

"Mom, the White Tank Mountain Park is a few minutes from your house and we can drive straight up to the path that leads to Petroglyph Plaza. It's only a quarter-mile walk from the parking lot to the ruins."

"A quarter mile? What's the matter with you? I'm not walking a quarter of a mile because your aunt has lost her mind. And what about the book club ladies? They're not about to get winded either."

"Oh, for heaven's sake, Mother, all of you walk farther than that when there's a good sale at Kohl's. Besides, I'm sure they'll arrange for golf carts or something."

"You know your aunt Ina and details. We'll be lucky if they remember to bring water."

I took a few slow breaths, something I'd learned in a Tai Chi class once, and answered before my mother could continue. "Don't worry. Aunt Ina will have all the arrangements made. Do you know why she picked that spot?"

"Seems she and her future husband wanted to get married where they met. We're just lucky they didn't meet on some footbridge that could have collapsed and sent us all into a creek."

I tried to change the subject before my mother took everything to the extreme. "So, where are Kirk and Judy staying?"

"Your aunt reserved some godforsaken place near

the mountain. Called it quaint. What was it? Oh yes, 'The Cactus Wren.' And they want all of us to stay there for the weekend."

"It sounds nice, Mom. A quaint little bed-and-breakfast overlooking the White Tanks."

"Quaint! Don't you know what that means? It means no air-conditioning, no cable TV, forget about a mini-fridge and a microwave, and we'll be lucky if they stick a fan in the room. There's only one thing worse than quaint, and that's rustic. Thank God she didn't pick rustic. That means no electricity and an outhouse!"

I quickly changed the subject. "I'm sorry your granddaughter can't make it. Too close to the end of the school year."

"Well, Kirk and Judy's daughter, your cousin Ramona, can't make it either. The navy isn't about to grant her leave and fly her back from Qatar because her grandmother has discovered eternal bliss."

I tried not to laugh, but the whole thing was pretty darn funny. "I'll take lots of photos and post them on Facebook. That way Kalese and Ramona can see the wedding ceremony. Did Aunt Ina mention who was catering the affair? I mean, it isn't just the ceremony, is it? You talk to her all the time. What's going on?"

"Your aunt may not be the wealthiest woman in the world, but apparently Louis Melinsky has money to throw around. They're having the wedding catered by Saveur de Evangeline, that fancy French restaurant on Bell Road, and if that isn't enough, they've hired La Petite Pâtisserie from Scottsdale to provide the desserts."

"Where? The invitation didn't say."

"Of course not. Why would Ina bother to let anyone know what's going on? Apparently they've rented out the entire section of that mountain for their reception. Some tent company will be setting up the shindig a few yards past that Petrowhatever Plaza."

"And you were worried for nothing, Mom. It sounds like Aunt Ina really organized this."

"Loosely."

"What do you mean 'loosely'?"

"I mean that whenever your aunt arranges something, it's in the broad sense. Mark my words, Phee, something is bound to go wrong."

I didn't feel like spending the next half hour listening to my mother moan and groan about how "spatial" Aunt Ina was and how my mother was always the one who had to step in and fix everything. I was hot. I was tired. And most of all, I was hungry. Promising to give my mother a call the next day, I hung up and walked into the kitchen.

All of the fixings for a huge chicken salad were in the fridge, and I began to move them onto the counter when the phone rang again.

Please don't let it be my mother. What else could she possibly complain about?

I had a good mind to ignore it and let it go to the answering machine, but if it was my mom, she'd know I was avoiding her. I walked over to the phone and checked the caller ID. Not my mother. Not a familiar number. I decided to let the machine get it when I recognized the voice at the other end.

"Phee, this is your aunt Ina. Give me a call when you get in. I have the tiniest, teeniest little favor to ask you."

I quickly put the mayonnaise and white meat tenders back in the fridge and picked up the receiver. It was the first in a long series of mistakes I'd be making.

"Hi, Aunt Ina. I, was . . . um, in the other room when I heard the phone. How are you?"

"Ooh . . . I'm as fine as any bride-to-be could be. I don't know how I ever managed the first time around. And as far as your cousin Kirk's wedding went, well, Judy's family took care of it. That's the trouble with getting married late in life, you have to do everything yourself. It's daunting. That's the word for it—daunting. Did your mother mention that her friend Shirley was designing a special hat for me for the wedding? It's too bad she closed down that cute little shop of hers near Sun City. At least she's taking special orders. I decided on a hat. I do think wearing a veil would be too extreme, even for me."

In the thirty seconds it took me to put the scallions and kale back in the fridge while cradling the phone, I realized my mother was an amateur blabbermouth compared to Aunt Ina. At this rate, I'd die of starvation. I had to move things along.

"Um, so . . . Aunt Ina, you mentioned a favor. A small favor. What can I help you out with?" *And please let this be a reasonable and normal favor.*

"I don't know if your mother mentioned it, but the entire affair is going to be catered."

"Uh-huh." I wasn't sure what she was getting at and I held my breath.

"You cannot possibly imagine all the odds and ends that have to go into something like this. No wonder people hire a wedding planner."

Oh, God no! She's going to ask me to be her wedding planner!

"Aunt Ina," I blurted out, "I don't know the first thing about planning weddings."

"Well, who does, dear? Now, to get to the reason I called you. Louis and I have hired a marvelous pastry company from Scottsdale to provide the desserts. Unfortunately, between the fittings for my gown, the endless bantering over the menu, and those dreadful people at the tent company, we're at our wits' end. Phee, can you please meet with Julien at La Petite Pâtisserie to figure out the dessert menu? I would ask your mother, but between you and me, Harriet would select an assortment of Fig Newton cookies and those tasteless sugar-free things she keeps in her freezer. So, will you do it?"

I didn't want to sound whiny, but Scottsdale was a good hour from my house, not to mention I had no idea where the pastry company was located. Before I could reply, it was as if my aunt could read my mind.

"Julien and his assistants will be at the Renaissance Hotel in Glendale on Thursday for some sort of evening exhibition. That's only a half hour from your house. You can meet him there. I'll call him immediately to let him know. You will do it? Won't you, Phee?"

I wavered for a second but finally caved.

"Yes, I'll do it. What about the wedding cake? Is Julien making that, too?"

"Louis and I decided not to do a wedding cake. Too mundane. That's why the desserts have to be spectacular. And one more thing, Phee."

"What's that?"

"Whatever you do, don't tell your mother, or the pièce de résistance for my wedding will resemble the potluck dessert table at one of her card games."

She thanked me at least three times before hanging up. I had suddenly lost my appetite for chicken salad and opted instead for popcorn and an O'Doul's. I spent the rest of the evening Googling wedding desserts and chastising myself for answering the stupid phone.